Preface.

An Extraordinary Boy was first published in 2010. It was envisaged then as part of a trilogy but over the last ten years it became increasingly obvious to me that the second book was too insubstantial to stand on its own. Two years ago, after a lengthy stay in Arizona, I decided to merge the remaining two books into the present volume. There are many bits and pieces left over from the imagined 'third' book and these may well find themselves used in subsequent work. Much of the impact of Malaq settlement is left unexplored, especially concerning the resistance of humans and the cultural and theological impact of human culture on Seeth identity. There is much that may prove interesting to explore later.

Seeth Nation begins with a double whammy, plague and infertility. Started long before the current COVID19 pandemic, I feel it necessary to explain that the use of a coronavirus in the novel predates the very real grief and loss of the current outbreak – fact is often stranger than fiction. Writers use conventions and tropes because they add realism, and an attempt at plausibility should be the hall mark of creative writing, science fiction or not. The 'killer' plague scenario is a pretty standard sci fi approach, but as I finished this final manuscript in Morocco in January of 2020, working on the Arizona draft of 2018-19, I felt uneasy about what may well look like opportunism. The emergence of HN51 is not about COVID19, and as writers of fiction usually state, the similarity between any real virus, living or dead, is purely coincidental.

Many people have assisted in the completion of this book, and I would like to thank the many readers who reviewed and commented on *An Extraordinary Boy*. I have tried to apply these critical insights to the current novel. I would also like to thank my friend and former colleague, Dr Torsten Michal, for reading through the entire manuscript and allowing himself to be subjected to an interrogation via WhatsApp, beset as he was with the emergence of on-line teaching at the University of Bristol, and the obvious frustrations of these bewildering times.

Vernon Hewitt. Bristol
April 2020.

Prologue: The New Peoples.

Murec throttled down the land speeder and eased it over to the edge of the road; evidently lost. Decades of erosion had fissured the tarmac into great zagged break lines and the verges had crumbled into deep groves of scrub and bush. Once this has been a major highway running through Arizona towards the Californian state line, but it looked now like some curious natural feature, a gully or oddly straight section of dry riverbed. He pressed the scanlens to his face and panned over the horizon, trying to get his bearings. The reservation should be three kilometers in front of him, although the beacon was down and there was no sign of activity. He leaned down, his blonde, cropped head neatly covered by the perspex windshield. He sensed already that something was wrong. Gripping the side of the bike with his muscled thighs, he spun the machine up and sped off, throwing up a smudge of dust as he accelerated.

Murec had once come here often, liaising with the settlers and ensuring that their needs were met, as much as they would allow, but that was many years ago. They had grown reclusive, shunning contact and making it clear they wished to be alone as the world changed – and the United Nations Commission on Human Welfare had rolled back its staff and obliged them their privacy. Twenty years or more later, the landscape was so altered that Murec recognised nothing. Wetter and cooler summers had transformed the semi-arid landscape, driving out many of the succulents and cacti and replacing them with stands of birch and great pastures of thick, lush grasses. The yellow gold of the tors had weathered quickly, and small thickets of pine were breaking and fragmenting the stones into fine screes of pebble. There had once been Joshua trees, but they had retreated south to what had once been the Mohave desert, leaving behind dead, solitary stumps like fossils. As Murec zipped almost soundlessly over the dead road, the machine blew away the loam and accumulated dust, revealing for a few hours the remnants of a yellow center line, an echo of a world lost. About him the morning haze thickened.

Within ten minutes he had passed the original boundary of the camp and entered the reservation. The main gates were open and clearly long abandoned. Once there had been security and scans and genetic identification; numerous warnings on how to proceed – no scans, no technology. But the guard blocks were now shattered piles of crumbling cement, their windows missing, with saplings and brush clustering inside. Murec slipped the bike away from under him and stood, puzzled and increasingly uneasy. He walked to a shattered, doorless entry; noting the graffiti on the walls shouting out the old defiance: *Earth for Humans*. There were derogatory drawings of Malaq, horned heads; many sheath less, with thick penises snaking up from their groin, ribbed like snakes with wide flat heads. Murec mused over these strange phallic images; a very human obsession with genitalia, reminiscent of the first decades of the arrival of the Malaq. It was something he had never entirely understood although others of his kind were intrigued. Leaving the land speeder, Murec walked through the gateless entry, broken glass crunching under his boots. He walked with the curious lope of the *Dura* Malaq; the second born, his tall sculptured body slightly forward; humans had called it 'lizzing', a once derogatory reference to their assumed raptor ancestry.

He walked on for about a quarter of an hour. Ahead the road became less ruinous, canalized by the remnants of houses and shops set back on either side.

'Hello!'

He shouted, self-consciously, his hands cupping his mouth. His voice slammed about the facades of the buildings, sending a cloud of pigeons up from a nearby roof. The only reply was bird song and a door somewhere, butting in the wind.

Murec pursed his lips plaintively, unsure how to proceed. His instructions had been relatively clear; but the pre-op briefing had been vague. He unzipped his tunic, peeling the fabric away from his chest, already gummy with sweat from the morning heat. His body heat alerted him to the start of his phasing: the shift from male to female. He ignored it as best he could; it would be a few days yet. Murec removed a small metal band not unlike an old wristwatch from an inside pocket and slipping it over his hand he moved it about, scanning ahead and observing the data on the inside of his retina. There was no humans present within range – and the range was set for over fifty clicks. There had been at least 400 settlers at the last census; where could they have gone? Suddenly anxious, he risked calling in the land speeder and waited, hunched down in the scrub, until the soft hum of the approaching vehicle stopped behind his shoulders. He stood and placed his hand on a rear panel under the seat, launching eight small surveillance drones from the machine's hub. To prevent obvious treaty violations these were disguised as small, intricate birds, although in the past they were easily spotted by the humans and often shot down. Murec found himself hoping that there would be a loud crack of gunfire, confirmation that somethings were still normal, but the small flock spiraled up into the sky and scrambled in different directions without incident. After several minutes the data streamed in; empty streets; no heat signatures except for some large mammals – bison – up on the ridge. Murec walked on, cautiously entering several buildings, some ruinous, thick with the smell of damp decay, others evidently lived in until recently.

Back in the center of the road, Murec took a risk and made a call to the Orbital, but it was still below the horizon. He recorded a brief description of his predicament and set it on repeat transmission. 'Just tell me what to do' he said to himself softly, looking instinctively to the east for guidance. After hesitating slightly, he pressed on, walking and observing. About a kilometer from the gates, the settlement hazed away into brush and prairie. Set back in a thicket of young juniper trees he saw the hospital and what appeared to be a school. Inside, the place seemed tidy and utilitarian; in a mess hall places were still set for food, but the plates and glasses were covered in a thick reddish dust. Murec risked shouting again, his voice loud and intrusive. Nothing. He walked through what had once been some sort of clinic; the cabinets still stocked with medicines and the desktops clear. He wiped his hand absent mindedly over the surface, his fingers leaving parallel lines of whiteness. Through an open door he walked into a garden, the beds neat and flush with roses. The lawn was a lurid green – and curious – Murec stepped over the shrubs to find it was synthetic, laid down like a carpet. The one story buildings closed in around him, producing a sort of cloister; chairs were set around low plastic tables, some still littered with cups. He found it oddly depressing, as if he was seeing something final, terminal.

He walked back through the deserted complex and stood where the road stuttered to a finish. A landslide had snapped the asphalt and ribbed it up on the far side of a gully. The nose of a rusted, shattered car poked up through the long grasses; its front windscreen smashed in a cobweb of break lines. He unzipped his tunic further, feeling the wind cool his lithe, smooth torso. Ahead, where the land fell away steeply, he looked down to a wide clearing, the ground littered with small white sticks. Scrambling down, he stood in what was obviously a burial place. Oblong mounds of earth stretched away on either side, some bordered with stones and the bottoms of broken bottles. Close to the twisted ribbon of the old road, Murec noticed that several plots had been filled recently while next to one solitary, open grave lay a spade and a curious metal bucket on wheels. He walked towards it, resting his boot on the wooden handle and glancing down into the neatly excavated hole. Narrowing his sparkling, fluorescent eyes he scanned the area and calculated; there were 399 plots. He stood for a long time working through the implications of what he was seeing, and then with slow resolution, he walked back into the hospital.

It did not take Murec long to find the grave digger. In the back of the infirmary building was a room that had once been an office. On the frosted glass door panel, the name *Professor Jamie Relph* could still be made out. Murec pushed the door open slowly, aware of a soft hiss as an unseen airtight seal was broken. Sensitive to smells, he lifted his face back sharply from the rush of ammonia, the deep burned smell of desiccated flesh and stale dead air. Breathing deeply, Murec pushed into the room. Sitting behind a desk was the body of an old man still in a white lab coat, his head slightly back and looking directly at Murec as if he were expected. The body had not so much decayed as dried out, the cheeks gaunt and mottled like old fruit. Murec stood, his neck and cheeks flushing luminous blue, setting out the intricate mottling on his forehead in bold relief.

When the first hybrids returned with the *Illuvatar*, the humans believed that they were without emotion, but they felt things deeply and often struggled when sharing feelings with each other, especially about how to relate to humans. The first born had been puzzled by human singularity; their inability to form associations and undertake collective action without dispute or endless debate. Yet they were also deeply moved by humanity's sense of wonder; its self-reliance; and ultimately its bravery. Murec knew who Jamie Relph had been. He was, to coin a humanism, famous. He had been a companion of the Qua Quendi and had been instrumental in pushing for compromise during settlement. He had been there at the beginning, the signing of the covenant, and had fathered one of the first *Dura* Malaq, coupling with one of the first born when such an act was perverse and treacherous. How it was that he had ended up here, in a reservation for segregationists, was a deep mystery: presumably the one he had been sent to solve. He walked slowly to the desk. Death held no revulsion to him but rather a grim fascination. Malaq experienced time differently to humans; one of the many problems they faced in the first decades of their arrival. Some similarities, but many differences. Looking at the body, it struck Murec suddenly that it had been a miracle that the covenant had held at all. There had been problems; many humans resisted, and some of the first born had decided to return to the stars with the Qua Quendi and the Illuvatar, unhappy or unsettled by their new home; of the first born that had remained, some had withdrawn from human contact. But the covenant held as the complexities of the new peoples unfolded, if mostly through people like Jamie, who believed in it passionately. The Earth had prospered.

There was a flicker and bubble of light to Murec's right and suddenly a holographic figure expanded into life; the Orbital had obviously just cleared the eastern skyline. Murec bowed to the image, which returned the greeting and then listened to Murec's brief report. The resolution of the signal revealed not just Murec but the contents of the room, and after he finished speaking, Murec watched the *Sallaq* looking at the remains of Jamie Relph, the smooth face clearly troubled. There would have to be a moot – a brief meeting of the Security Council. Murec was asked to bury the body, as was the human custom on the reservation, but in such a way as to facilitate its later removal to a more appropriate site. Murec was also informed that he must find and remove any personal affects before the Illuvan Curia arrived. This news surprised Murec; absent as it was from the earlier mission brief.

'With respect, what possible jurisdiction can the Curia have here: this was a human territory?'

The Sallaq, expressionless, was looking at the human body. 'That is unclear to us and the council. It is possible they believe Jamie Relph has some sort of record of the arrival that the Curia wish to examine.'

This did not strike Murec's logically attuned mind as an answer at all, but etiquette required he accept it.

'It will be an unpleasant business, Murec Malaqii; but we request that you stay on the reservation until the UN can dispatch a team. Given the Curia's interests, and the need for the moot – this may take some time. Is all well?'

Murec answered in the affirmative; the image wrinkled and folded away and he set about his task, fetching a gurney from one of the wards, and placing a sheet gently but firmly around the body in case it disintegrated, eased it onto the trolly. He theorised that Jamie had been dead for almost a year, possibly two, the hermetically sealed office made calculating the exact time almost impossible. Jamie had clearly buried the last survivors as they had succumbed to age and illness and had been thoughtful enough to dig his own grave. Death had messed with his plan.

Outside the heat was growing over the cemetery and Murec removed his tunic, clearing the bottom of the rectangular hole to make it more even. His powerful physique made short work of the digging, and after several minutes of stabbing the spade into the hard, rocky soil, his body was polished and glistening with sweat. When satisfied with the grave, Murec placed the body into the ground, curled on its side in a fetal position. It seemed to him a barbaric act, atavistic in its simplicity. He backfilled the grave with loose gravelly loam, enough to deter predators but not enough to complicate a possible future disinterring. Afterwards he stood wondering if there was some ritual, some phrase, that he should speak over the body. He had seen humans do this, praying to a God for their souls or the resurrection of their body everlasting. The Malaq burned their dead, and since they were intimately linked through telepathy, no one individual ever died. And most of the Malaq did not believe in God; taking a rather naturalist view that their bodies returned to the Earth and would manifest themselves in different forms through deep time. Some however – the Illuvan Curia – practiced a spiritualism that had become increasingly religious and doctrinal, worshipping the Qua Quendi and remaining, through their devotion and meditation, in a constant state of maleness. So it was said. It was also said the Illuvans mummified their dead and entombed them in the walls of their monasteries. Murec had, of course, never seen any of these things for himself.

After ten or fifteen minutes, standing with the hot sun on his back, he put the spade upright into the soil at the head of the grave, slung his damp tunic over his shoulder and returned to the road and eventually the hospital. Back in Jamie's office he looked delicately over the desk and carefully inspected the draws to a cabinet. In the bottom draw he came across a series of data cubes and a few yellowed sheets of blank paper. In the middle draw was a thick filing box; an old fashioned thing made from vegetable pulp to hold hard copy materials. He took it out and lifted the flat lid. Inside was a thick wad of paper. Intrigued, Murec lifted the heavy metal clip and placing the manuscript on the desk, examined the first few pages. They were filled with a dense typeset, imprinted by keys; something he had never seen before. On the first page was a poem:

Tell to the King that the cavern hall is fallen in decay

Apollo has no chapel left, no prophesying bay,

No talking spring.

The stream is dry that had so much to say.

He narrowed his eyes, pressing his lips together, thinking, recalling. The wording was reputedly the last utterance of the sybil of Cumae, an ancient human prophetess who had been asked by the Roman Emperor Julian whether his restoration of the old Pagan faith would succeed over a decadent Christianity. The answer, evidently unequivocal, had not been to the Emperor's liking. Jamie's use of the expression seemed unequivocal too – and from a human who had lived with and fought for Malaq settlement, particularly odd. Troubled, Murec flicked through the rest of the tome and saw what was clearly a lengthy testimonial, what the humans called an autobiography or recollection. He ran his tongue over his full, elegant lips and although trained well in the matter of futile speculation, suspected he was holding in his hands the subject of the Curia's interest. He placed the manuscript back into the box. He messaged the finding and transmitted several scans back to the orbital. He received a short acknowledgement but no instructions. Depressed by the lingering stench of death, he walked back slowly to the land speeder, snapping open a small compartment containing food and water. As he sat drinking, the surveillance birds fluttered back from their wasted journey, settling neatly at his feet, and then sitting motionlessly, the illusion of life gone. By late afternoon he was still alone, and conscious that the Orbital would soon be out of range, signalled again. He was not superstitious or uneasy with solitude, but he was anxious to return to his own kind and to leave what had become a necropolis. Just as the Orbital was dipping below the western horizon, underlit by brilliant, golden sunlight, he received a recorded message saying he was to remain and 'ensure the body was secured' since the council was awaiting the arrival of the Illuvan Patriarch himself. He would be briefed again in the morning.

Murec had no idea why Jamie's death could cause such a flap (a human expression he was fond of using), or why no live transmission had been made to explain the situation. Somewhat exasperated, he switched the land speeder to flight mode and returned quickly to the hospital, landing quietly on the fake grass. He set up a silent perimeter alarm out of habit and set off to explore his surroundings before it fell dark. Murec found behind the mess hall a kind of improvised dormitory; evidence that towards the end the humans had moved in and lived in the hospital, abandoning their homes as if seeking solace in company. He brushed away dust from a neatly made bed and lay down but felt uneasy; partly because, typically human, it was off the floor and level, partly because he could not help thinking about the people who had lived and died here, a choice made to avoid Malaq such as himself. In the end he camped out in what had once been a utility room; fitted with shelves like a closet and containing sheets and blankets. Once cleared, Murec used cushions from the mess hall chairs to make himself a reasonably comfortable bunkbed, his head above his feet and on the ground. He showered in the garden, finding a hose still connected to and pressured by an elaborate watering system. He felt as if he were committing sacrilege. Later, he sat as the moon flooded the garden and thought about Jamie, what he had been like, and how it must have felt to live through such turbulence and fear. Towards midnight he climbed under his shelf, and with the ease of the Malaq, fell quickly asleep.

Around 4 am, he was awoken by the repeater on his wrist band flashing noiselessly, relaying a message from the proximity alarm on the land speeder. He rolled silently into a sitting position, listening to the gaunt silence, the strobing light filling up the small room. Malaq had near perfect night sight and standing by the opened doorway he could see the corridor clearly, despite the near total blackness that would have rendered human eyesight useless. He stepped out silently, feeling the cold tiles on his bare feet, and moved quickly to the mess hall and then towards the garden. He had no weapons, only a taser which was still in the land speeder. He listened again, holding his head slightly forward, bird like; still nothing, not even the wind. His wrist band showed something 30 meters ahead and stationary; a slight heat signature but not big enough to suggest a bear. Possibly a mountain lion. 30 meters put it outside the hospital, down on the road or even possibly in the cemetery. Murec relaxed slightly, irritated that he had not protected the body well enough; the signal was probably coyotes. He returned to the utility room, picked up a broom and removed the brush head. Holding the wooden stave like a spear, he walked quickly up onto the road. At the lip of the gully, he saw the path down to the cemetery like a pale ribbon, worn through an embankment and curving down towards the clearing, grooved by long use. There were no coyotes. He would have heard them yapping and whining over the burial. Instead there was one solitary figure standing over Jamie's grave, its back turned to him.

Murec felt a flush of surprise; not alarm. His instinctive reaction was one of curiosity, not threat. He stood contemplating whether to call down or summon the land speeder. After a moment of indecision, he did neither but walked down the slope casually, deliberately using the sides of his feet to shift the loose shale noisily, announcing his approach. The figure did not move. As Murec drew closer, he saw that it wore a long cloak in the way a Malaq would wear one, one side thrown back over a shoulder, the hood half up. Murec felt momentarily irritated – the moot had clearly sent someone else and had not thought to advise him, or worse still, the Curia had sent someone even while the council was in session. He drew level with the mysterious figure, as tall as he was, and said curtly '*Tela ca qua serek ha?*'

The hooded head turned, and Murec caught a glimpse of deep golden eyes, glowing steadily, flexed with amber.

'I am not from the Curia, Murec Malaqii.'

Bemused, Murec walked closer and turned to look at the grave. The voice was deep, human and male in intonation, but the eyes were not. His posture, such as Murec could decern through the cloak, was not of the Dura. Murec had not seen such an obviously young human for decades; none existed. Sensing his confusion, the man said softly, 'I am here to say goodbye to an old friend. This was good of you; to bury him, incidentally.'

'I fear that the moot may well wish to remove him. And there are some complications with the Illuvan Curia.' Murec spoke in english, his curiosity deepening. 'You knew him?'

'Long ago.' The voice was thick with emotion. Then, pushing back the hood, the figure crouched down, one arm outstretched towards the clods of earth and stone. Thick strands of hair cascaded over a chiselled, handsome face and Murec, aghast at his earlier rudeness, realised he was standing next to none other than the Qua Quendi. For the first time in his relatively young life, he was speechless and as the Malaq say *nela qua* – thoughtless. He considered whether he should bow or show some form of deference but then he heard the man laugh quietly at his consternation.

'Be still, Murec Malaqii; you do not bow to me. I am the 'complication' that is troubling the moot, as well as my rather devoted followers, but I am not really here.' The Qua Quendi stood abruptly, pulling his cloak about him. 'You say he is to be moved?'

'I believe so Quendi Sa. The council were unaware that he was ever here. This was the last humans only settlement; and he was its last occupant. What puzzles me is why he would come here at all. Were these not his enemies?'

Max said nothing for a while, then sighed deeply, glanced up at the brightening sky. 'I suspect in the end he felt the need to be with his own kind. He probably thought that, close to their end, they might still embrace the covenant. And he was a skilled physician, they might have needed his help. Who now will ever know? The Curia are looking for something.' It was not a question.

'Yes. There is a testament in his office; something I believe he wished to be found; perhaps the Curia feel otherwise? There are also some data cubes.'

'Very interesting.' Max stood. Murec saw that beneath the cloak he wore a simple white darshi, the long sleeveless dress of the first born. Still startled by the presence of the Qua Quendi, Murec watched him carefully. To the majority of the Malaq, Max was their human progenitor – a male with hybrid characteristics, longevity being one of them. That his sexuality was fixed was of no interest to a majority of them, but to the Illuvan movement he was an emissary, almost a god. The aesthetic appeal of his permanent masculinity ran deep in their faith; despite their isolation from humans with their bewildering dimorphism. How the Illuvan had come to worship a male human was a mystery. Murec's curiosity got the better of his training.

'You are worshipped by the Illuvan; a significant section of the first born that did not lie with humans; shunned human contact, and yet you seem so human to me. Forgive any offence, for none is intended.'

Max looked at the young Dura Malaq and smiled whimsically. 'And none taken. The world I helped create is full of irony; and that I am worshipped is an abomination – but the spiritual, religious imagination of the humans runs deep in all of you, even those who have no faith. And alas some of us encouraged it, without understanding the consequences.'

Murec mused briefly over the cryptic comments. 'We are many and tolerant; Quendi Sa.'

Max laughed, and turning, stood facing the Malaq. He placed his hands on each firm shoulder.

'And long may it be so.'

Murec awoke with a start, banging his head on the shelf above him. A thick blade of brilliant sunlight fell through a broken skylight in the corridor outside, sending a dusty beam, tight as a laser, across the floor of the closet. He checked the wristband and then pushing the door wide, ran to the garden. The land speeder glistened in the early morning, and a cursory glance showed there was no record logged of an intrusion. Murec then ran out along the road and stood looking down at the cemetery. Jamie's grave was open. Scurrying down, Murec saw his own footprints and that of another stamped about on the reddish soil. There was no body in the open pit.

Chapter One: Jamie Relph.

After Max's disappearance in 2006 the human world began to unravel. To some, the escalation of the climate crisis, the pandemics of 2019 and the resulting crisis in human fertility was all just coincidences; to others they had been foretold in some complex, esoteric way through the apparent revelation that the Earth had once belonged to another sentient species. The successful resurrection of the Seeth through human DNA was taken as a sign that the time of our dominion was coming to an end. For those of us susceptible to apocalyptic imagery, Max's disappearance was also heavy with symbolism, either the cause of our fall or the promise of our restoration. Photos of Max spread like a virus; the beautiful, muscled alien boy who turned into a lizard and blazed away into the stars: it should have come as no surprise that he quickly became a cult, an obsession heavy with sexual longing or simple, unadulterated fear. That the Seeth had failed to reappear since 2006 hardly seemed to matter: there were endless 'sightings' and rumours of secret agreements between governments and aliens, lurid accounts of alien experiments and abductions, and the internet spawned a vast series of intricate conspiracies that required no evidence or discussion. As the world slipped into crisis these rumours and apparent 'facts' infested our understanding of how to save ourselves; and when the hybrids did finally return in 2022, we had already lost the basic premise of reasoned argument. With the hybrids among us, religious movements and vigilantes sprang up like fungus after heavy rain; condemning, consoling, worshipping. The end is all about us now. It is one of the reasons that I am writing this. Recently Julian Grey said to me that he had expected the world to end in fire; it was his generation's zeitgeist; not a slow slipping away of reason and fecundity. I, of course, had never expected it to end at all, but one thing is clear to me now: this is our madness, not that of the Seeth *Malaq,* we did this to ourselves.

It is difficult for me to remember the period immediately after Max departed from Leicestershire. I had been shot but had somehow recovered; my stomach darkened with a whirl of healed skin like a fist with clear entry and exit marks still showing like scabs. After being airlifted to a local hospital I, along with all the people involved with Max, were sent off to an all-expenses paid detention facility just outside Cambridge and interrogated politely for almost a fortnight. Ministers resigned and governments fell. In its immediate shock the international community sought cooperation where there had been secrecy and competition. An entirely new UN agency was created under the eventual leadership of Dena Small to coordinate efforts and pool resources – it had the unwieldy title of the United Nations Commission on Seeth and Alien Contact: known colloquially as the skink brigade, presumably after the lizards that shed their tails. Rockets, probes and satellites were launched in various directions, with particular interest in Tau Ceti, the only star Max identified in one of his last coherent conversations before he left. Archaeologists looked for evidence of cities and structures and palaeontologists examined the shredded and often incomplete genomes of raptors dug up in the Badlands of Nevada and Wyoming to confirm some ancestral linkage between the Seeth and terrestrial therapods.

The dying Earth yielded clues. The sudden collapse of the western Antarctic ice shelf in 2018 exposed the edge of a vast circular base, rendered from what appeared to be triangular sections of geiss, polished and jointed with engineered precision. At the centre, a single shaft was found to contain the fossilised remains of up to 1,000 Raptor like creatures, identified as Utahraptors. Dated at just over 70 million years, when the continent would have been situated just adjacent the equator, the discovery was explosive; taken as the first clear evidence that fitted the theory that the Seeth had originated from Earth before being forced to escape some planet wide disaster. To many of course it was a hoax, a US cover up of a secret installation. To others it was an alien temple, the ossified bodies evidence of some ancient atrocity; quickly it became a prophecy.

My recovery was slow; tediously slow. I kept myself going on the diminishing hope that Max would return soon, but after a year; two years; five years – my life had to resume somehow and in some reasonable direction. I had friends, boyfriends now of course, and sex was a consolation if not a joy but every man I touched I compared to Max; sometimes to my embarrassment I even called them Max. In 2009 I was well enough to resume my plans to study medicine, but it was impossible to stay in Oxford; everywhere there were memories of Max, stark reminders of that fateful year and the root of my own loneliness. I went to St Thomas' in London to eventually qualify in epidemiology; an ironic delay in my education which ensured that I was employed in a major research institute when the first pandemic arrived in 2019. Coincidence again or prophecy? I am no longer sure of the difference. I stayed in touch with Jonathan of course, and not surprisingly I developed a sort of crush on my former nemesis. It was not just our shared love for Max that drew us together, but Jonathan's peculiar singularity. Of all the people whose lives had been touched by Max, Jonathan's seemed the least affected by his absence; so much so that he was the only person who talked about Max in the present tense, as if he had just gone out on some errand and would reappear at any moment. Freed of Max however, Jonathan lost the gaunt zombie boy look, filling out handsomely into a tall, lean man of few words but much meaning; and not surprisingly he had many secrets. He studied to be a social worker and finally acquired a girlfriend of sorts, although Jonathan succeeded in making even this mysterious. For someone who was indelibly straight he also acquired a bewildering familiarity with the gay world I was now living in, including the right to implicitly vet any guy I was sleeping with.

Julian never talked about his son, not even after he married my mother following the final collapse of his marriage to Sally in 2008. Another irony, of course, not lost on Jonathan. I had become the stepbrother of my alien lover in absentia, and the stepson of one of the world's most famous scientists. It brought some consolation and lots of jokes from Jonathan about gay incest. Julian had retired from Green College, Oxford in 2010 and although they had planned to move away from Farndon Road, they remained of course. My visits there were few but bittersweet and both Margaret and Julian – always sensitive and supportive to me – developed the habit of coming up to London to see me instead. By 2009 my mother was a successful academic in her own right, supporting Julian in his unmentionable grief and even managing to salvage some sort of friendship with my father. I stayed in touch with my sister, but our relationship was strained by her belief that Julian had broken up our parents' marriage. I also stayed in touch with Daniel Lockwood. He remained on his farm at the top of the Kirby Lane despite his plans to escape after the drama of 2006. He became a local celebrity throughout the East Midlands but despite clearly enjoying the publicity, he remained loyal to Max and to many of the details of that final, desperate day. Once, saying goodbye at Kings Cross railway station he had kissed me on the mouth, a clumsy gesture that aligned his beard with my lower lip. He had been appalled but I was not surprised, not because of any immodesty in my looks, but because I had always sensed in him an interest in men and a need to be in their company. Our friendship survived perfectly well.

In 2016, at the age of 28, I met Garen Lane at a gym just off Russell Square. I was living in Marchmont Street in a dysfunctional gay household constantly arguing about utility bills, Brexit and cleaning, but it was close to where I worked in Charlotte Square, and close to the fleshpots of the west end. Garen was exotic: half Jamaican, half Russian, beautiful and clever if not at times evasive and indirect about his life before me. He worked as a graphic designer illustrating websites and book covers and was particularly good with his hands. After years of hedonistic adventure, I was ready to settle down and although the prospects of monogamy remained unappealing, he moved in with me in the autumn after a detailed cross examination by Jonathan. He also survived the prurient interest of my two male housemates as well as the (inevitable) faux paus of being called the wrong name during the sexual christening of our joint bedroom. In hindsight, that should have been some sort of warning: even the most promiscuous of men usually take offense when, at the point of orgasm, you confuse their identity. Garen was intrigued, although later I was to find out that he knew about Max before we met and that it was my connection to Max that had attracted him to me in first place. I was still naive when confronted with a muscled, toned body and some decent foreplay. Interestingly Jonathan had his doubts; he thought Garen's artwork not just needlessly pornographic but misogynistic. I did not see it like that, at least not at first. Garen clearly liked images of bondage and sadomasochism; many of his drawings were of young men trussed up in elaborate knots, presumably inspired by Japanese homoeroticism. Like many of my sexual fantasies, while in certain circumstances they appealed to me, I had no actual desire to be hung upside down in a cellar dribbling from a ball gag. Garen, on the other hand, clearly enjoyed it immensely.

In the autumn of 2018, a series of flu epidemics broke out in Southern China, centred initially on Hong Kong. Pre-existing political issues and disturbances in the territory complicated the immediate response and by the spring of 2019 a particularly potent coronavirus appeared and spread rapidly. The outbreak occurred several months after the discovery of the Antarctic platform, a fatal coincidence as it turned out. By the summer, the World Health Organisation issued a protocol on treatment using vaccines developed during the H5N1 outbreaks of the previous decade, but the intervention was ineffective, and the virus continued to mutate and migrate. I had been working on the uses of quantum computing for the synthesis of antiviral agents and found myself suddenly co-opted by the CDC to head up field studies in what was clearly now a serious pandemic. In its early stages the virus had an incubation period of about six days and an infection index of about 4: meaning that one sick person was likely to infect four others. By early 2020 this had shifted to an index of 10. The fatality rate was high (between 10 and 12%) and climbed higher before a successful vaccine was finally produced by the Paris based Institut Pasteur in 2021. In the final analysis the WHO and CDC projections on the fatality rates were conservative: by June 2021, as the treatment began to bite into the pandemic, over 400 million people had died, around 4.5% of the global population.

The impact was immediate and devastating. While concentrating on the poor and the vulnerable, the virus seemed increasingly indiscriminate, proving extremely hard to quarantine areas believed to be free of infection. Mass population movements were triggered and resisted, increasingly by force, and the collapse in world trade led to a deep and sudden economic recession. Cities and large urban areas became prisons; travel became something exotic and remembered, an indulgence we lost almost overnight. The political impact of the crisis was to shift popular sentiment to the right and to extreme forms of nationalism and self-protection. International cooperation collapsed as states scrambled to close their borders and protect their citizens from a disease that was increasingly blamed on immigrants, and then by almost imperceptible turns, the existential threat posed by the unearthing of the Antarctic artefact. The first public assertion of such a bizarre connection was made by a group of American right-wing activists calling themselves *The Earth For Humans Movement*. Their nonsensical claim that the virus had originated from the alien structure spread as quickly as the virus itself. It proliferated across the internet just as print media and accredited journalism collapsed under the economic fallout of the pandemic.

Worst was to come, however. In the winter of 2021 – the warmest on record – virologists in Paris, Geneva and Atlanta met in secret to analyse a puzzling side effect of the HN71 virus. People who had survived the initial infection had been rendered infertile, and the cause of infertility was spreading even to those who had not been infected with the virus. What were believed to be isolated incidents soon became general: the parallels with the presumed fate of the

Seeth, although conjectural, were not lost on anyone. Fertility rates plummeted, especially in men, while still births and miscarriages rose to almost medieval levels. The impact on population growth was not just to invert the age distribution, but to cut it away with a steep, precipitous step that looked disturbingly like an extinction event. In countries where the demographics were already skewed in favour of aging populations the predicted outcome was that mortality rates would rapidly overtake live births. The UK, Japan and most of north western Europe would be depopulating in less than a decade. I had been working in Atlanta; separated from my muscled and contoured boyfriend by regulations and restrictions on movement: even talking over the internet was rationed to the availability of power. Our data sets outlining the extent of our crisis were heavily classified, but they leaked, fuelling the *Earth for Humans Movements* assertion that the Antarctic find was a plague pit. The events of 1993-2006 were for them a reconnaissance, a sign of plans being made. It was absurd but, like all good stories, it appealed to a mood of fatalism.

The existential threat of sterility unleashed new horrors; initial denials by governments proved useless since of course by now everyone had heard of the empty paediatric wards, the still births and the deformities. Women were kidnapped and live babies when found were horded away. Abortion was made a criminal act across most of the old democracies. There were lurid stories of fertile men being imprisoned and used for breeding. Underground clinics proliferated. Already undermined by the pandemic, governments struggled to contain panic and outline policies. Many turned to 'voluntary' donations of egg and sperm cells to store until a cure could be found. Under increasing pressure, I was reassigned to head up clinical trials to find the cause of this mysterious and fatal blight, working out of New York, under the vague direction of the UN and WHO. In January 2022, after a dismal winter stuck in downtown Manhattan, I had the privilege of meeting Dena Small. I recalled her from the debriefing sessions of 2006 and was struck by her warmth and interest in me after all these years. We had all managed to defy snow and storm surges and get to New York for an emergency brief with the US President and a special meeting of the UN security council to discuss a global response to the fertility crisis. Dena was still in charge of the skinks but confessed it was not long now before UNCSAC would be moth balled if not closed completely. 'We have more terrestrial concerns to deal with.' She had sounded resigned, almost defeated. I asked her about the Antarctic find and whether she believed there was any connection to the virus; a stupid question, like asking whether the Earth was flat.

'Well it's a bit beyond my expertise, Jamie; more yours or your mothers. The whole story is fake, yet the more we deny it the more it is believed. Myself and your stepfather visited the site; the remains in the ossuary were not just completely fossilised, they had been compressed by millennia under ice. Nothing could have survived. And no one working on the case had any contact with Hong Kong. What do you think?'

The presence of Julian Grey in Antarctica surprised me almost as much as my question; partly because I had no recollection of him going, but mostly because I could not imagine him flying all that way. There had been recent cases of anthrax being released from the exposed carcases of woolly mammoth in Siberia, but these creatures had died within the last 70,000 years and in conditions that had preserved tissue and skin. Moreover, a bacillus was considerably more robust than a virus. It had been a stupid question.

'Besides, I was there explicitly to look for any signs that might signal danger or a warning.' Dena had added, 'I'm a cryptologist remember!'

As she stood to leave, she said something that implied she thought I knew far more than I did.

'I know pretty much for a fact that Samuel Davies is funding *the Earth for Humans* madness, and most of this lie came from him. I told Julian back in the summer. I just don't understand why, and now he is in the President's cabinet for god's sake!'

I did not have enough security clearance to attend the UN session, but it was clear that drastic remedies were adopted to turn around the inescapable fact that within 75 to a 100 years the human population would drop below the levels required to sustain the species. The scheme to create a human seed bank was adopted, to be stored in specialised facilities and, if necessary, for humans to be bred in vitro. The idea was to create a repository diverse enough to buy time for the discovery of an eventual cure. Constitutional and ethical issues; such as the thorny question as to who owned the germ cells, the donor or the state, were irrelevant given that the courts had been suspended during the worst days of the pandemic. All the permanent members of the UN Security Council agreed to implement similar policies. I heard all this incidentally not from Dena, but from Garen, who I managed to get about twenty minutes with on-line later that evening. How the content of the debate could already be known to him was deeply mysterious, but I tried to make light of it. Before we lost the connection, Garen also informed me that the British government had devolved power in the UK to five regional commands for the duration of the crisis. The Prime Minister was to address the nation at 8 am the next day, no doubt to inform the public about the new policy on harvesting fertile haploid cells.

I was staying over on 73rd E street for the night before heading home to the UK. My mother, with Julian's help and no doubt that of his former wife, had secured me passage out on a military transport plane – there were no civilian airlines running at all by now. Manhattan had the semblance of a city slowly returning to normal, despite the bitter cold, despite the wrecks of cars and burned out apartment blocks off to either side of Fifth Avenue and the flooded spectacle of the UN Plaza. I felt numbed and fatalistic as I walked down the snow trenched walkways. Later, aroused by the sight of Garen sitting naked in all his glory, I met up with a guy at a gay bar in the East Village. We went back to his place, a still relatively intact apartment overlooking the empty and unlit expanse of Brooklyn bridge. The sex was desperate and rather bestial but therapeutic. He had been in the Army engineer corps and was trying to find the rest of his unit. Jed's body was veined and tough and smelt of gasoline and sweat. I played with his dog tags as I contemplated the end of the world, how it would play out exactly: no more young men, declining levels of testosterone, the eventual collapse of internet porn; a gay man's dystopia.

We fell asleep under a mountain of blankets until, at about two a.m. – six hours before I was to get escorted to a military base and sent home – I awoke in searing pain. We were spooned together in a ball, gummy with shared body heat, although outside the room was probably -12 C and falling. My initial thought was that I had been stabbed. The dark warm fug of the blankets was lit up with a livid, twisting brilliance and it was only as I lay writhing on the floor, with Jed scrambling to help me, that I saw my old wound was glowing, pulsing from within like a clenched hand opening and closing. It strobed Jed's handsome, stubble coated face as he coaxed me to lie on my side, exploring the scars with unlooked for tenderness. The pain ebbed, the blue-green light dimmed to a blood red shimmer and then stopped completely. We lay stunned, leaning into each other as if we had fallen. I knew instinctively that Max was back. The thought rushed up on me, stinging my face and chest with excitement, perhaps even panic. When Jed finally spoke, he was looking at his hand on the side of my lower torso. 'You're the guy who got shot in 2006? The guy with the alien. I've read stuff about you.'

'Really? It was well over a decade ago, and most of the accounts were bollocks.' I was sitting on the edge of the bed, holding my side although the pain had gone completely.

'Shall we get you to a doctor?' Jed sat at my feet. Military tattoos and mysterious insignia slid and rolled over his smooth muscled shoulders and forearms.

'No, it's fine now – I'll check it out when I get back.'

Jed rose and sat down next to me, thigh to thigh, his arms back. 'I'm guessing you know what it means?'

I nodded my head without looking at him. 'Yeah, I think I do.' My lips and mouth were dry. Jed was watching me intently.

'You think the aliens are back?'

My silence was confirmatory. Jed whistled through his teeth. 'That's kind of weird. I read a blog recently about that, about the aliens returning.'

I half heard, my mind elsewhere; fogged by tiredness, bewilderment; residual lust. Jed leaned back and fumbling under the bed, produced a brandless packet of cigarettes and lit up. 'He claims to know you, incidentally.'

'Who?'

Jed laughed not unkindly, shaking me gently. 'The guy who writes this blog.'

Through a kaleidoscope of images and emotions I thought of Dena's curiously oblique reference to Davies; a name still notorious in the Grey-Relph household.

'I doubt it. The whole cult is just another form of fascist tribalism; even the title *Earth for Humans* has a sort of Nazi ring to it.'

Jed blew plumes of blue-grey smoke from his nostrils. 'Not those fuckers, this is another group.'

'Which one?' I had not kept track of the proliferating blogosphere; it was too full of hate and hedonism.

'I'll show you if the internet is up. Hold it. It's kind of cool.' He leaned over to the bedside lamp, clicked it; his torso beautifully bunched to one side as he stretched towards the bedside lamp. The light blinded us. 'We have power!' He retrieved a smart phone lying face down on the floor. I leaned in, waiting for it to connect, listening to his long dark fingers flicking over the on-screen keys. 'Here: have a look.'

The blog's homepage was a stunning photo of Max, taken just after he had come out of hospital in 2006. Unprepared for it, the image shocked me. It must have been taken about May – one of the last photos that Jonathan took, and it was one of the many images I had spied Julian trying to burn on that fateful evening in the back garden of Farndon Road. I took the phone out of Jed's palm. The blog was called *The Reconfigured Man*. Stubs of sub-menus were situated down the left side of Max's beatific, watchful face: *blogs, devotees, news, events.* Under devotee were endless thumbnails of slim, wide eyed young people, mostly men, stripped down to the waist and staring blankly from the screen.

'This is definitely a cult!'

The images were oddly unsettling; the testimonies spoke of abductions and sex and *revelation*. I skimmed through one post; ten days old, talking about the emergence of 'fused identity' and the coming reconfiguration of the human body through the union of human and Seeth. I thought it obvious rubbish, a pastiche of hallucinatory ideas stoked up by the fear of extinction, but professional in its own way, glossy, footnoted to 'references' which gave it the sonorous air of an academic article. One of the stubs linked to a paragraph on the power of the male orgasm led to a piece on accelerationism, a term I was then unfamiliar with. Female orgasms seemed irrelevant.

'I've never come across anything or anyone remotely connected to this!' I scrolled down a disturbingly long list of members; some had tattooed themselves with the speckled bands seen on Max in the final few hours.

Jed stubbed out his cigarette and rubbed my neck. 'I wouldn't call myself a devotee, but I do kind of like some of the images!'

'Yeah, I can see! So, who is the guy who runs this?' I looked down to the bottom of the last blog. The name was set in smaller text than the rest and italicised. *Garen Lane*. Jed saw my expression change.

'You know him?'

'Yeah.' My mind was blank. 'It's my boyfriend.' Jed had gone to laugh, impressed by what he initially took as a prime example of British irony. When he saw my face he stopped, his mouth frozen.

I tried to contact Dena Small, but it was impossible. Someone in her office said she had been called away in the early hours of the morning and I took this as quiet confirmation that Max had indeed returned. The arrangements to get me home were chaotic but ultimately successful. The British consular office in New York passed me over to a NATO unit leaving from Long Island 'for Europe'; a vague term in the context of Britain's departure from the EU. To my civilian eye something seemed wrong; but after several delays I was packed into a Hercules transport plane, surrounded by crates of heavy equipment, and watched over by a clutch of smooth faced, curious men bundled up with kit and equipment. They seemed to me ridiculously erotic, like action dolls, and incredibly young. Three had been posted overseas before, but the rest were basically raw recruits. I was referred to throughout the endless, cold flight as 'Doc' and quizzed quite knowledgably by many of them. We landed in Iceland, circling over Keflavik in great wide sweeps. Lined up below was an impressive armada of huge transport planes, grey-green, massed like insects.

As soon as the plane was down, the soldiers disembarked, cheery and bright eyed, spilling briskly across an airfield obliterated by fog on some mysterious purpose. Ground crews swarmed into the plane to unload and reload before we continued to Brize Norton. By the time we landed in Oxfordshire I had lost all track of time, numbed and fuzzy from what later turned out to be a fifteen-hour journey. I tried to call various people; Garen, my mother, Julian; but the reception was too weak, and the phone battery then typically died. I tracked down the base commander to request a lift to London, shouting over the thundering, whomping buzz of Atlas planes taking off above us. Dusk was falling. After some officious irritation at my presence he became suddenly apologetic and asked me my name.

'Ah yes – yes: that man over there.' He had pointed across the concrete apron to a grey citron parked up next to a hanger. 'He's been waiting for you for some time.'

I slung my bag over my shoulder and walked towards my lift. As I drew close I recognised Jonathan standing by the passenger door, wearing a long grey coat over a hoodie and a torn pair of jeans.

'Finally! Where the fuck have you been!'

'I took the long way around – and am I glad to see you!'

We stared at each other. I could make out the freckles on the tops of his ears and over the bridge of his nose, vivid in the chill.

'Is he back?' My voice faltered. Jonathan, not a tactile man in normal circumstances, walked over and hugged me, his lips close to my ear.

'He is indeed. He's with Dan Lockwood.'

'He turned up in the wood?'

'Yep, his favorite place. How did you know?' Jonathan let go slowly, pecking my cheek. I could smell his smell, weed, a strangely pungent aftershave, soap.

'The old war wound – the gun shot – it lit up like a Christmas tree.'

Jonathan's eyes narrowed; a sign he was both impressed and taken by surprise. 'Ah, ok. I hadn't thought of that.'

'And you – how did *you* know?'

'Usual juju; I saw the wood suddenly, like a hallucination; it literally leapt out at me. Come on, get inside.' He swung the passenger door open. 'Before that commander tows us.'

Jonathan started the engine, easing his foot on the accelerator to rev the engine gently. 'I don't think Max is alone, either.'

'What do you mean he's not alone – you just said he was with Daniel - what's going on?' I looked across the airfield, the lumbering transport planes rolling forward, their high shouldered wings lined with propellers like wind turbines. It had not occurred to me to think why there were so many, either here or in Iceland, or where they were leaving to. We passed under a red and white barber's stick of a security barrier. Suddenly it all seemed ominous.

'Jonathan?'

'Relax. Max arrived at about 9 pm yesterday evening, dropped into the wood. Around the same time there were numerous UFO sightings across Scotland as well as southern Europe, China and Australia. All in all, six landings have been confirmed. There could well be more; since the pandemic, the deep space network has been patchy at best, and many states are no longer sharing information with UNCSAC. Julian had already left for Edinburgh before I got Daniel's phone call, but I am pretty sure Julian's worked out that Max is back. I've been trying to get hold of Margaret.'

I swallowed hard. 'Has Julian gone with an UNCSAC team?'

'Yeah, Dena winked him out of retirement. She is on her way with him.'

'I met her just the other day – in New York!'

'Really?'

I watched the hedges rush by, the roads empty for the most part but in some places partly blocked by storm debris, branches and rubbish. As always, I was both impressed and intimidated by Jonathan's information, mystified as to how he acquired it. His tone was an attempt at neutrality, casual interest, but it warned me that I was being excluded from something.

'She told me that she had visited Antarctica with Julian; to investigate the alien site – which was obviously untrue, since Julian would never fly that far.'

'Well he might have done.' Jonathan sounded evasive; evidence I suspect that he knew. 'You ok?'

'Yeah sure – sorry – I'm feeling a bit sketchy.' I changed the subject. 'Do we know which *version* of Max is back; our Max or the lizard Max?'

'It's our version of Max, in fact..' Jonathan's voice faltered, his eyes shifting to his wing mirror. I was bemused by the pause.

'In fact?'

He glanced at me sideways again, the fingers of his right hand drumming the steering wheel.

'He's still eighteen.'

I didn't understand at first, assuming that Jonathan was using a metaphor, a reference to reassure me. It was only when he said it again that the penny dropped.

'You mean he hasn't aged?'

'Exactly. Daniel is quite sure, his eyes are weird, and he has the tats and a few shoulder bumps but essentially no scales or tails, and lots of muscles so yes – our Max is back. Dan has been trying to pump him for information but without much success. *Why* Max's return has coincided with the Seeth landings is the million dollar question. I had always assumed that if the experiment succeeded, Max would just return alone.'

'Could it be that the experiment failed?'

'All this looks different from 1993; no one saw anything land then, not even as the children were abducted. This time round, shit loads of people saw them. If we had any news media running, they would be swamped already with all those grainy dash cam and mobile phone videos! Perhaps we never really understood what the experiment was for?'

I sat listening, sieving through the information, arranging it. I had waited as patiently as I could since 2006 because I believed that when Max returned it would be over; all the alien stuff put aside, the new Seeth hybrids happily restored to their planet, and Max back with us. He would be different of course, as would I; but we would resume our friendship, freed now hopefully of my obsession with him. Now it felt like something else was happening, a beginning, with Max suddenly sixteen years younger than me and part of some wider, alien arrival. As we drove into the ochre browns and greys of the Midlands, a long distant curve of planes filed off into the lowering sky behind us. I felt a sudden dread.

'Don't overthink this, Jamie. We'll know soon enough. Perhaps they've come back to thank us for helping them, or perhaps they've turned up to help us: fuck knows we could do with it.'

'Perhaps they've come to donate semen.' I said, deadpan. Jonathan snorted a laugh and then grew serious.

'So, I gather from the US announcement on harvesting, no one at the CDC or WHO is nearer a cure?'

I nodded. The heat in the car was making me sleepy, and I could still feel the ghostly slip and tilt of the plane as it had started its final approach. I felt nauseous and hungry. 'We've haven't the faintest clue where to start. We're dealing with that most evil of bio-chemical phenomena; a syndrome.'

'A concurrence of factors without any obvious causal relationships?'

Despite my tetchiness I smiled. 'Clever and handsome, Jonathan. Exactly. In fact, some of the disputes mirror the old controversies between HIV and AIDS, and the conviction amongst some pathologists that the HIV virus was not the cause of AIDS. In this case, antibodies to the HN71 virus are present in around 80 percent of those patients diagnosed as infertile: but there is a significant incidence of sterility in people who were never ill. The causes of infertility are also bewilderingly varied to be tracked back to one discrete pathogen. We have had some success reversing it in women, where the trigger appears to be an excess production of follicle stimulating hormone – but in men the damage appears to be to the cellular structure of the sperm itself.'

'And in plain English, Jamie?'

'Sperm cells contain numerous mitochondria; the power that drives the cell to the egg: in all the samples taken from infertile men the sperm have none.'

Jonathan pulled a face. 'You mean it's not so much they're firing blanks as not firing anything at all?'

'Basically. I've seen something like it before – dioxins can cause malformed sperm and can also affect the endocrine system and hormone production: but none of the patients show abnormal levels in their bloodstream. My suspicion is that we are dealing with long term exposure to man-made industrial pollutants but that is not a popular view now: most of the scientists I have been working with want a straightforward diagnosis with a quick fix. Artificial insemination might prove useful in the short term, but I have my doubts.'

We moved through an eerie landscape of growing darkness. The anthropocene's hallmark of light pollution; the bluish haze over cities and towns had gone with the first mandatory power cuts over two years ago. Night had returned as a primordial entity, absolute and annihilating. We were heading out towards the M42 having passed about four cars since we left the airbase. 'Garen told me the Prime Minister was going to make an announcement this morning on the fertility crisis – what did he say?'

Jonathan was lost in thought, looking at the arc of light thrown forward by the car.

'What? Oh, he didn't say anything. Our boyish PM sent out some unknown newsreader to announce the landings. No doubt he'll follow the Americans on 'harvesting' later – I hate that word by the way. How did Garen know?'

'I'm not entirely sure. We need to talk about Garen at some stage. I think I might have seriously under-estimated him.'

I saw Jonathan cast his eyes over me quickly and then return his concentration to the road. 'I doubt that, Jamie: he's mostly dick and no brain.'

'Let's just say I discovered he's the creative genius behind a rather bizarre website. We can leave it at that – I don't think it's a hanging offence, but he clearly helped himself to photos of Max – some of the ones you took, and I kept. He seems preoccupied by a particularly homoerotic version of God.'

Jonathan said nothing for a moment. I thought this surprising given his dislike of Garen. Again, my paranoia, of being out of some intimate loop, itched inside my chest.

'God in a jock strap?'

'Yeah. He's been running a website called the reconfigured man, it's basically about Max and aliens, and from what I saw, a lot of weird shit about a new humanity, minus the women I think, or at least women who don't look like boys– I lost the will to read any more once I found his name. A friend had mentioned it.'

Jonathan nodded and parried the topic. 'Well as you say, we'll have to talk about Garen at some stage, but I think the biggest issue is the Earth for humans brigade; there's a rumour that they've started a militia.'

'Perfect! Just what we need – more men with guns. I think we need to talk about a great deal, Jonathan, but let's get to Leicestershire before we start.'

Catching my tone, Jonathan glanced at me and pressed his lips together tentatively but wouldn't be drawn. I was too exhausted to have what would be an argument; too volatile at the prospect of seeing Max again; we implicitly acknowledged a truce.

'Try and get some sleep Jamie; you look exhausted. I don't want Max thinking I've tired you out.'

We merged with the M42 in total darkness. The only traffic we saw were rows of abandoned cars shoved off into the shoulder, many charred and blackened, others already rusting, leaves and debris heaped over windscreens. Free of working speed cameras and police patrols, Jonathan put his foot down. As I fell into a light, ambient sleep I thought briefly of a world we had all taken for granted; computerized, mechanized, lawful even if at times pedestrian, bleached of imagination; but a world of certainty and predictability; safe too if you were the right colour and lived in the right place. Within two and a half years this world had vanished almost without trace. At one stage Jonathan pulled off under a bridge to refuel the car. He had gasoline in the boot and stood filling up the tank with me keeping watch. It was dark and stormy; the wind moaning fitfully under the concrete pylons. Water sluiced down from the road above. We climbed back into the warm fug of the car, Jonathan smelling of petrol. Wisely, he left the pre-rolled spliff behind his right ear unlit.

'Not far, Jamie.'

Chapter Two: Julian Grey.

The helicopter shimmied and lurched over the loch, conveying to Julian's stomach the sensation of being in an elevator. He looked sideways to where Dena sat, bundled up in what appeared to be an army greatcoat, reading a pre-apocalypse copy of *Vogue*. He had not seen her for many years and even now was not convinced that she was here. There was another lurch; an incoherent apology from the pilot shouted above the noise and rattle, and Julian eyed the absurdly small vomit bag with studied resentment and closed his eyes. Only the prospect of Max's return could have dragged him out of Oxford. Margaret had wisely chosen to stay behind.

'Julian, relax: this is nothing compared to a twelve-hour flight over the pond in a military transport!'

'I'll take your word for it, Dena. Sorry.'

He gathered his strength and peered out. They were skirting the northern edge of Loch Ness heading in roughly an easterly direction. Glimpsed through shredded fog and low cloud, the black waters were mirror still, lined by white threads of current. Dena folded the magazine and put it down the side of her chair.

'I'm sorry about Jamie; I had no idea he didn't know. Perhaps he didn't pick up on anything.'

'It's alright, Dena: if this is indeed what we think then it will make no difference, besides this is on me and Jonathan. We both decided to keep him out of any Seeth work – he took Max's departure hard, harder than the rest of us; I didn't want him getting involved before he had to.'

'Well he is heavily involved with the fertility crisis – he has some disturbing theories all of his own and he thinks that the current US policy is pointless.'

Beyond the long wide finger of peaty water, Julian spied a road and the beginnings of high moorland; further north high purple mountains marched off into the gloom, their peaks lost in thick cloud. It was intensely cold. 'If the Seeth are indeed back, and in numbers, what can this mean?' asked Dena.

'It means we got something wrong, somewhere.'

Julian willed himself to relax; cupping the hope that somewhere below Max was back and willing life into the idea so he could actually see his son in his mind's eye, standing tall and dark with his arms outstretched. But his thoughts ran on to his nemesis, Samuel Davies, and the odd developments of the last few years. Julian disliked coincidences, they made bad science and led to bad decisions. After 2006 Davies had vanished, reportedly arrested by the US authorities and his lab had been closed. Louis DeMarr died on the eve of Max's departure, and then James DeSilva had died in a car crash in 2009. The old conspiracy around the children had been broken and the emergence of a new UN commission answerable to the general secretary seemed to bode well for future transparency. Yet it had not lasted. Even before the discovery of the Antarctic artefact, there was a rumour that Davies was out and to some extent rehabilitated. The sudden outbreak of the HN71 pandemic further revived his reputation and his access to funding, and then had come the allegations that the virus had originated from tissue samples removed from the Antarctic site. Despite being a blatant fabrication, there had then emerged a website linked to a series of social 'activists' who claimed that the Seeth had never left Earth and had indeed been here all along, tirelessly working to take the planet from us. Insidiously linking hysterical accounts of sightings with his previous obsession with alien invasions and biological attacks, Davies seemed to have masterminded a coup. By 2021, even as the pandemic seemed contained at last, political movements emerged demanding action to safeguard human society from 'alien occupation'. And a year later – the aliens appear to have arrived.

'I challenged him every step of the way.' Dena said eventually, as if reading Julian's thoughts. 'Even as they stripped away my budget;

not one piece of evidence, just the old obsession. I doubt he ever read a damn thing UNCSAC published! Davies isn't a prophet – he just stuck to his old obsession until the Seeth returned to vindicate him.'

Julian nodded; his face twisted to watch the shoreline slip under them. 'Well, let's see what we can see, Dena. The fact that he is still alive when so many good people have perished is bewildering.' Julian had met Davies once, around 1996 when DeMarr was dragging him about Oxford like a personal trophy. He must have then been in his seventies at least. The helicopter bobbed playfully and then clearly started its descent.

'So UNCSAC have jurisdiction here? Have the Scots played up at all?'

Dena pursed her lips. 'We'll have to play it by ear. Logistics are poor and we only have a few operational assets – we've had to let national agencies investigate the other sightings and just hope they call them in. The Scottish government will cooperate if the English stay out, but since they still claim sovereignty here, I doubt they'll stay out for long: it depends on what we find, of course.'

'I think I'll just keep quiet!' Julian had turned now to have a better look at the landing site. Something had clearly come down on the north side of the loch, having cleared the Perth A road and the first low hills of the Invermorriston estate. A ridge of pines had taken a direct hit and from the air Julian could see a deep black gash in the treeline and then slightly beyond, a cairn of rubble still smoking in the morning gloom. Debris – strangely white and vivid from the air – lay scattered on the ground and as they closed in, he could make out groups of people, a yellow earthmover and a series of dun green military vehicles. One had UN stencilled prominently on its roof. A tarmacked area emerged almost below them; cluttered with soldiers. Julian saw under the nearby trees a collection of wooden chalets, probably the old estate office, and what appeared to be some guest lodges set back at right angles. The ground closed in and a man, gesticulating wildly with two fluorescent sticks in each hand, made a cutting motion with one hand. The helicopter bumped down, whining and shuddering as the engine slowed.

With evident relief, Julian dropped out of the craft and instinctively bent down as he scrambled towards a middle-aged man in uniform and two female civilians. Dena, diminutive and almost rhomboid in her thick coat, followed bear like. The man in uniform stood forward, initially mistaking Julian as the head of the UN commission. There was a moment of indecision until Dena took charge, sticking her hand out; her greying hair frizzed and mobile under the slowing blades.

'Major Sinclair – head of operations; and this is Emily Long of the Scottish government. With her, is her *British* – counterpart, Linda Bowen.' Sinclair did a half-hearted salute. Emily shook Dena's hand warmly and then took Julian Grey's with less enthusiasm. Linda somewhat glacially did the same; clearly all was not well. Since the first major crisis the situation north of the border had been complicated by Edinburgh's unilateral declaration of Independence in 2020 and the co-opting of most of the British civil service and the British army stationed in the lowlands. A majority of the regiments had been locally recruited but the staff officers were all English; obviously Sinclair, and there had clearly been a recent disagreement over protocol. The air was thick with tension.

'Very good to meet you, and many thanks for getting here so promptly. I appreciate the difficulties, but since we're all still in NATO and all signatories of the UN, let's all put our shoulder to the wheel.' Dena straightened her hair as Sinclair, appreciative of her tact, led the way towards the estate office which Julian now saw was, somewhat incongruously, a former giftshop. Inside, the counters and displays of stuffed Loch Ness monsters and Scottish tartan had been cleared away and great banks of computer monitors blinked in anticipation.

'So, Major – is it safe to proceed to the site immediately?'

'It is ma'am. Your team is up there now. The initial assessment shows little or no risk; no radiation and no biohazard. We are expecting a mobile lab at any moment since we don't necessarily want to move anything.' Sinclair glanced sheepishly at Emily, who looked stoically into the middle distance.

'Excellent. Have we established communication with New York yet?'

Sinclair looked somewhat crestfallen. 'We're having a few problems, but we should get through shortly.'

'It's the bandwidth; we don't have nearly enough.' Added Emily cryptically. They all moved at once. Julian followed alongside Linda as they started to walk up a drive and into the tree line. Yellow tape closed off the verges and small plastic numbers appeared next to the small white debris that Julian had spied earlier. The air was resinous with pine and as the road snaked and climbed, Julian saw that thick mats and veils of lichens and mosses coated the branches, bearded and grey like seaweed. After ten minutes or so they came to a sharp, steep bend where the trees had been snapped back with sudden force; a deep furrow line veered off into a small rise and a white tent had been hastily placed over an object buried in the hillside. A grey mass – not unlike a boulder – rose out the rear of the canvas.

'What are we looking at?'

Sinclair paused, indicating that they were to leave the road. 'Mind your footing. This is the outer casing of an object that landed here about fifteen hours ago; the impact crater is surprisingly slight, evidence probably that it was on a controlled descent.'

'Propulsion?' Dena asked carefully.

'No obvious engines – it might have been assisted by some sort of parachute. It's all too early to say.'

Dena clicked the top of her mouth with her tongue thoughtfully. 'Any telemetry?'

Sinclair pulled a face. 'Not as yet. We have virtually no network in this sector. It appears to have come in from the north Atlantic. If the other objects conform to this, then it might well be they were all in a similar orbital trajectory, but it's anyone's guess at this stage I'm afraid.'

Several people in white isolation suits were moving about the impact site. Dena toed shards of the white material scattered in the dead bracken.

'What is this?'

Someone came out of the tent and seeing the party outside, peeled back their respirator.

'We're not sure yet. It looks like some sort of ceramic – it's quite harmless.' The man – dark skinned, youngish, smiled as Dena looked at his suit, frowning. 'It's ok, we just like dressing up! Victor Lall – we met in Antarctica.'

'Of course – I didn't recognise you!' Dena visibly relaxed. She introduced Julian but ignored the others.

'Probably some kind of heat shielding. Come, you'll want to see these.' Victor lifted the tent flap. The two civilians paused alongside Sinclair back on the road, seeming reluctant to proceed any further. Julian and Dena walked forward looking at the ground and then stooped to go inside, walking into the end of an elongated egg-shaped object, the top of which had come away on impact. Lying on the floor were three silver grey cylinders, about eight feet long and about three feet in diameter, snub nosed, secured to the bulkheads of the ship by what appeared to be brackets. Julian paused before slowly extending his hand and touching one. It was warm, slightly moist; he left a handprint on the wet surface. Dena, practical as ever, removed her mobile phone and using it as a torch, examined them closely.

'Metallic?'

'No. My guess is that it's some form of organic compound, probably the same as we found in the artefact all of those years ago.'

'Ribose?'

'In part, possibly. The arrangement of the carbon is not to say unusual, but here; look at these.' Victor crouched down next to Dena, guiding her light to the end of the cylinder where three distinct grooves appeared incised into the base of the object; the middle shorter than the other two. Julian saw Dena's face change; tense with excitement. She had waited sixteen years for this. She shook her head gently.

'It's unbelievable.'

Julian tapped the cylinders, chilled a little by their appearance. Victor fished about in a pocket on the inside of his suit and produced a stethoscope. 'There's a cardiac rhythm in all of them; very faint.' Julian looked horrified; intuitively thinking of Max sealed up, but Dena patted his arm affectionately and Victor, seemingly oblivious to his distress, put the earpieces of the stethoscope over Julian's head.

'Don't be alarmed. It's clearly some sort of suspended animation; the pulses are slow – under 5 beats a minute – no sign of stress. I suspect the cylinders are full of fluid. We're going to get them down below once the lab is functional.'

They contain bodies; Julian thought slowly, tracing out the words in his mind, but bodies of what? He looked at Dena, her eyes wide in the gloom, glancing about, trying to take it all in. This is not how he had expected it to happen. Somehow Julian had anticipated a re-run of the return of the abducted children in 1993; the sudden appearance of the Seeth without any obvious technology or instrumentation. There was a movement at the tent flap and Sinclair's head appeared, his officers cap askew.

'Sorry to disturb, but we've finally got New York – they're confirming six landings.' He glanced down at the cylinders. For a moment Dena did not react and then, with sudden resolve, she placed her hand on Victor's arm.

'We need to get these objects in an isolation unit. Do you have anything you can add at this stage Victor?'

The young biochemist ran a hand somewhat proprietorially across the nearest cylinder. 'I think we need to move them quickly. There is some obvious exothermic reaction taking place, probably following their exposure to the air. We should try for a level four biohazard containment protocol, but we won't have such a facility here. The best we can muster is a level two.'

'Where is the nearest lab?' Julian spoke slowly.

'We'd have to move them to Edinburgh, but I don't think we'll have time. I think we'll just have to improvise.'

'OK, improvise – I don't think the British will like us going to Edinburgh.' Dena walked out and headed for the road. Sinclair was standing slightly back from the tent flap, his arms folded in the small of his back. Julian stayed for a while, watching Victor examining the brackets that held each cylinder in place, until turning and walking out into the clearing morning. Sunlight was catching the tops of the broken pines, turning the drapes of moss a bright gold. Sauntering down to the carpark, Julian passed three squaddies pushing metal gurneys up the hill. One had what appeared to be cutting equipment on his back. Above the requisitioned gift shop a chinook helicopter thundered and roared down a heavy payload – probably a generator. Surrounded by the organised chaos of the military, Dena appeared to be in the middle of a protracted argument between Emily and Linda; no doubt over who was going to pay for this. Suddenly exhausted, Julian felt redundant; in the way. Sinclair, sensing something was amiss, walked over to him briskly.

'If you fancy some shut eye, Professor, we're using the chalets – I've billeted you with Professor Small. Nothing much doing until they get the stuff out of the craft.'

Julian smiled, brushing back a wisp of grey hair out of his eyes. Shut eye was just what he needed.

He awoke at just gone 3.30 pm; disorientated and cold. Outside the light was already fading in the folds and pleats of the wooded valleys. Dena was sitting on the opposite bed, a blanket pulled up over her knees, tapping away furiously on a laptop. She peered over her glasses as Julian sat up, stiffly.

'Good timing. You fancy something to eat?'

'Definitely – and some coffee if there's any.'

'That's one thing the army have in spades.' Dena shunted off the bed and walked into a small open plan kitchen, once the preserve of tourists walking and shooting in the glens. She reappeared with coffee and a plate of sandwiches covered in clingfilm. 'Tuna, and tuna.'

'Tuna's good.'

Dena watched him eat. 'The labs up and running by the way; the brackets were easily removed, and Victor thinks we have about two or three hours before the cylinders open. We've got locations now of four other landing sites, but the Russian's are playing hardball and we have no confirmation from China. Presuming they contain the same cylinders, we're looking at eighteen' her voice trailed away, 'eighteen visitors.'

'Any pattern or commonality in the sites?'

'No. At least nothing obvious – they're all pretty unpopulated. One came down in the middle of the Gibson desert in Australia's northern territories – I had to google it!'

Julian chewed thoughtfully, his ears popping. 'Well we planned for almost every contingency except this one!' He smiled, fishing out a mobile and checked for messages. As soon as he could he had texted

Jonathan and then Jamie. Nothing. Margaret had texted to say the BBC had just announced the sightings.

Dena sat back on the bed. 'Any thoughts on what is actually going on here – apart from a level three contact?'

Julian put down the plate and rubbed his hands together vigorously. He looked at Dena affectionately, aware that they had been together at the beginning; she was the first person he had told about Max and the mysterious plates of chromosome 21, driving through the rain to Heathrow in 1993. It seemed infinitely long ago in a world that had inexplicably vanished before their eyes.

'If we base these events on what we *think* we know; it's a good bet that the experiment has managed to hybridise the repaired Seeth genome with Max as the human donor. The cylinders probably contain hybrids, but why they have returned to Earth, and not Tau Ceti as we supposed is unclear.'

Dena sighed, looking thoughtfully out into the dusk. 'To be honest I was never entirely convinced of the Tau Ceti thesis: despite managing to persuade NASA to send up some very expensive probes, there is way too much debris around the star – why escape one meteorite impact to suffer a lot more! And the only testimony came from Jamie and even he said Max had sounded unsure. Drake had exhausted Tau Ceti as a possible source of extra-terrestrial intelligent life as long ago as the early 1960s. It made no sense to me given the probability that the Seeth could have settled somewhere in the same solar system – god knows they had the technology.'

There was a knock from the porch and Julian, lost in thought, jumped slightly; much to Dena's amusement. She walked over and opened the door; peering into the face of Sinclair who was standing, a cane in his hand, the wide collar of his coat pulled tightly around him.

'Dr Lall would like you to join him in the lab.' Sinclair's voice was tight. 'And there is something else I'm afraid.'

Julian was pulling on a coat but caught the tone, glancing across at Dena. 'And what's that?'

Sinclair held back the outer screen door as the two scientists emerged into a deepening fog, sleet spitting fitfully about them. 'We've just managed to receive a message patched through from NASA, it's from the ISS.'

'We still have people up there?' Dena sounded incredulous. Arch lights had been placed around the giftshop, and a solid white prefabricated building had appeared attached to one side. There seemed many more soldiers and Julian noticed back down the road towards the loch a barrier had appeared. A group of people, muffled up against the cold, were standing about taking what appeared to be the odd selfie.

'We do. Apparently, there are still four astronauts – one has been up since 2018, which is of course a record. ESA managed to get a supply vessel to the station before the epidemic broke off communications, and NASA managed to resupply late last year: but they've had a rough time to say the least. The fact is they have identified a large object moving into earth orbit – they're sending data now but of course it's anyone's guess when we get it.'

'More cylinders?' Julian asked, glancing again at the roadblock and at the people gathering. It seemed unlikely to be the press.

'No – it's much larger than the craft that came down here. Several times larger than the ISS; apparently triangular in shape. The US want it all kept under wraps for now.'

'Quite.' They walked into the improvised headquarters; throbbing now with activity. Victor waved them over to what was an improvised airlock leading into the lab. The door sealed behind them with a distinct hiss. They pressed through two plastic screens made of interlocking strips before arriving in a wide, evenly lit space containing a separate see through tent situated in the middle of the room with its own dedicated air supply. The cylinders – clearly visible – were resting on the gurneys Julian had seen earlier, each one surrounded by a bank of blinking, anonymous instruments. Julian and Dena peered through, with Sinclair standing a little behind. Victor had been joined by an UNCSAC team made up of one biochemist, one physicist and a woman who introduced herself as an astrobiologist, 'formerly known as an exobiologist – but they keep changing the nomenclature. Debora Ewing.'

'And we're ready to stream this live?' Dena looked at a bank of monitors containing a mosaic of conference calls; some occupied with individuals messing about with earpieces and hurriedly going through notes; others showed empty desks and a variety of national flags.

'Are you sure this is a good idea, Ma'am. We could record and transmit it later?' Sinclair was brushing a small moustache rather whimsically; Dena had not noticed it before.

'I do, Major – if we transmit this later, we shall be accused of a cover-up, and besides if we go public, we might shame some of our international partners to come clean and do the same.'

Julian pressed up close to the inner tent. The cylinders were much changed since he had seen them in the wreckage of the ship. The tops and sides were translucent, showing a mass of dark webbing spooled around what appeared to be a tall humanoid shape. Dena, noticing his anxiety, reached over and rubbed his shoulder.

'Let's just hope they don't explode.' Sinclair added dryly, standing back as both Victor and Deborah climbed into isolation suits, open at the back, and connected to the inner tent on metal runners. They moved forward and thick plastic sheets concertinaed out behind them. A technician checked the Wi-Fi hubs. The tension in the room was palpable. The technician pursed his lips.

'We're running this on what is in effect 3G, it's the best we've been able to rig up.' He addressed Dena in a thick Scottish brogue. 'If we get too many hits the site will crash, so if it looks like that's going to happen, I suggest you allow me to restrict the show to the conference calls?'

'Sure – whatever you think necessary.' Dena stroked her face. 'And whatever we do, don't mention or comment on this object that's appeared in orbit – NASA or someone else can do that – we've got enough to think about. Victor:' she raised her voice 'can you do the honours and narrate?'

She saw the heavily wrapped figure nod.

'That's my boy.'

The webcams filled up with officials; even the Russians had appeared although the Chinese square was blank with 'no connection' flashing fitfully across the bottom. Cameras zoomed in on Victor, who was standing now alongside a cylinder holding what appeared to be a Geiger counter; everything was covered in thick plastic; each control panel and bank of instrumentation, gleaming as if brand new and unpackaged. A white, heavy vapour was cascading from the top of each container, snaking to the floor. Victor spoke calmly into his head mic. Suddenly the lights flickered, and several screens went blank but quickly rebooted. Dena swore under her breath. The top of each cylinder appeared to glow and then disintegrated, forming a coarsely grained white powder blowing down under the ventilation system; three heads, necks and shoulders appeared, seemingly identical but it was hard to see clearly. Julian pressed even closer, screwing up his eyes: the faces appeared male, high cheeked and well boned like marble effigies on a sarcophagus; the foreheads were pronounced, ridged with fine muscles spreading into a faint, blondish hairline. The images were unsettling if not mesmerising; Julian thought he could see a clear resemblance to Max, but again the lights flickered, and the screens dropped off momentarily.

'Victor what the fuck is that!' Dena spoke into a microphone. 'Can you stop that happening?'

Victor mimed a gesture of incredulity; 'it's some sort of electromagnetic interference; we're on it.'

Slowly each cylinder broke down, revealing three bodies that settled evenly onto the gurneys. Their arms were at their side, and despite Victor and Deborah crossing back and forth, the monitors showed clear and powerful musculature; a thick boss of pectorals framed by heavy solid shoulders, the body tapering down through ribbed abdominals to powerful thighs and buttocks. Hesitating slightly, Victor attached several white disc shaped ECG plugs over the bodies and appeared to take their pulse. He began speaking slowly.

'Each subject has a resting pulse of 56. They appear to be in delta sleep.' He leaned in, placing a small thermostat in an ear. 'Their body temperature is 39 C.' Victor glanced down the naked body, removing a smart phone and snapping shots. It struck Julian as insensitive, but the ethics of any examination would only get more complex once they regained consciousness.

'The subjects have – wait – .' there was a pause, a flash from the phone. 'They appear to have no navels and no visible genitalia. Deborah come over here a moment.'

The astrobiologist edged around the nearest gurney and stood next to Victor. On the monitors the assembled authorities of several governments were silent, watching the live feed intently. Victor tapped his visor.

'The neck and shoulders of each subject is covered in what appears to be a find boned cartouche.' The voice was Deborah's. 'A faint exoskeletal structure like cartilage. There is distinct mottling across the top of the pectorals and down the side towards the waist.' She lifted an arm carefully, bending her head to trace the pattern and to direct Victor's phone.

Dena walked and stood by Julian but spoke directly to Deborah. 'You think we should rehydrate them?'

Deborah shook her head. 'No – not until we can test their serum, we might mess up their electrolytes: they look in pretty good shape to me. Definitely humanoid. Seemingly identical. Age is hard to guess but I'd put them in the earlier twenties. And –' she moved what appeared to be a small flat square not unlike a cigarette lighter over each one, starting at the feet, 'they are all 6 ft 6 inches in height.'

A silence fell, the sleepers lay perfect and immaculate; their bodies still except for the visible rising of the chest as they breathed in unison.

'Clones?' Dena asked Julian, quietly; conscious of the pastiche of faces on the monitors behind her.

'Possibly. We know the Seeth were capable of advanced cloning, but I would be surprised if they were genetically identical. When Max departed, he contained millions of hybridised genomes, a majority consisting of 52 chromosomes: humans have 46. We'll have to map their genetic code and compare it with the data we have on Max – but I have little doubt that these, these *people*, mark the successful completion of the experiment.'

Dena shook her head gently, breathing in deeply though her nose. 'Jesus. Ok, guys –do what you have to do to prepare a preliminary report; can you take a tissue sample without a blood test?'

Victor nodded. 'Sure, we can do a cheek swab.'

'Good – I'd rather not stick any needles in them yet, first contact and all that.' She turned again to Julian; he thought she looked tired, on edge. 'If you could suit up and help these guys, your expertise on Max will help speed things up – I'll go field any questions and comments from our gathered diplomats.'

'Good luck with that.'

Dena rolled her eyes and turned to face the various conference calls. The first question came from the Russians who asked for clarification as to whether there were any biohazards; an unanswerable question at this stage, as were most of the others. The Australian authorities confirmed that they had three identical humanoids in an isolation facility in Perth. So far, they remained unconscious. Greece, Jordan, and Thailand also confirmed they were in possession of seemingly identical humanoids all in deep delta sleep. According to NASA data this left one landing and three subjects unaccounted for – presumably in either China or Russia. Julian listened as Dena managed to chair what threatened to become a chaotic and accusatory meeting, conscious that it was also being observed by endless social platforms and media outlets. He was deeply impressed by Dena's ability to stay calm; he recalled her in 1993, hesitant, a little emotional: she had grown into her role. As he stood listening, a technician handed him a white biohazard suit and directed him how to wear it. He was looking at the sleeping forms, searching for Max in each serene face; he could see him everywhere. The technician led him to a third aperture and guided his feet into yet another protective layer of thick plastic. 'Just move forward, Professor – the suit extents out like a corridor – don't yank it.'

Dena eventually wrapped up the conference, ending on a long chat with the acting UN general secretary. Sinclair had stayed throughout, standing stiffly at the back of the room. He seemed troubled. At just gone 11 pm, several hours after the cylinders had disintegrated, Deborah, Victor and Julian went through a decontamination procedure and returned to the main lab. The hybrids were still deeply asleep; something which puzzled Deborah, who have covered each one in a sheet to their chests and placed their heads on plastic covered pillows. Julian left for the chalets, strangely depressed, pulling the collar of his coat up against what was now heavy falling snow. There were still people in the road, and as Julian crossed the car park someone shouted at him.

'They're from God! Leave them alone!'

The voice was strained, youngish. Taken aback, Julian peered into the gloom and the youth shouted again. Two soldiers, situated behind the temporary barrier that sealed off the approach to the lab, moved up and moved the man back. His head bobbed up, calling out his incoherent protest. Julian half turned but then, seething with sudden anger, marched carefully across the freshly drifting snow. The arch lights gave the scene a ghostly, chilly tint of grey; the figures of the youths a rag tag of people in an assortment of coats and blankets, bleached out in the gloom, like a photo negative. There were about eight or ten of them.

'Release them – stop experimenting on them! They've come to save us!'

One of the soldiers, recognising Julian, stood back and then said quietly. 'I'd leave it Professor, we've got this. Just a bit of juvenile excitement.'

Julian had drawn level with the youth, who appeared suddenly indecisive. Julian fought down waves of irrational anger. For a moment he wasn't sure he could speak.

'No one is torturing anyone – did you not watch the process yourself – on your phones!'

'We saw what you wanted us to see, we're not being taken in by this shit. God has sent his angels; you need to let them go.'

Angels. God. Julian's rage boiled up from some deep wound; an inexpressible anger at the boy's stupidity; at not finding Max. It was all he could do to stop himself seizing him by the collar.

'Millions of people have died, but you; you somehow survived. Do you not think you owe it to them to use your intelligence, such as it is, and consider the facts: these visitors have been through an ordeal which saw them suspended in some sort of cryogenic state, and they have yet to regain consciousness after crash landing. Do you understand anything I have just said? They are not angels, and no one is torturing them!'

'Don't fucking patronise us – we know who you are.'

It was almost impossible to see the youth's face in the light. Julian could just make out the top of a shaved forehead exposed by a woollen hood. He looked absurdly young. There was a tattoo or a birthmark on his cheek.

'The world is going to be remade, old man, washed clean.'

'Is that so – then I look forward to watching you all flushed away.' The soldier touched his arm gently.

'Come on Prof, let's get back to the chalet.'

Julian breathed hard; conscious of his behaviour, struggling to make sense of it as much as the youth's strange obstinacy. He half turned and then stopped and said something he had not intended.

'You deserve extinction! All of you – why would God save you!'

The soldiers hand grew firmer on his arm and Julian turned abruptly, wrestling with his own spite. Once in the chalet – blisteringly hot now – he sat on the bed and to his own surprise, sobbed uncontrollably. Dena found him later, his hands pressed hard into his face. She stood for a moment thinking how little she knew him, despite their long years together. After Max had left, and after Julian had retired from Oxford, he had become something of a recluse. His marriage to Margaret had helped in that Dena knew her well and she had often volunteered to work on UNCSAC matters – such as they were, then. But in many ways Julian remained a mystery to her; almost as much as his ex-wife. Dena sat down and with some difficulty, stretched an arm over his shoulders.

'Come on Julian, it's been a surreal day – you're emotionally exhausted – we all are.'

'Sorry – I don't know what came over me.' He removed his hands, his face ashen and tired.

'Sixteen years of waiting is what came over you. I think it's time to take a leaf from the late DeMarr!'

Dena stood up and wrestled with an enormous handbag discarded earlier on her bed. There was a distinct chink and Julian smiled as she produced a bottle of Martel and two rather large shot glasses.

'Dena Small! Is this the secret of your unimaginable tenacity?'

She winked conspiratorially, pleased to see him grinning. 'Actually I miss the old bugger.' There was a satisfying glug and a smell of honeyed vanilla. 'He'd be invaluable now, walking about in one of those ridiculous hats and saying that everything was 'extraordinary!' She raised her glass. 'To Louis!'

Julian tapped his glass to hers. 'To DeMarr – we could do with his indefatigable optimism, that's for sure. You know he left me several boxes of cravats in his will?'

Dena laughed. 'I didn't – do you wear them?'

'No – they were far too flamboyant for me: I gave them to Jamie who sold them on eBay'

'God I miss eBay as well! The last time I used it all you could buy were vaccination kits to save you from the plague – stolen as it turned out from the CDC.'

Feeling calmer, Julian sipped back the cognac. 'So what do we do now?'

Dena stood and pulled up a chair, nursing her drink. 'Well, I've just got off from an interesting chat with the Australian, Greek and Thai governments: Jordan is having connectivity issues. It looks as if they hybrids are all pretty much identical and seemingly male – which is curious. None of them have yet regained consciousness.'

'And what happens when they do? What's the protocol?'

'We try basic communication; mathematics probably, then simple visual prompts, but the fact that they are in effect hospitalised complicates things. Deborah and Victor are working up a short statement, but we'll need to acquire some form of consent to examine them physically if we want to really understand what they are, let alone what they are doing here. And the last thing I want are alien probing stories leaking out!'

'They've already started – as I came out some youths were shouting about angels and god!'

'The camp commander got them moved back down to the A road. First contact of this kind is going to be difficult, Julian – we must accept that. It was going to be hard enough even without the pandemic and the infertility crisis – it's unfortunate that they have arrived now and not five or ten years ago. But – there it is.'

'Any news on this mysterious object? The one reported in by the ISS?'

Dena rolled her eyes. 'ESA and the Russian Space Agency have released photos – NASA haven't said a word, I suspect because what's left of the federal government is breathing down their necks. You'll find this interesting though.' Dena returned to her bed which was a veritable nest of papers, books and print outs. She fished out the laptop attached to a charger and pulled down a pair of glasses from her head.

'It's big – and we've seen something very much like it before.'

Intrigued, Julian leaned in as Dena's hands flashed across the keyboard. A grainy low-resolution photo loaded slowly. Dena angled the screen towards Julian for a better view. The object was a wide triangle, the outer, wider edge slightly curved. It was impossible to judge the scale of the object, or its thickness, but Julian recognised it immediately.

'But how is that possible?' He took the laptop from Dena and held it close to his face. The Antarctic artefact was a wide circular structure consisting of 12 triangles, fitted and jointed almost seamlessly like slices of pie. There had been extensive excavations until the pandemic forced governments to recall their teams, but no instrumentation had been found and nothing by the way of technology. Nor had any sections of the rendered gneiss been missing, but essentially the object now in orbit conformed to the shape almost exactly. It even had the same decorative cartouche around the outer edges of the triangle.

'This is just what we wanted!'

Dena scrolled down. The image had been reposted 1.2 million times from the ESA homepage alone. 'Apparently it appears to be settling into some form of geostationary earth orbit, so whatever it is, it's going to be very visible. You'd think NASA would do their homework. This is just the kind of mess we were supposed to avoid; government denial when everyone on the planet with a smart phone already knows we're lying!'

Julian sat and drained his glass. His mind was blank, foggy. Images – almost memories – ebbed back and forth in disorderly vividness. He found himself wondering if what they were looking at was the experiment itself, finally made manifest, the mysterious implacable force that had searched tirelessly for a donor to repair a destroyed species; a machine – an intelligence – presumably built by Seeth for that sole purpose of resurrection; a force that had outlived its makers. There were two almost instantaneous pings on Julian and Dena's mobile phones. It was an identical WhatsApp message from Deborah: 'come to the lab – the visitors are awake.'

They stood promptly, lost in their own separate thoughts, and stepped out of the overheated chalet into a wall of intense cold. Julian felt suddenly incredibly emotional. Ahead of them, crunching across the rapidly freezing snow, a figure approached them slowly, a small blue torch angled down at their feet. It was Deborah.

'Sorry it's late but I thought you'd want to be there – it's going to be easier than we thought.'

Dena's small figure wobbled and slipped between the two scientists. Julian took her arm.

'In what sense, Debbie?'

'They've come preloaded with the necessary software, so to speak. They speak fluent English and they know all about Professor Grey, you and UNCSAC. They asked to see you both – and I say 'they' literally. They appear to share a telepathic link which makes individualising any of them difficult. Victor named one of them Adam – so we have three Adams!'

Julian steadied himself as they turned into the blue white sheen of light thrown out from the lab. Above, dimly visible through a pale fog, he caught sight of the constellation Orion, glinting brilliantly. He turned to Deborah.

'The name is unfortunate: we should try and avoid anything too biblical – I'll explain later.'

'At least I don't have to brush up on my prime numbers!' said Dena.

As they approached the lab Julian noticed that indeed the road and the barrier were empty, except for several soldiers, clouds of breath pluming from their faces.

The gurneys had been replaced with three folding cots, too short for the hybrids whose wide, pale feet stuck out in perfect symmetry. They were all sitting up and had been dressed, somewhat haphazardly, in green hospital gowns; again, somewhat too small, bunching around their necks and gathered up the thick muscled forearms. The inner tent was still intact but much of the equipment had been removed and as Deborah ushered them in past an armed guard, she commented that only a few precautions remained, mostly for the protection of the hybrids. Victor was nowhere to be seen, presumably having decided to snatch some sleep.

Deborah handed out gauzed masks and unzipped the inner lining, ducking through after Julian and Dena: the complex double skin and separate air filters had already been discarded. 'I'll leave it to you – I'll be hovering if you need me.'

Three youthful, androgynous faces looked at the scientists; the hybrids had a short blush of stubble appearing on their heads, but otherwise appeared to be quite hairless. They were almost mannikin like. Julian stood alongside Dena looking at each face, trying to smile, to look relaxed but his mouth was dry and for a moment he had nothing to say. The hybrid opposite frowned, his brow creasing together briefly in such a facsimile of humanity that suddenly, emboldened, Julian stepped forward and introduced himself and Dena.

'It is a great privilege to meet you both; and we thank you for receiving us. We have been called Adam.'

The three hybrids spoke together, their voices were deep, masculine, but there was an ambiguity to their beauty that seemed accentuated when they spoke. To Julian's irritation he thought of the youth's description of them as angels, shouted out in the darkness like a challenge. It seemed disturbingly accurate. Had he not once likened Max to Ariel?

'The privilege is entirely ours; and we have waited many years for you to visit us.' Dena said carefully, her voice betraying little of her sudden awe.

There was a silence. The three seemed to confer, their heads slightly down, their lips pursed and sometimes animated. The hybrid sitting up on the middle cot suddenly spoke alone.

'We shall have difficulties speaking as individuals for a while; you must – bear with us. There is much we need to discuss.'

Julian caught Deborah shaking her head discretely in the background.

'Of course – but we have plenty of time, and it is important that you rest.'

'We have less time than we believed.' Said Adam, without emphasis, so much so that Julian was not sure he had meant it to sound so ominous. The other two dipped their heads in silent agreement.

Dena pulled up a lab stool and invited Julian to sit, wheeling over for herself a chair from a now empty desk. 'Then let us have a brief discussion.'

'There is, first of all, the matter of the missing three Malaq. We cannot sense or detect them. Do you have any information on their whereabouts?'

Julian glanced across at Dena, who asked politely. 'We are unfamiliar with the term Malaq – is this your designated identity?'

'Yes. We are Malaq, which is a derivation of a Seeth term for hybrid: we are hybrids of Seeth and humans, your son Max is one of our progenitors.' Adam looked directly at Julian.

Julian fought down a sudden impulse to ask about his son.

'Your landings took us by surprise. We have, as you might be aware, experienced a series of –' Julian watched as Dena shifted mentally through various words and expressions; he presumed that Adam was probably as much aware of her thoughts as he was of her actual speech. 'Of catastrophes. These have made many of our people suspicious and uncooperative. We believe that the – the Malaq – are being held, much as you are here, in either the Russian Federation or the Peoples Republic of China: these are geo-'

'Yes, we are familiar with these nations.' Adam interrupted but without any evident impatience. Nonetheless he seemed to sense that he had trespassed on some matter of etiquette. 'Forgive me, I thought it would save time: we have a relatively complete understanding of your history and culture; provided for us by Max; and we were aware of the pandemics. The issue for us, as I am sure you will understand, is to ensure the safety of the pod.'

'The pod?'

'A trinity of hybrids; hatched together –' Adam sensed the confusion, frowning again with elegant simplicity. 'Born together?'

'Not born.' Corrected the hybrid on his right. 'Incubated.' An almost identical face looked with obvious enthusiasm at Julian and Dena.

'Yes, ok – I think I understand. And we attach great importance to their wellbeing as well. UNCSAC is in contact with both the Russian and Chinese authorities; my government and' Dena turned to Julian, 'Professor Grey's government are going to call a meeting of the UN security council.'

The hybrids moved their heads gently. 'We see. But is not the UN, as we understand it, a forum not an agency however, incapable of collective action – do you think this will work?'

Somewhat taken aback, Dena found herself agreeing before adding some necessary caveat. 'I have every confidence that we can get you information in the next few hours and that we can identify their location. Is that acceptable.'

'Yes, it is acceptable. If any harm comes to them, it will complicate the situation.'

'I agree entirely.'

There was a pause; animated by the soft murmur and click of machines. Julian, unable to restrain himself any longer, looked directly at the lead hybrid.

'Do you have any news of my son, Adam? Do you know if Max is alive?'

Adam found the question puzzling; or rather, his brilliant grey eyes narrowed momentarily. The Malaq conferred again in their silent intensity.

'Your son is here, Professor: he is with Daniel Lockwood. He has returned to the place where this began.'

Dumbfounded, Julian let out a small cry, standing abruptly. 'What! But there were no sightings reported over England!'

Adam, aware of the sudden intensity of Julian's feelings, leaned up and reached out a long, toned arm, the hand extended. Almost unconsciously, Julian took it in his, struck by the warm flesh over his own mottled fingers.

'The *Illuvatar* has returned Max in human form, as was required of us. Forgive us, we thought you would know this, although we were surprised to find you here: you must go to him. He will explain what is happening.'

Again, unaware that his use of English conveyed some hidden foresight, an intonation of prophecy, Adam smiled. Dena turned and hugged Julian. 'Go, go now – we can get you a transport! Contact me as soon as you get to Leicestershire.' Dena then looked over to the hybrid.

'What *is* happening, Adam?'

The smile stayed on the lips of the hybrid; pursing them sensuously. For the first time Dena was aware that the wide clear eyes were luminous, laced with different colours ebbing across the iris.

'We wish to return home, Professor Small.'

Chapter Three: Daniel Lockwood.

Driving back from Leicester there is almost a pre-pandemic feel to the journey. The houses that flank the Hinkley Road are free of stacked body bags and someone has removed most of the car wrecks that littered the drives and pavements. I see more people about, hooded up against the sudden, unusual cold and there are even a few shops open; their entrances barred by armed guards from the Territorials, as well as youths wearing blue tunics – some sort of militia or perhaps just special constables. I clatter over the cattle grid with a sense that I have survived, somehow, in some miraculous way and pull up next to the farmhouse feeling emotional; tearful. So many of my friends died that my existence numbs me. There is still several hours of power before the mandatory blackout, so I dress up warm and walk up Brascote lane towards the Windmill pub. As I approach it from the direction of Kirby Mallory the evening comes on quickly. Cold low fog curls up over the hedges and spills over the road. I push open the door to the tap room gratefully. We have all survived, even Marston's bitter, although the Windmill's supplies are long past their sale by date.

The conversation at the bar pauses as head turns and then nod in recognition. Jim Ridgeway is leaning up against the bar, looking already the worst for wear. I dislike him but realise that the last two years have been hard: he lost his wife and three children along with many neighbours and friends from the village. Jim has the bewildered look that many survivors wear, myself included, bewilderment. Leaning next to him is the tall, solid frame of John Gardiner, his back turned to me, playing with his phone. In the last few weeks connectivity of a sort has been restored.

'Come and listen to this, Dan. Jimmy has a real corker of a story!' The landlord – Bertie Pennington – pulls a pint for me as I drag up a stool and sit. He winks as I take the beer, turning to include Jimmy.

'It's not a story, Bert. I was told it by Dave Henson who works for the Blue Jackets. He told me that they are going to start quarantining fertile people.' He lowered his voice. 'They're taking samples.'

I say 'cheers', lifting the glass to the room generally although it is far from crowded. People are still cautious about congregating in public; some people still wear masks. The wind, picking up from the north east, snuffles and ruts about the back of the pub like some forlorn animal. Jim is about as reliable as a deck of Tarot cards, but his tone worries me.

'Samples of what, Jim?'

Jim leans towards me, lowering his head. 'You know – semen and eggs. These Blue Jackets aren't making it up, Dan; it's happening!'

Bert laughs and winks again. Jim scowls and drinks deeply. I notice his right hand is shaking.

'I doubt it Jim; Who are the Blue Jackets?' Instinctively I recall the youths hanging about with the soldiers, smoking; bored but clearly somehow official.

Jim is shaking his head but not in a belligerent way. 'Some new militia the government have drafted in, they're linked to the Earth for Humans Movement. But you don't get it Dan; you don't see. No one is having any babies anymore – not live ones – it's to do with the bug, what they call a side effect. They're testing and taking fertile people into custody.'

There is some derisory laughter. At the far end of the bar the back door opens to a blast of air and Michael Gardiner, John's younger brother, comes in still doing up his flies.

'You look after that tackle, young Michael or they might lock you up for it!' quips Bert. More laughter. At just turned eighteen, Michael is the spitting image of his older brother but prettier, his body tall and well made, still blooming out around his shoulders and chest. The cold has flushed his long, pale face red. He looks down at his groin and removes his hand.

'What's that, now?'

'Nothing Mike, ignore them.' He pushes in between me and his still standing brother.

'Alright Dan?'

'Yeah, can't complain.' I look back at Jim who is chewing his lower lip. There have *been* rumours, lurid accounts of young men and women being taken, and if tested fertile, spirited away. But since the pandemic there had been so many rumours it is hard to keep track. During the initial outbreak there were urban tales of immigrants deliberately infecting people; people being tested on un-trialed vaccines; the classic tropes of fear and loathing. I look at Jim and have a sudden feeling of compassion.

'Don't worry about it Jim, I'm sure it's just a load of balls.'

'And fertile ones at that!' adds Bert to more relaxed laugher. Even Jim smiles weakly. In the silence that falls we all hear a rumble growling in from behind the pub; vague, resonant, close. People look up vacantly.

'What was that?'

The lights flicker and a distinct tremor sets Bert's collection of metal jugs rattling on the shelf above the draught bitters. The ceiling lamps swing, casting arcs of light over my head and back up against the far wall. More flickering and then the power fails, plunging us into darkness.

'For the love of God! We've got hours before lights out!' In the instant pitch dark, I can see the back of John's head lit up by his mobile. For a moment he is distracted by what he is reading.

'John, go see if the village is out or just us, would you? John?'

John looks up at Bertie and seems to notice the power outage for the first time.

'Uh? Yeah – sure.' He stumbles and curses towards the front of the pub, there is the sound of wood scraped hard across tiled flooring. He ducks out into night. Through the open door comes a smell of earth and dampness and the sound of rain striking tarmac hard. I put my pint down carefully, feeling out the top of the bar first with my left hand until my eyes adjust. Jim is trying to call someone on his phone but announces there is no reception. I catch his unshaven face in the phone light.

'Probably those aliens back again, Dan.' Bert's voice carries clearly in the silence. 'And I'm not talking illegal ones either, Jimmy my lad!'

'Now you keep your sarcasm to yourself!'

I can see the silhouette of Jim's hand still trying to make a phone call.

There is a bang from the saloon door and Jenny, Bert's wife, appears holding an electric torch. She is wearing a dressing gown over her clothes. 'What have you done now, Bert Pennington!'

'Nothing my sweet; it will come back on soon I suspect.'

'Not if you've blown something it won't!'

'John's out there now seeing if it's just us, baby – it's fine.'

Michael turns to me. His hair is shaved away from the sides of his head giving him a curiously military profile. 'I didn't get the dick joke, what was that about?'

I pat his knee absent mindedly. 'Forget it, Mike.'

John reappears, stomping water off his boots. 'Yeah, it's not just us. The whole village looks out. Brascote Lane is in total darkness.'

'You think it was lightening?' Jim says, but without conviction. 'You got any candles, Bert?'

John has appeared next to me, looming suddenly out of the dark. I can smell the cold rain on his jacket. The landlord mutters under his breath and starts searching under the counters. John leans down and whispers 'come with me Dan, come out the back.'

His tone is neutral, but his face is tense. I drain my pint and follow him towards the rear exit.

'Where you two off to?' says Michael.

'None of your business. You help Bill find those candles.'

We walk outside, the wind whipping across our faces. I squint into the driving rain. At the rear of the pub I catch sight of the beer garden, chairs turned over and covered for the winter. The toilets are to our right. Somewhere a door is slamming and whining. John is holding his phone up in front of him, scrolling down.

'I don't think there's any reception.' I look at his downturned face, the strong nose and lips. The light casts a bar of shadow over his eyes and forehead.

'Yeah, it's not that Dan; look – it's this.' He passes me the phone. Luckily it's one of the big smart phones released just before all production ceased during the worst days of the pandemic – even I can read the screen. Since 2021 the only media outlet that has remained active is the BBC although there are doubts over its reliability. John is pointing to a red banner, cached before the connection went down, stating that British Prime Minister will be making an emergency statement at 8 am tomorrow.

'People will be expected to cooperate with all announcements.' John reads, frowning attractively, the corners of his lips drawn into a pout that reminds me of his brother. 'What the fuck does that mean? You think Jim is actually onto something?'

'That would be a first!'

There is another distinct tremor. The sensation is weird, a sudden inertial jolt, rocking us forward. John looks up and away, focusing on something behind me. He is looking in the general direction of my own farmhouse, about three fields away to the east. The sky is veined and luminous with light. I catch my breath. To the left, blocked by trees and hedgerows, it pools into a peculiar intense. 'That's your wood, Daniel, and that's not lightening.'

A haze of blue and white glower behind heavy clouds. It is moving slowly downwards, as if descending; landing. The motion creates an illusion of veins cast out, like the rune line of trees and branches, but it could be veins inside my eye; some curious optical illusion. I have a mild sensation of vertigo. Without any electricity, the sky seems especially brilliant and the lights are probably visible for miles. For a moment we both stare in silence. When I look at John, he is looking at me carefully, almost thoughtfully.

'Did you bring a car, John? I left mine back at the house and walked.'

'Sure. You want a lift? Come on.' He pulls a hoodie over his head and strides out towards a battered Toyota truck, the flatbed littered with building materials; a stepladder hangs out of the back with a red cloth tied to the end. He climbs in, turning the engine and opening the passenger door. 'You think this is a good idea?'

'No but let's go mate; I'm suffering from a distinct attack of déjà vu.'

Someone shouts behind us, and in the glare from the headlights Michael's face is fixed on the distant glow as he runs towards us.

'Michael you get back inside right now! I'm driving Daniel home.'

'No you're not!' The youth springs through the passenger door and shoves me up into his brother, wedging me between another argument that John loses simply because he can't muster the energy to get out and drag Michael back into the bar. As we pull out onto Brascote Lane, I see Bert and Jim crowding into the doorway of the pub, with Jenny strobing her light about as if signaling.

It is a short drive to the wood, a sharp left as the road bends close to the entrance of Selkirk's farm and then along the road to the top of the Kirby lane to another sharp left: three sides of a square, with the main village always to our left, still inked out in darkness. The clouds are veined with luminous silvered threads, their edges tinged with purple. All I can hear is the blood surging in my ears and the sound of heavy rain overwhelming the wipers and thundering on the cab roof.

'What is it, Dan? You think it's that lad? The boy who turned into an alien?' Michael speaks breathlessly. John drives fast despite the appalling visibility, his gaze fixed ahead. Mike is looking at me, his eyes wide and excited; probably scared. 'Dan?'

'Yeah – I think it might well be.'

Mike turns and leans his face up against the windscreen, straining to see. His movements are lithe and animated despite his height. The blue white light is reflected in his eyes, striped across his face as the hedgerows flash by. 'Shouldn't we call the police or someone, the army?' The truck bounces close to the verge and a sluice of water sprays up the passenger window. Michael jumps back and John laughs nervously. 'I told you to stay behind!'

His brother scowls. 'You think he'll still be a lizard, Dan?'

'I don't know. Hopefully not.'

'Why do you think he's come back now?'

'Enough with the questions, Mike! We'll find out soon enough.' John sounds on edge.

We pull over into a turn in and Michael jumps out to open a gate set back in thick, dripping hawthorn. A track leads off into darkness. I see him illuminated by the headlights, head down, the thick boss of blond hair hanging raggedly over his face. The water is hazing up off the ground as he pulls the gate wide. John idles the car forward as his brother climbs back in; he is soaking wet, his shirt clinging to the line of his back.

We heave and bounce over the ploughed field and confront another gate; opening into the field with my infamous wood on the right. Michael is out again, there is a clank and whine of metal and John parks up not far from the edge of the spinney, angling the headlights towards the trees. He roots out a flashlight from under the dashboard, dislodging a flotsam of empty beer cans, a screwed up map and – I am not surprised to see – a crunched up pack of condoms. We walk briskly, bent down from the waist as if under gun fire. I have no coat and John's hoody is already plastered to his face and head like a mask. We pass the first tapered birch trees, pale and smoky grey under the ghostly light. It is coldly brilliant, casting our shadows behind us; highlighting the dips and furrows on the ground but already it is fading, rippling upward and away. John casts the beam of the flashlight about although it is difficult to see in the stinging rain. I head for the remnants of the mound where the last two children were found in 1993. I have no doubt in my mind that Max will be there. John has drawn away to my left, sweeping the torch over the watchful runes and creases of tree bark. The light has all but gone and the darkness is disorientating. It is Michael who sees the man first, his white body caught in the beam of his brother's torch, lying in the pale wintered grass like a log. He cries out, grabbing my arm with unexpected strength. We run the last few yards to where the man is lying on his side; naked, the thickly pleated muscles of his back and buttocks plastered with leaves and mud. But it is the hair I recognise, corded black around the top of his shoulders.

'Oh my God! Max? Max!' The name is ripped from me; I am shocked by the sound of my own voice. Michael has dropped behind, his eyes wide in disbelief. I crouch down by the head, touching the face and turning it to towards me. I feel the cold, sculptured cheeks and wipe the hair from his forehead. The body has a curious texture, tacky, like cold clay, as if freshly rendered.

'Max?'

John crouches down on the opposite side to me, practically feeling for a pulse. I see his eyes casually glance over the prostrate body, taking it in.

'Jamie?'

The voice is faint, but hearing it freezes my blood.

'No, no Max, it's Daniel. Daniel Lockwood. Do you remember me? You're back in the wood!'

'His pulse is very weak! He feels like bloody ice! We should get him out of this weather before he gets hyperthermia.'

'Or before someone else turns up!' Mike has slowly moved up alongside me, watching Max sheepishly and looking about him as if he expects to see things in the tree. He is understandably spooked. John slips his arm down Max's back and under his arm. I take the other, rolling him slowly onto his back. With effort, we hinge him up from the waist. The eyelids flutter and there is a sharp intake of breath.

'Max it's Daniel – you're back in the wood where I first found you. You're in Leicestershire!'

'Daniel?' The voice carries a tone of dim recognition and he lifts his face to mine slowly, like someone who is blind. I hold him close to me; hugging his frigid body, rubbing his arms and shoulders vigorously. I can feel each groove of tendon and muscle under the dimpled skin. But something is wrong. I part his hair and look at his face. I can sense John watching quizzically.

'What is it? Dan?'

I move my legs, cramping in the cold. I look anxiously over Max's shapely, contoured body. I notice he has a cut near his navel and another, deeper gash on his shoulder.

'Is it Max?' John whispers urgently, confused by my expression. He looks up at his brother. 'Mike run to the truck and get the blanket off the back seat – come on, off you go!'

Mike runs towards the smudge of headlights. John turns back to me. 'Well?'

'He hasn't aged a day!' My voice is scarcely audible above the storm.

'What?' John tactfully flicks the torch over Max indirectly.

'Max left from this wood in 2006 aged 18. He should now be in his mid-thirties.'

'You sure? Well, that's just fucking weird.' John examines Max's face. 'Yeah, I think you're right. I've read about this – something to do with travelling at or over the speed of light? Time passes differently.'

We hear Mike running back, tripping and swearing over the wet grass. John takes the blanket and we manage to wrap it over Max's back like a cape. Holding him I can feel his body beginning to shiver.

'Max, you think you can stand? We have a truck nearby.'

'Sure.' Max says quietly. I am suddenly too emotional to hide the waiver in my voice. 'Jesus Max, where have you been!'

'Come on, at the count of three we're going to heave you up and get him to the farm.' John half slaps my back. 'Ok Max? We're going to lift you now.'

'Sure.' Max says again, and I sense him fighting to gather the strength needed to animate his body. Suddenly he opens his eyes and they are a deep, luminous blue, the irises flecked with red and orange. The pupils are dark and wide, but as John struggles with his weight the torch catches his face and they snap almost shut into narrow vertical slits like a cat. I sense John tense, but we are too preoccupied with dragging him to his feet to think. After a huge effort, Max is hauled up and guided towards the open field. He turns and looks at John as I fold the blanket over his front, hitching it around his neck.

'Who are you?'

'I'm John Gardiner. I'm a friend of Dan's. That's my brother Mike.' He nods towards the edge of the trees. Max mutters something, inaudible, lost in the chattering of his teeth. He turns to me. 'Daniel. We have lots to talk about.' His voice trails away as if he is close to fainting.

'We sure do Max, but not just yet. Come on. One foot at a time. I'd forgotten what a heavy bugger you are!'

There is a fleeting smile, or perhaps it is a trick of the darkness, the scudding flashlight and the beams from the truck, strafed by rain. With further effort we manage to get Max up into the front, squeezed in between me and John. Michael volunteers to sit up on the flatbed.

'Let's get him inside.'

'Shouldn't we get him to a hospital?' John reverses, the gears whining loudly. He waits while his brother wrestles once more with the gate. The rain is beginning to ease. As we rejoin the Kirby Lane Max's gimlet eyes close and then snap open.

'What year is it?'

John looks sideways at Max and then at me.

'It's 2022 Max, the day is the 25th January; you've been gone sixteen years.'

'2022' he says quietly. 'And Jamie? How is father? And Jonathan – why is Jonathan not here?'

'Ssssh, Max; all in good time. Everyone is fine. We can talk about this later when you're in the warm.' John looks at me; the look is almost accusative. It says, 'when are you going to tell him about the shit show he's returned to?'

Max drops his head onto my shoulder, his wet hair thick against my face. He is trembling now with deep agar. He turns his face to me and says once more, almost whimsically, 'We have lots to talk about.'

'We're nearly there, Max.' John says quietly, as if he has known him all his life, rubbing his knee affectionately.

The rain sleets up for a few seconds and then slows. As we turn into the long drive from the road to the farmhouse, the sky behind us resumes a sudden yellow haze as the power comes back on, popping and flickering the yellow soda streetlamps back to life. We trip a security light as we pull up outside my front porch. It takes all three of us to get Max inside, and there is something vaguely comical about it as if we have retrieved a body or committed some mysterious crime. We get him into the sitting room by which time he is a dead weight.

'Let's just put him down on the sofa, lads.'

'He's caked in mud, Dan.'

'It's ok, Mike, let's just put him down here.'

We swing him, sack like, onto the sofa where he lies soiled and wet as if he has been fished out the sea. Mike leans down and tactfully re-arranges the blanket to cover Max's genitals. I have a sudden, distressing image of a body in a mortuary.

I run to the kitchen to collect some towels. I see John and Mike looking at each other in bewildered fascination, communicating in the way that siblings do. I go to say something but John's phone springs to life, snarling and shrieking out an elaborate ringtone. He goes out of the room; I catch strands of random conversation. Mike has perched himself on the arm of the sofa at Max's feet. He is shivering now.

'Mike you better get out of those clothes.'

He nods vacantly and then says with quiet understatement, 'I've never seen a body like that; it's amazing.' Mike stops, blushing suddenly. Before I can reply John comes back in. 'That's mum, she wants us back. Dan, that ok?'

'Of course – you've both done more than enough. I could never have moved him on my own.'

'I can stay if you want – give a hand?' Mike looks at his brother hopefully. John chews his lip but is shaking his head. The boys still live with their aging mother who has taken the last few years hard. Mike worries she is showing signs of dementia. She is overprotective of her sons, especially Mike. Nonetheless I could do with the help.

'I could use Mike to be honest; I think we're going to have put him in a bath.'

John mulls it over, his black eyebrows knotted in a frown.

'Ok, sure.' His face is still troubled, drawn down; a haze of black stubble textures his cheeks. 'I'll get back once I've put mum to bed and settled her. It might take a few hours. Just do what Dan tells you, ok?' He casts his eyes once more over Max, nods to himself, and then leaves quickly, crunching over the gravel. We hear the truck burst into life and pull away. Freed of his brother's presence, Mike looks incredibly young and rather hyper. I towel down Max's face; he is stone cold, and his skin has a curious greyness to it.

'Mike, you need to change – we don't want you catching a cold. There are some clothes in my bedroom; help yourself. Then we'll run a bath.'

'Ok.' Mike jumps up and bounds up the stairs. I sit by Max looking at him; it is almost impossible to comprehend what I am seeing; that he is here, unaged, restored. I take out my mobile and try and call Jamie, then Julian, then Jonathan: all go to voicemail. I hesitate and hang up on all three: what message could I leave? I run my hand over Max's forehead, troubled by his appearance: even if I rang for medical assistance there is no guarantee it would get here – many hospitals remain closed and the call could bring the police or the army. Above me I can hear water running into the bath. Mike appears, wearing one of my shirts and a woolen cardigan. He sticks up a thumb enthusiastically. As kids, the Gardiner brothers helped on the farm in the school holidays and then often between jobs. Watching them grow up was a form of vicarious fatherhood but I was always conscious – especially once John got into his twenties – that I had a thing for him, a desire, hidden away and unacknowledged. If he sensed it he never showed unease and by then of course he acquired a reputation as a ladies man; gentle, thoughtful, but something of a lad. In a small village people knew these things. There was never a Mr. Gardiner, or not one I ever knew about. They are the closest I have to family; apart from Jamie perhaps, or Jonathan: but they are coloured by Max; by the extraordinary events that changed our lives. I had the Gardiner boys to myself, no complications or concerns. I stroke Max's head, preoccupied.

'Max, listen; we're going to try and raise your body temperature. We're going to put you in a tepid bath for a bit ok?'

Max nods as if massively hung over. I feel for a pulse at the base of his neck. It is slow and glacial. I stand above his head and try to hook my arms under his, pulling him upwards toward me. He is even heavier than in the wood. Mike bounds down the stairs again and grabs his feet, slipping them slightly self-consciously up to his knees over thick muscled calves.

'He's like a fucking bag of cement – no offence Max!' Mike grunts. Somehow, we manage to get up the stairs, it is more farcical than getting Max out of the car but more troubling. Guiding his almost inert body towards the bath I am aware of an array of scars across his body, red and scabbing from the arrival in the wood. Mike puts his arm in the water, considers it too hot, and pulls the plug out and starts filling the bath up again with cold. 'It's got to be just warm to start with, otherwise we might give him a heart attack.' His face is so earnest I can barely suppress a laugh.

'Since when have you been an expert on hypothermia patients?'

'I saw something on the National Geographic channel.'

Satisfied that the temperature is right, we manage to get Max into the bath but not before we douche water all over the floor and ourselves. Max makes the bath look absurdly small, and we must bend his legs and rest them over the sides to get his shoulders and chest low enough. The fringes of his black hair float like weed. With incredible care Mike keeps adding small spurts of hot water, until the bath level gurgles into the overflow and splashes more onto the tiles. Finally, Mike leans back on his haunches looking exhausted. 'That should do for now. Someone had better stay though.'

'You ok with that? Let me go get some food on, before we lose the power.'

'Good idea – I could eat a horse!'

I leave Mike squatting on the floor, his clothes soaked again. Exhausted myself, everything seems vaguely surreal; too bright; too loud, as if I am having some hallucination. It is just gone 9.30 pm. In the kitchen I open and close draws randomly looking for something easy to cook. I have been fortunate to stockpile food, able as I was to barter with local farmers during the worst of the crisis. Since the end of November things have slowly improved but there is still a great deal of violence and robbery; especially if people think you are hoarding. I turn on the TV in the living room. Only one channel works and as I start lighting the hob all I can hear is some absurd patriotic music playing over a photo of the current Prime Minister. As the bottom of the screen a message informs us that he will address the nation at 8 am tomorrow. I calculate I have about forty five minutes to cook before the evening blackout. Strangely I think of Mike, not Max. I wonder whether the world will ever right itself and if not, how he will look back on the experiences of his childhood and early adolescence. He was probably about fifteen when things started to come apart, devolve; to run down. The fault of my generation? The one before mine? None of us were worthy caretakers. We took the place for granted and wrecked it. Over the sound of frying meat, I hear the music from the TV stop abruptly. I turn the gas down and put a tin of opened potatoes next to a saucepan. The inane photo of the PM has been replaced by a live shot of an empty news studio – a novelty in itself – partly because news broadcasts stopped in early 2020. My stomach tenses. I go to call Mike down but decide to leave him on his vigil. A newsreader appears, walking from behind the camera. I do not recognise her. She sits down at the desk, looking over a prepared statement. Were it not for the times in which we live, it seems almost like a parody; a comic sketch. Settled, the camera zooms closer and the woman starts to read from a clip board. I turn the volume up.

'Over the previous six hours the British government has received numerous reports of UFOs over these islands, southern Europe, the Middle East, China and Australia. As of 9 pm this evening, the government can confirm that there have been six landings globally, including one in the vicinity of Invermorriston, Scotland. Following the protocols established in 2007 with the setting up of the United Nations Commission on Seeth and Alien Contact (UNCSAC) we are in communication with our allies and partners and will keep you informed of all developments. People are advised to stay in their homes until the situation can be clarified. In the light of these developments, the Prime Minister will not – repeat will not – be addressing the nation tomorrow on matters relating to the current national emergency. Further announcements will be made when available. Thank you.'

The camera wobbles and then refocuses as the announcer leaves. It then blinks out and the channel resumes the Elgarian tribute to our once elected leader; this time with no photograph, however. I stand staring at the screen in disbelief until I notice the smell of burning pork. Mike calls from the stairs – John is on his mobile and wants to talk to me. Unwilling to let Max out of his sight, I climb up to the landing and take it from his outstretched hand: Max has not moved, but I notice the pallor has gone from his skin and his complexion looks darker.

'Did you see that shit on the TV?'

John sounds breathless, excited.

'Yeah I did – I thought it was a sitcom for a minute. I don't understand what it can mean but it has to be connected to Max. He's still out but we should get some answers from him by morning. I've been trying to call his father and stepbrother, Jamie, but I can't get through.'

'Has anyone come to the farm, Dan?'

I walk past the opened bathroom door and rather theatrically peer through the window towards the distant road. 'No one. At least the government seem upfront this time; that's encouraging.'

'Let's hope so. They didn't mention Leicestershire. I'll be over in a few hours. Is Mike ok?'

'He's a regular miracle worker!'

Mike's head is sticking out around the bathroom door. John has clearly told him about the announcement. I walk into the bathroom. I feel for Max's pulse again. It is steadier now and stronger. I notice a line of mottled patterns running from Max's neck into his shoulders. I part his forest of hair and see the same markings appearing slowly under his hairline, emerging like a secret code. Seeth markings. I had seen these in 2006. Is he changing or have these markings been made visible by the warm water? I feel queasy with impatience. 'Let's get Max into the spare room.'

'You think this is an invasion?' Mike is leaning against the doorframe.

'No I don't. I don't profess to understand any of this, but.' I hesitate, unclear in my own thoughts. 'When Max was taken there was talk of invasion then; it's just panic, Mike, it's what people do when they don't understand something.' My confidence sounds unconvincing, but Mike seems placated, walking in and removing the plug from under Max's feet. After a cursory rub down with a towel we finally get Max under a duvet with his head propped up on several pillows.

'You think he needs food or something? You got any brandy?'

'I think we let him rest, Mike. Come on, I've got some burned offerings downstairs.'

We sit down just as the power fails. Luckily, candles are already on the table. I light them and think suddenly that it looks like a date. The thought embarrasses me. We spend the next few minutes scrolling through our respective phones, both still connected – although I have forgotten to charge mine when I could: the battery is low. Mike eats voraciously.

'You think of the future Mike? What you want to do when this is all over?'

'Nah – what's the point?' he chomps noiselessly. 'I mean things seem to be getting back to normal, but I hardly remember normal: and this doesn't look like it is going to end soon. They closed my school when I was 15; I don't have any education, no girlfriend, no money – not that there is much use for that. You?'

The question has never occurred to me. Somewhere, in the middle of the pandemic when the lights literally went out across the country and people were shot in the streets for violating quarantine, I stopped thinking at all. I just hung on for no other reason that the instinct to survive. I remember being surprised by my own tenacity, and then later, by its pointlessness.

'No, not really. Before this happened, I had planned to sell up, move down to the south west or back to London. I'd just put this place on the market when the first deaths started.'

'No woman in your life, or man?'

The observation is canny; it would once have taken me by surprise, but Mike is intuitive, observant.

'Nah – just you and John, Jamie Relph who was – is – Max's best friend, and the boy who was taken with Max in 1993, Jonathan Price. We stay in touch – Jamie is a scientist, an epidemiologist.'

'What's that?' Mike's plate is empty.

'The study of infectious diseases, how they spread.'

'Good line of work! He must have been busy.'

I laugh. 'You want to finish off my pork – it's like cardboard.'

'You sure? It's delicious!'

I hand him my plate, worried when he last ate a proper meal. My affection for him is suddenly acute, protective, quite selfless.

We take it in turns to go upstairs into the spare room and check in on Max. I am touched by Mike's thoughtfulness; taking up water, adjusting the duvet which Max seems to constantly throw off. He asks me about Max, about the day I collected him and Jamie from the train station in Leicester; I haven't thought about it for years. We then talk about UNCSAC – Mike is well informed, clearly a bit of what John would call a nerd. He is impressed I know so many people. At about midnight, John turns up in the pickup. He stays for a while since Mike is reluctant to leave, but it's best he goes home amid all the uncertainty. I ask John if he has seen anything unusual in the village; police or soldiers and he says no. We walk out. The night has turned cold and frosty. Above us the sky is thick with stars. John pulls open the driver's door and then pauses; looking up to where a dim cloud of light marks the center of the milky way. Without light pollution the sky seems enormous, a vast upturned bowl. There is something bright, almost wedge shaped, steady against the deep sweep of the cosmos, seemingly poised about the wood like a dagger.

'Is that Venus?' asks John, casually.

'No.' Mike is looking too.

'What the fuck *is* that?'

'Hold up.' I walk over to my patio and fetch an old pair of field glasses; strategically placed long ago when the wood was a shrine for UFO hunters. I had long given up trying to keep people off my land, but I could keep an eye on them: most got bored quickly when they found nothing except birch trees. I walk up to John, slinging the strap about my neck, bringing them to my face and focusing. Stars dance and bobble and then suddenly, quite clearly, I focus on a triangular object, the tip pointing down earthwards. Its luminosity is probably from reflected light; an even silver sheen, but it is dazzling.

John, impatient, is already putting his wide calloused hands on the binoculars.

'Don't strangle me!'

'Sorry man.'

I hand them over. He angles them up, whispering expletives. 'That is weird – is it a satellite? I've heard some have been coming down.'

'Wouldn't it be moving?' Mike is next to us now, waiting his turn.

The object is clearly stationary, fixed in place; it's scale and height impossible to measure. 'John, pass them back a sec.'

Mike complains as I use John's shoulder to steady the glasses. I lower the binoculars and look briefly with the naked eye. In March 1993, the night I found Max and Jonathan, I had seen something over the wood. It had been dark, utterly black, and yet the shape had been similar, side on as it was then, I had seen – or thought I'd seen – that one end of the shape was wider than the other, like an arrow or flint head. I try calculating what the same object would have looked like at a different height and position.

'Something not right, Dan?'

I shake my head. 'I'm not sure.'

'Like fuck you aren't – is it a ship?' Mike is pawing at the strap, making John snap at him and then typically apologise.

'Yeah – I think it's a Seeth ship.'

I hand the glasses to Mike soundlessly, screwing up my face. Mike looks, his jaw dropping, and then asks, 'You think they've come for Max?'

'No, I think it's how Max got into the wood – that's his ride.'

'Why's it still here – it's definitely not moving.'

John whistles gently, shaking his head. 'I think we better get out of here. Someone is definitely going to see that and come looking – it might be another landing, like the ones they've been reporting.'

Mike picks up on John's panic and heads into the car. 'Let's get home.'

'Dan – what's the plan – with sleeping beauty up there?' John gestures towards the house.

'I'll give him a few more hours then I'll try and wake him – clearly people will know something is going on here.' I glanced up at the sparkling, glistening shape.

Our parting is chaotic; we discuss meeting in the morning, but the pickup is already moving. I watch it track down towards the road. I look up through the binoculars one more time; alone, I have no doubts now what I am seeing. I turn and walk briskly back into the house. Inside I try texting the usual suspects, desperately hoping that someone will pick up. Jonathan is the last one I call. It rings and I can feel myself sweating despite the cold house. I am about to shut it down to save the last of the power when I hear Jonathan snap; 'Daniel! Is he back?'

'He's back. He's in my house – I need you to get here, Jonathan – there is some really weird shit going on.'

'Sure, sure. Listen I'm on my way to collect Jamie who's coming back from the US. I have no fucking idea when he arrives but as soon as he does, we'll come straight to you. Have you contacted Julian?'

'I've tried, he's on voicemail.'

'Yeah, he's gone to Scotland to the landing near Loch Ness; I'll try and get a message through to Margaret. Hold tight. We'll get to you as soon as we can. Is their official activity – do they know he's with you?'

'No, nothing. But listen, Jonathan, there's something up in the sky that looks pretty familiar – '

'Don't say anything more, Dan: get inside and we'll be with you. You need anything text me on an encrypted ap.'

'I don't understand –'

'WhatsApp – don't use the phone to make calls.' He disconnects.

Jonathan's voice had been immensely reassuring, but the reassurance was brief. Jonathan sounded as if he was on some obscure mission and the way he ends the call leaves me feeling suddenly exposed, vulnerable. I lock the doors and replenish the candles smoking on the still uncleared table. Stupidly I keep going to the window, watching the drive and now glancing up at the object which, if anything, seems closer and more distinct. I light a fire in the sitting room, stacking up logs. I consider just going upstairs and waking Max but drop the idea and after a few beers retrieved from the cellar, I go to bed. Unable to sleep I lay in the intense cold. Since the pandemic, my house has felt permanently cold; permanently damp. Oddly I think of my parents. I live in their world now. They were the first people to have central heating installed – it must have been the early 1970s – prior to that we lived in a house in which you were never warm enough, regardless of the season, unless you were on top of a fire, and even then the chill clung to your back. My father lived in a variety of dressing gowns. I see him clearly, shuffling about the house, convinced that radiators and hot water were an extravagance, a sign of decadence much as I thought mobile phones were later until I eventually bought one. I nod off, dreaming vividly that I am helping John fix something, a car or truck, jacked up over an inspection pit.

Something wakes me. I pull the nearby mechanical clock up to my face – it is 5 am. The wind has shifted, and I can hear an old aerial cable whomping on the side of the house. I turn to lie on my side but think I can hear something else, someone talking. I sit up. I can definitively hear Max having a conversation. I reach out to my side table and feel the cold slab of my mobile, but it is quite dead. Puzzled by the sound I wedge my feet into my slippers and walk quietly to the door. The spare room is opposite mine. The door is slightly ajar, and not only can I hear him quite plainly, I can see that there is a brilliant light in the room – beading under the door jamb and along the bottom, spilling a bluish glare into the hallway. The hairs rise on the back of my neck. I go to walk out and knock the door gently but merely stand in silence.

Max says 'I told you it was a bad idea. We need to stick to our agreements in future.' I hear a sort of reply, a deep sound like a human voice but liminal, on the very threshold of my hearing. I move forward silently. The light ebbs and distorts, and I think it is part of the same light seen over the wood earlier; the same purple veined shimmer that brought Max home. The thought frightens me. I shift slightly to the right and try to peer through into the room. My eyes squint painfully into the glare.

Max is sitting on the edge of the bed, seemingly naked despite the cold. His hair is sticking up like a crazy halo, each thick strand silhouetted against the brilliance.

'All I am saying is that you should have waited until I had contacted UNCSAC – the landings will arouse suspicion. I am the human expert here, remember! I am in charge of tactics.'

The light dims very slightly, and to my surprise I hear Max laugh, a deep bark. 'Exactly. I'll go now and talk with Daniel; you go back over the telemetry and locate the missing pod – let's try and keep to the plan.'

I watch intensely. Max seems to be shaking his head, but the gesture is one of amusement. He stands suddenly, and I instinctively step back but as I do so I catch a glimpse of what he is talking to. Behind him, at the head of the bed, there is an obelisk of blue-whiteness, mirroring his own outline, even to the details of the hair and the solid curves of his arms and shoulders. It appears to be a projection of himself, but its brilliance obliterates any detail. It is as tall as him, definitively human in shape but it is at the same time something so profoundly alien that I feel something akin to a deep shock, like a hard slap to my face. Holding my breath, I walk backwards into my room, my heart racing. Suddenly the light fades and darkness returns. I blink, forcing my eyes to adjust, and climb back into bed. I hear Max trying the light switch in his room, cursing as he hits his foot on something. There is a sound at my door and as I feign waking, Max jumps onto the bed with a great whomp of joy.

'Daniel Lockwood!'

The Max I met in 2006 had been changing; probably painfully, into something he could barely comprehend. His silence had been stoical, especially once his sight had failed him on that horrendous final drive to the wood. He had been beautiful and unapproachable, like an oracle. We had been forced to split up and I of course was arrested long before Jamie and Max made it to the rendezvous point. As Jonathan said to me later, I had missed all the fireworks. The Max that is bouncing on my bed, stark naked and boyish, is someone I have never seen, an intimacy I have never experienced. Once he calms down, I tell him that Jonathan is on his way with Jamie. I explain that Julian is in Scotland, incognito, but he evidently knows this. He climbs under the sheets without a second thought and sits, with his knees up, smiling blissfully with his brilliant, lizard eyes looking at me and asking endless, breathless questions; especially about his new 'step-mother': he is interested how that came about and what Sally made of it. Had I not, a few moments ago, seen Max conversing with his own alien ghost, or seen a ship hanging Damocles like above the frosty fields of my own farm, I would feel his joy as keenly as he does. All I do is lie there, spinster like, clutching my dressing gown around me and trying to keep up with him and to nudge him gently toward telling me his story, where in God's name he has been for the last sixteen years, what the Seeth landings mean – but he will have none of it.

'I always knew Julian was having an affair.' He says, half growling out the words, a secretive smile on his lips. 'He was so bad at hiding things!'

'Most of my understanding of this comes from Jamie, who obviously didn't know.'

'Do they get on? Father and Jamie? They should do – they have a lot in common.'

'They do, very much so, and Jamie still sees Neville, his biological father – it was he who walked out, he couldn't get his head around Margaret's involvement with the alien stuff. Apparently, he had no idea.'

'That doesn't surprise me. Did you ever meet him?' Max rests his head back, exposing a thick muscled neck. The mottling on his throat has turned blue-black, speckled like a robin's egg. 'Incredibly dull.'

I confess I never met him, and we lapse into silence. My stomach rumbles. 'You must be hungry, Max? You should eat something.'

'Sure – but let's just lie here for a bit, if that's ok. I've been pretty isolated, what with me and just the experiment for company.'

'The experiment is alive? I mean an alien?' I try not to rush in, fumbling the words out. Max is clearly being tight lipped for a reason.

'Yes – and no. Look.' He bounds out of bed like a giant dog, standing at the window, pointing up into the sky. I stand next to him. We are looking at what I had presumed was a ship. Bizarrely, cheekily, Max waves at it irreverently. 'It doesn't like too much levity.'

'How can it be alive and yet not alive?'

'Oh Daniel – it's a form of AI, or it was originally. It has been sentient for millennia and is a bit cranky with it as well. We've spent the last sixteen years in conversation, it was infinitely lonelier than I was.'

'But where have you *been*, Max? And how is that you haven't aged?'

Max is silent for a moment, contemplative. 'Let's wait for the others to get here. I only want to have to tell this story once, otherwise I will get it all mixed up in my head: it's not a linear story, and sixteen years passed very quickly. It's all a bit of a rush; if that makes sense.'

It doesn't but I say nothing. He turns and unexpectedly pinches my nose.

'The aging thing is about general relativity; I've been moving somewhere very fast and you haven't. Come on, let's get some food. Nothing too heavy.'

The qualification mystifies me, but I get out of bed and manage to persuade Max to dress. Wherever he's been he appears to have spent most of the time naked because he looks at the offered dressing gown without initially recognising what it is for. In the kitchen Max examines each cupboard and shelf like a crime scene before settling on porridge. I tell him that all we have is condensed milk; he undoes a tin with effort and adds water to it. He asks me about the epidemic, and I give him an abbreviated history. He knows about it, but the details shock him.

'It sounds almost incomprehensible; you must have been terrified.'

'People wouldn't travel and then couldn't; most of the food disappeared and people fled the cities. Power failed because people were too sick to work or too afraid, hospitals closed, and the government moved out of London. The military were everywhere. Everything I had taken for granted ground to a halt within weeks.'

Max pauses, a spoon close to his mouth. 'Things were always so precarious, so delicately balanced. I suppose the more complex things became the more vulnerable they are to some systemic failure. Did you lose many people, Daniel?'

'A lot of friends, but never having had a family I was spared that: over half of the village here died. There was other stuff that started to impact on us. The climate for one thing, the collapse of industry paradoxically increased global temperatures, something to do with dust.'

Max nods, his mouth full again. The porridge is hot, and he spools it about his mouth with evident discomfort. He swallows. 'Yeah – atmospheric pollutants actually reduce the amount of light reaching the planet; when they're no longer produced the radiation increases even though the overall greenhouse gas emissions are reduced. Julian had a colleague at Green College who was working on that.'

'And now a vast majority of us appear to be infertile – as a probable side effect of the HN71 virus.' I watch Max eating; already the bowl is empty, the question causes him to frown slightly, looking at his spoon.

'Yes; I've been looking at the data.' He says cryptically and I lose the will to press the point. No doubt this is part of Max's non-linear story.

'Not that I ever wanted children. Bringing them into the world always required an act of faith I lacked. Even if we hadn't been decimated by some super bug, we've been running out of road for some time. It was just a question of time until we fell off the end.'

'You think so?' Max sounds intrigued.

'Sometimes I think we're the virus, or some form of malicious malware. How can you fix such stupidity? I'm not sure we deserve to survive. I think we are a nasty, vain little race full of spite. Even before people started dying, something wasn't working. People didn't believe in governments, didn't believe in facts, yet they wanted stronger governments to protect them.'

I feel that my rant has spoiled his mood, but Max is looking at me intently with his luminous cat eyes.

'Come on Dan. You're an adaptive species; there is much good that can still come from all this. You are an honest man; all it takes is one.' Mischievously, he picks up a candle and pushes it towards my face as if examining me.

His self-exclusion from humans is hardly surprising, as is the reference to Diogenes. And he is evidently still hungry. I point out my secret stash of frozen meat.

'Dan you are *such* a good man – but I'm not sure about meat just yet. This is the first solid food I've eaten in over a decade.'

There is a sound of a helicopter, the ebb and flow of the blades chopping through the air as it approaches. I stand and walk through to the lounge, squinting my eyes up into a blue milky sky. The fields and hedges are deep in frost.

'Who's this?' Max is already towering over me, pressed up against the window.

'I'm not sure – I think the news is finally out that something happened at the wood last night. It might be a good idea if you go back upstairs for a while; keep out of sight.'

I turn but Max is already outside looking up at the metallic silver green glint of what looks like an old AH1 Gazelle. It circles over my drive. Max is waving his arms; his open dressing gown flashing his perfect nakedness to the world.

'Oh fuck. Max!' I run out towards him. 'Max this isn't a good idea – you need to keep a low profile: I'd get inside.'

'Dan it's ok – it's Julian! In a helicopter!'

'It could be anyone – it's probably the army.'

Max is cheerfully adamant. Further protests result in him snaking an arm about my waist while waving with the other. 'He hates flying' he whispers to himself.

The helicopter turns its nose towards us, then tilts down dropping carefully, its rear blades sparkling in the vivid, golden sunlight. The glass fronted cockpit glares like the eyes of some giant insect. It bobs down, bounces forward slightly, then comes to rest. I hear the pilot cut the engines. A door slides open and a pair of brogues stick out tentatively, bent at the knee, feeling blindly for the ground.

'Julian!' Max lets out a huge cry and runs. I stand, hands on hips and I see Max bend slightly, rushing under the slowing blades. Julian Grey is standing, blinking in disbelief and unspeakable relief as a dark youth grabs him by the middle, lifts him, and swings him about like a scarecrow. I still think this will all end badly; there is something I cannot quite grasp about Max, about the experiment, but I am surprised to find that I am crying, the first time for many years; certainly the first since the epidemic. Perhaps now we can all be saved.

Chapter Four: Reunions and Complications.

The closer we got to Daniel's farm the greater my anxiety grew, my longing. There was also some bizarre fear of disappointment; that Max would be different, that he would not recognise me and that the power that had been between us would have gone. It was irrational but logical. Jonathan was probably having similar thoughts because as we approached Brascote lane he fell silent, chewing his lips and muttering things to himself; something I had not seen him do for years. As we approached the farm however, more immediate concerns crowded in. There were two helicopters parked casually in the field in front of Daniel's house and a bevy of soldiers standing at the entrance to the drive. The Kirby lane had been cordoned off.

'Shit.' Jonathan pawed behind his right ear, but we had already smoked his last spliff. He slowed the car to a stop, winding the window down. Overhead, flashing by in a cone of intense noise, two Lockheed Martin F 35s seemingly grazed the roof of one of Daniel's outhouses before banking and roaring off towards Newbold Verdon. As I followed them, my gaze was dragged upwards to a black triangular object suspended in the sky, obviously at high altitude, since it was partly obscured by wreaths of cirrus clouds.

'Jonathan – look.'

He had gone to protest, concentrating on the two soldiers were already walking towards us, but he looked suitably shocked as I angled his head upwards by grabbing his jaw.

'It's like a fucking air show! Gentlemen!'

'Get your eyes tested, son.' A female soldier wearing a UN arm band over her usual insignia leaned in and looked us over. She ignored Jonathan's attempt at small talk, playing with a small mobile device strapped to her wrist. She glanced at us again, the inscrutable stare of the military, and then standing away from the car waved us through. Surprised, Jonathan rattled over the cattle grid. In the centre mirror I could see she was speaking into a radio.

'UNCSAC by the looks of it.'

We could see Daniel and Julian Grey walking together out near the barns. Julian had looked up at the sound of our approach: that Julian was here did not surprise me. Somebody came out from the house, a tall dark shape, of course we both recognised the hair; pushed back and away from the face like a stork's nest. Jonathan stopped the car someway from the house and climbing out, we ran towards Max. It must have looked absurd, theatrical: but even as I thought that, as I resolved to not cause a scene and wail like a banshee, Jonathan was hugging Max. I slowed, watching the intensity of their reunion. Once I was jealous, insanely jealous of Jonathan: in my addled dependence on Max I had construed that they were lovers, excluding me from their secret life; I had been right of course, but the secret was an enormity that Max had tried to protect me from. Jonathan stood with his back to me, and I could tell that uncharacteristically he was sobbing. Max kissed the top of his head, and then dragged him towards me. Sixteen years in the abyss, sixteen years of denying that each day I woke with the hope that Max would come back to me, to us, and suddenly his smell was all about me. Later, after various jokes about our respective ages, and after watching Max deep in conversation with his father, I had thought him changed; more open, more visible, somehow more intense than I remembered. And I was haunted by the fear that what I was looking at was an avatar of Max; a copy.

After a feast of tinned food, Jonathan slumped down on the sofa next to me and we watched Max discretely as if he was a rare, mythological animal, unable to take our eyes off him in case he might vanish. Jonathan, more out of intrigue than spite, asked me if I had told him about Garen.

Once the excitement died down, we found ourselves in the middle of what was, to all intents and purposes, a sort of conspiracy. We had been joined by Sally Grey, the very last person I expected to see and who was, as she explained enigmatically, 'not really here.' She was different too, however, thawed out around the edges and suddenly tactile; to me, to Max and even Julian. Daniel looked bemused but well, presiding with an evident sense of disbelief. Jets continued to dash low over the fields. It remained unclear whether this was to protect or scare us, and then one of the helicopters took off, chuntering over the house. Finally, as the afternoon quietened, and reminiscent of a meeting in the kitchen of Farndon Road on a June morning in 2006, Julian sat down next to me, patting my knee and said that we should get down to business. He evidently meant Max. Looking back on the meeting many years later, there were things that Max did not tell us, perhaps because we did not ask him. But there were other things on which he was deliberately evasive over. Did he lie to us? I am not sure. Is an omission a lie? I say this because I loved him always, and because I was not the only person in the room who thought this at the time. I have often wondered if he was disingenuous because he realised that if he told us the truth, he would have compromised the experiment's mission, but like all disingenuity it came out in the end.

'Dena Small is unable to join us, but I have arranged to brief her later. She is in the process of examining three hybrids. Altogether there are fifteen hybrids accounted for. Three are missing.'

Julian had hesitated, playing with his eyebrows. 'I suppose what we need to understand first is why the hybrids are here, Max?'

Max stirred as if from a doze, his eyes flashing dramatically. He had seemingly rehearsed this scene in his head because he started out clearly and precisely, with just a few pauses and no interruptions. He started the story at the beginning, with himself. Obviously, in 2006 Jonathan appeared just in time to save him, and the device long buried in the wood and mostly ignored until it was almost too late, managed to extract Max's human DNA before he was cannibalised by his hybridisation with the Seeth genetic material he had been carrying inside since 1993. Max's next memory was of being alone with the experiment in deep space and over time he came to realise that the experiment was housed on a vast spaceship or was indeed the ship itself. It was, of course, the ship we could all then see from the comfort of Daniel's sitting room, in geostationary orbit at the top of the thermosphere, about 55 miles up, glinting in the low winter sunlight.

The experiment told Max the story of the Seeth; how they had fled to a giant gas planet following the meteor impact on Earth that had destroyed their civilisation. Although he did not expand on this point, he did confirm what Julian and many scientists associated with UNCSAC had suspected, that the Seeth were a therapod race, related to raptors, that had evolved sentience and acquired extraordinary mental abilities through which they were able to build advanced and enduring technologies. The gas planet proved disastrous for resettlement however, it was too cold and did not respond to the Seeths attempt at terraforming. Even worse, it exposed the Seeth to a deadly radiation which over several centuries poisoned the Seeth genome with devastating effect, destroying their ability to reproduce and limiting their abilities to manipulate physical matter, an essential prerequisite to their continued adaptability and survival. In a final effort to stave off extinction, the Seeth constructed the experiment to return to earth and to find a donor to provide the coding to repair their damaged chromosomes. The experiment was essentially a sentient AI which was also the repository of Seeth culture, charged with the task of saving them. Over millennia, the experiment carried out its primary function but was continually frustrated with failure, until in 1993 it abducted the 24 children suffering from Ewing's sarcoma. As DeMarr and my stepfather had theorised, the cancer was the key to enabling the integration of Seeth and human DNA, retaining the telepathic abilities of the Seeth progenitor combined with the physical form of homo sapiens. The amount of human DNA in the hybrids was however to present a problem, since in effect the experiment created a new life form that was more human than Seeth.

This had, of course, already been anticipated by the experiment – it was why the experiment sent the device that would restore Max to human form once the extraction of the Seeth genomes had been complete. It took sixteen years for the hybrids to be incubated to the experiment's satisfaction. However, as the experiment was returning Max to Earth, it became aware that the planet was facing a sustained ecological and political catastrophe, culminating in the HN71 outbreak and the infertility crisis. The experiment and Max spent many months discussing the probable fate of the human species, as well as the likelihood of finding a new planet for the hybrids. Given the experiment's provisional prognosis, the human race was facing extinction. Max asked the experiment to help, suggesting that the two problems be solved simultaneously. In the light of the suitability of the Earth for the resettlement of the hybrids, and the robustness of the hybrids reproductive capacity it was concluded that they should negotiate with UNCSAC, a suitably internationalist body, for an exchange. Technology to reverse the damage done to the planet and to prevent further environmental degradation, fertile hominids to reverse the onset of sterility and both for the right to settle a hybrid population, which the experiment calculated would need to be about 30 million to provide the necessary genetic pool. The experiment had further proposed, and Max had accepted, that it would be useful if he returned to Earth to head the negotiations. The experiment knew of his relationship to Julian and Sally Grey, and his friendship with other leadings scientists associated with UNCSAC.

Max paused at this stage, gathering himself elegantly as if he were relieved to have finished. The day was already waning, cold late afternoon sun shone through the back of the farmhouse and for a moment there was an intense silence. It was Sally who broke it first.

'It's a sound proposal Max, but in the current climate 30 million might be considered too many too soon. Also, if I am not mistaken, the genomes are incompatible to rule out interbreeding; it that is what you are suggesting?'

'The genomes of the hybrids have been modified further to make them compatible to fuse with a human gamete of 23 chromosomes.'

'How do fertile hybrids solve our fertility crisis?' Daniel asked, bemused.

'Sex with aliens.' Said Jonathan.

'Max – this is a radical suggestion – the implications are unprecedented; even if it's possible.' Julian spoke quietly, almost to himself.

'There are precedents, father: Neanderthals and Homo Sapiens interbred, as did probably other hominid sub-species approximately 200,000 years ago.'

'But the Neanderthals went extinct if I recall.' Sally said, playing with her necklace, her face inscrutable.

'They survive in our genome to this day.' Max smiled at his mother almost playfully.

'Our genome? Darling – don't misunderstand me, but how human are you? There are clearly physiological differences that you have retained, despite the success of the device in saving your original coding. Secondly, why did eighteen hybrids arrive at the same time – would it not have been wiser to have started the negotiations first?'

Max had nodded, an expression of exasperation momentarily clouding his face, a half wince. Unconsciously he was tracing out the mottled banding across his hairline.

'I have retained several distinct features but if you map my complete genotype you will see it is human. I have some telepathic abilities, which the experiment retained in order to facilitate communication, but I do not possess the ability to manipulate matter and nor do the hybrids. What Julian and the committee identified as the tags in the abducted children was a natural anatomical characteristic of the Seeth, it enabled them to visualise places and past events, and even transport themselves, if necessary, to other Seeth. This is how

Jonathan of course arrived in the wood, since the device was made up of the same material as the tags, and I had become sufficiently Seeth to connect with him. The hybrids have lost this characteristic, although they remain telepathic. As for their arrival, I am afraid that the experiment acted impetuously, anxious that the hybrids should be seen and experienced: it believed it would expedite the negotiations.'

'So there are 30 million hybrids napping up there, on the ship?' Jonathan asked, craning his neck back towards the window.

'There are 29,999,982 to be precise. There will be no more landings. I promise.'

Julian asked Max if there was a reason behind the areas chosen for the landings. Again, Max had looked vaguely guilty, a slight narrowing of his lips, an expression I was deeply familiar with.

'Possible settlement sights.' He said quietly. 'I know how that sounds, as I say it won't happen again: but the hybrids will be useful in reassuring people that they are not green lizards with tails that eat people!'

'And something they'd be prepared to have sex with?' Sally said, half in jest, but shaking her head in silent disbelief. She looked at her ex-husband. Julian changed the subject.

'Which brings us to the missing three. Does the experiment have any idea where they might be? Dena is in discussions with the Chinese and Russian authorities who deny that any landings took place on their territory.'

By this stage Max was sitting crossed legged on the floor, his hands folded on his lap. He looked up at his father. 'The experiment is looking into the telemetry now. I'll check in on it later. But they are definitely not in Russia or China.'

I had sat silent throughout, despite bursting with questions. As the room fell silent, I asked about the infertility crisis. Surely there was a less radical solution to solving it than a massive inter-species breeding program.

Max's reply surprised us all with its bluntness.

'There is no cure. The experiment has run the numbers millions of times: you have about 100 years before you go extinct.'

'Max that can't be right!' Sally snapped. 'I've been working on the WHO data, it's complicated but there is no reason to assume the worst. How about in vitro from stored gametes?'

'It won't work – not with sperm; possibly with eggs but only after extensive hormone therapy. Jamie?'

Max looked at me, the eyes wide, questioning. Everyone in the room turned towards me.

Jonathan nudged me. 'You're on.'

'He's right, Sally. The damaged gametes degenerate in stasis; the storage time for fertile semen can be measured in months not decades. And a 'cure' begs the question as to whether infertility is the result of a discreet pathogen. There isn't any, and believe you me, we've looked.'

I had expected Sally to protest further but she merely nodded briskly. 'That confirms some of our observations, the chromosomal information degrades and doesn't recombine with the female gamete, and if it does the embryo is deformed. The damage to the sperm cells appears to have multiple causes, possibly environmental or chemical. We have no idea. However, I'm not sure I'm willing to go on record that there is no cure. Not yet, at least.'

Another silence, longer; more thoughtful, filled up the now darkening room. Since without Dena, Julian was in fact representing UNCSAC, Max looked at him directly. In the gloom, his eyes shimmered and sparkled. Julian finally stirred.

'Well this is just extraordinary, Max. Frankly, in the current climate, your proposal will shock many. If the deal is refused, I presume the experiment will leave with the hybrids?'

'It will. You have my word.'

Julian seemed to consider his next words carefully, fussing with his cuffs. 'Ok. Then I think we should take you to New York, as quickly as possible. It's Dena's call but I cannot imagine she would disagree. I'll run it past her. A security council meeting has been called for the day after tomorrow. I'm not sure if you can attend in person, and the more usual appearance before the General Assembly is difficult because, since the epidemic, so few countries have maintained diplomatic representatives in New York. We can sort out the details when you are there. I also think it might be wise to try and assemble the hybrids with Max in one place; including the missing three which I hope we can find very soon. Thoughts, anyone?'

Daniel stood and put the table lights on. 'We've got about four hours of power.'

Sally spoke first. 'I think we should obviously get Max over the pond, but I have some misgivings about assembling all the hybrids in the US. Too many aliens in one basket.' She spoke cautiously, either because the thought was tentative, or it derived from something she alone knew. Julian's eyebrows bunched together quizzically.

'Are you able to give us any reason for your misgivings?'

She sighed, frustrated; glancing down at the top of Max's head as if she were fighting some instinct to reach out and touch him. She stood up abruptly.

'I wish I could Julian, but you know as well as I – you all know – that the political situation in the US is not good. It's not particularly good here either, whatever the government is saying about the restoration of power and essential supplies. I am not convinced we could ensure their safety.'

Still she hung back, her reluctance to expand on what she had said was almost palpable.

'Mother?'

Max's voice, the classic growl from his beautiful, precocious childhood seemed to startle her. I remembered Max when he was eighteen first time around, it was impossible to resist him once he had set his mind to something. I had always thought Sally was immune to this particular ability. Her resistance lasted about ten seconds.

'I promised myself that I would *never* use this expression; but if I am to be pressed on this matter what I have to say is classified.'

'You're a spy?'

'For God's sake Jamie, of course I am not a spy. I work for the Foreign Office.'

'Oh. I thought you were the chief medical officer.'

'We got a little shorthanded. Regardless of what I am, the fact remains that, well, there is good reason to believe that the missing hybrids are in the US.'

Jonathan's thigh, which was pressed up against mine, jumped distinctly and Julian opened his eyes in clear surprise as if someone had stuck a pin in him.

'And I would be appreciative, Julian, if you could manage *not* to tell Dena this until we have confirmation. Max, get a move on with the telemetry data - then you can discover it for yourselves.'

'Will do!'

'Just to be clear, are you saying they're being detained?' asked Julian slowly.

'Yes – that's what we've been hearing: mostly through back channels, nothing we could go public with at the moment. The missing ship came down in Arizona, not far from the Californian state line near the Aboy crater.'

'But why would they detain them?' My question was naïve. Jonathan rolled his eyes.

Julian stood up, re-arranging his tweeds. '*Davies*. That's why. Some little covert operation I suspect.' He looked at Sally knowingly, shaking his head in disbelief. 'Dena warned me about him last year.'

'Samuel Davies – he can't still be alive – he was like 107 in 2006?' I remembered seeing photos, a smooth anonymous face, tight as if tucked up in a knot behind his ears.

Max sprang up, making me jump, lithe and suddenly very tall in the dark room.

'He's very much alive, Jamie. He is behind some xenophobic, unpleasant movement called Earth for Humans, and that since the US administration evacuated Washington DC he's been in the cabinet. Sally?'

'Yes – he's been appointed undersecretary to Homeland; but given that the secretary is dead, it gives him cabinet rank. And yes, we've been monitoring the Earth for Humans Movement for some time, especially their new militia – which had grown dramatically in the last few months, both here and in the US.'

'Blue Jackets? I saw them out with the territorials a few days ago – I wondered who they were.' Daniel looked troubled, running his hand over his beard and face. 'Hasn't the PM just invited them into the government?'

'He has, yes.' Sally's voice still sounded guarded. 'Unfortunately, I should add and with considerable reservations.'

'I need a smoke, sorry.' Jonathan sprang up from the sofa and walked out into the kitchen. I watched him squirrel out a pouch of tobacco. There was a sense of indecision in the room, of sudden complexity. Julian was standing by the window, hands in pockets, clearly thinking over what he had heard. It was Max who broke the silence, sounding oddly definitive, implicitly in control.

'Sally I know about Davies; I and the experiment have been watching him for some time, but Julian is right; the hybrids have to come with me. I am after all in a sense their only surviving parent and the experiment is quite capable of protecting us.'

'And it would have the advantage of looking as if we didn't suspect anything.' Jonathan called in from the kitchen door.

Julian nodded in consent. 'I think they're right Sally. I appreciate the heads up, but having the hybrids spread out in five different countries is probably more of a risk than having them all in downtown Manhattan.'

Somewhat impatiently, Sally acquiesced. 'It's probably for the best. I don't know how long Max and the Scottish hybrids will be safe here either, if truth be told. The PM is holding onto a position of international cooperation, but the cabinet is hardening against him; especially with the new intake. They might try and detain him.'

I looked at her quizzically, but it was all she was prepared to say. I thought of the jets snapping about earlier, clearly it was widely known Max was here. I suddenly felt anxious for Max's safety.

'Well, they tried it in 2006 – half-heartedly – so I wouldn't rule it out.' Julian noted, turning from the window.

'It is something to bear in mind. OK, get UNCSAC arrange to get Max over the pond, Julian– it would be easier. When the security council convenes, we can get our Ambassador to formally propose the motion on Max's offer of technology and – babies - for land. It's true that we suspect Davies is working with the tacit consent of a cabal around the President, a suitable arrangement which gives the executive plausible deniability, but the situation could change very quickly. I'm afraid I must get back to Nottingham now.'

'What's in Nottingham, mother?'

'The remains of the British government darling.'

Sally hugged Max with genuine emotion, and Julian followed her out into the darkness. As they squeezed past Jonathan, I was surprised to see her rub his arm affectionately. We heard the remaining helicopter starting up its engine. Before she boarded, Sally stood having a conversation with her ex-husband, animated, not quite an argument but forceful, emotional. Julian reappeared in the kitchen as Daniel was putting out candles.

'Daniel I am afraid I will need to stay with you tonight. I hope that's ok.'

Daniel winked. 'Already sorted Prof, although it's going to be a bit intimate. Jonathan and Jamie can sleep in my bed, you can have the spare, and I can have the sofa: and I insist!'

'What about Max?' I asked.

Clearly adept at timing, Daniel had lit the last candle just as the lights went out. 'Since his arrival he hasn't slept much at all.'

'He can always get in with us.' Mocked Jonathan, smiling. To my embarrassment everyone got the joke, even Julian, who laughed nostalgically. 'Where is he, by the way?'

'He's probably communing with the experiment.' Daniel whispered, half seriously.

Later, both unable to sleep, Jonathan and I lay in the spare bed like an old sexless couple, although I had thought it prudent to layer up before I climbed in beside him. Daniel, thoughtful to the last detail, had allowed Jonathan to smoke without going outside – mostly on account of not disturbing him on the sofa. The subject of conversation was of course Max and sex with aliens. About Max, Jonathan thought that apart from the disorientating age difference, he was much the same. I wasn't so sure. I also confessed that Max's account of his time with the experiment struck me as vague and contradictory.

'What do you mean?' Jonathan had passed a spliff over which I had taken, not because I enjoyed it, but because I knew it would be wet from his lips.

'Well firstly, why would the Seeth settle on a planet that seemed so eminently unsuitable for them?'

'Come on, Jamie – they might have looked at hundreds of planets. Admittedly we now think there are thousands, millions of worlds out there capable of supporting life, but we might be wrong: a lot of the Hubble data was based on huge doses of speculation, let alone those fucking stupid 'artist impression' mock-ups that made them all seem like Kent. Perhaps space is emptier than we think.'

I passed back the spliff, already dizzy.

'And Max's '*I'm human*' line – look at him, his physique is more pronounced and well – *unbelievably* defined than ever – and he's covered in dots and his eyes flash!'

'I can see this has been a trying day for you. They might just be superficial differences, something the experiment couldn't correct. Fuck knows. He does seem rather thick with this AI don't you think?'

'Ah the experiment.' I shifted down the bed, stabbing the pillows down with me. 'It sounds more than an AI to me. Max is probably up there now, plotting, discussing mating rituals.'

'Green eyed over a computer now are we! Perhaps Max is Mohammad to the experiment's Allah?' Jonathan had laughed and I had sighed, smiling, but the image had bothered me, a little too close to Garen's religious mania. I lay in the dark, my mind whirling.

'Isn't all of this – the breeding idea - a bit too close to the *reconfigured man* shit for comfort?'

'Yeah. Your boyfriend seemed oddly prescient on the sex – but since that's all he ever thinks about, it's probably less sinister than you think.'

There was more I wanted to say but I was suddenly tired and anxious and before I could say anything Jonathan had turned his back to me. I did manage one last query before Jonathan lost consciousness: his ability to sleep in any place and under any circumstance was legendary.

'How did Sally get here – did Julian invite her?'

'I guess so – she's a dark horse – did you notice she pecked my cheek? Anyway, I'm glad she turned up, although something is clearly not well here as well, never mind the US. She is always at the heart of things, thank god.'

Max did not reappear until the morning, just as Julian was preparing to leave. I had snatched a brief conversation with my stepfather; he had described the emergence of the hybrids and how it had troubled him; he didn't elaborate why. He had also been disturbed by a run in with a group of youths outside the lab, claiming that the hybrids were angels and that they should be set free immediately. Again, I had thought of Garen and his sinister blog but said nothing. Later, we had all watched from the breakfast table as Max and his father said goodbye, pacing about together outside. Max seemed restless, touching his father a lot, holding his arm, hugging him. I thought Julian looked suddenly old; existentially tired. They both walked to a car that had appeared on the driveway, and Max stood for a long while after it had left, watching the empty road. As he walked back to the house, I saw him cast a glance upward in the direction of the ship, although low cloud had made it invisible. Next minute he was sitting down with us, his hair drawn up in a ponytail.

'Daniel we've eaten all your supplies – are you going to be alright?'

'I've got plenty more squirreled away Max, don't you worry.'

I asked after Julian and whether he had slept ok, although I was more curious as to where Max had been all night. One thing Max always disliked about me was my habit of interrogating him. I was old enough finally to control it, but it was still difficult.

'He's ok – it's just weird seeing him older, more fragile. I worry about him; I don't think he's well. I wanted him to come to New York, but he says he wants to stay with Margaret: I can understand that. It would be good to spend more time with him.'

'When do you leave?' I tried not to sound needy. I had hardly spent any time with him, and none alone. Max, of course, was well ahead of me.

'When do *we* leave you mean; you and Jonathan are coming with me. And before you fake some protest Jamie Relph, you can carry on your work there as much as you can here; and I need you Jonathan, all the old stalk and stealth! It is decided.'

I had no intention of finding an excuse but tried to look put out anyway. Jonathan faked a salute. 'Yes boss!'

Satisfied, Max bound up the stairs. Jonathan had raised one solitary eyebrow. 'Won't Garen be disappointed that you're leaving for the US again so soon?'

'I'll think he'll live.'

'You wanted to talk about him, back in the car yesterday?'

'Yeah – sorry about that, I was feeling tetchy and excluded. I presume no one told me about the return of Davies or Julian's little jaunt to the southern hemisphere to make sure I didn't relapse or something.'

Jonathan sighed, rolling his eyes. 'Something like that, and it wasn't as if you weren't busy saving the world. But yes, we thought it wise – but Max is back and we're off to New York so don't go all petulant on me.'

'But unless my paranoia has finally got the better of me, you know something about Garen – and given what Julian told me about the demonstrator outside his lab – I'm sure he told you as well – the reconfigured man is more than just Garen's porno version of first contact. What do you know, Jonathan Price, and no bullshit!'

'Fuck you are incorrigible!' but he had smiled, a good sign; since unlike Max, Jonathan was prone to fly off the handle if prodded too much. He looked at me thoughtfully.

'I always thought Garen was weird; I know you're pretty weird but apart from the kink there was something quite coherent to the site really; a sort of consistency that I didn't think Garen was capable of, even a degree of imagination.'

'He's quite imaginative, I can assure you of that.'

'I meant out of the sack, Jamie: and clearly if someone mentions it to you in New York, and some dudes turn up in a snowstorm up in Scotland, it's got followers, more dedicated than I would have thought, more political, I guess. I've kept my eye on him.'

I looked vaguely scandalised. 'You mean you've had him followed?'

'I wouldn't put it quite like that. What do you know about him?'

I sat eyeing Jonathan suspiciously. What did I know about Garen other than he was immensely good at sex? Almost nothing. I made several silent gestures with my mouth, wracking my brains for some biographical detail.

'He's got a degree in fine art from the Courtauld Institute.'

'And?'

'He's ex-catholic – which explains some of the erotica, I think. Ok, what do *you* know?'

'He gets shit loads of funding from an international bank account in Switzerland, linked to endless shell companies that hide the identities of his sponsors. Most of the recruits are gay, bi-sexual or pan-sexual – I have no idea what that means, by the way. His father was quite a well-known academic, working on social activism in the digital age. He was fired from his job – the reasons are obscure – and he started his own think tank on something called accelerationism.'

I was watching Jonathan with an expression of admiration and annoyance. 'I've seen that term used, on Garen's website. What does it mean?'

'Fuck knows, Jamie. Some sociological term, something to do with social radicalism and political activism – presumably he was fired because people thought he was condoning terrorism or violence. Anyway, his think tank disbanded, and many went off to Far Right organisations and movements – some even ended up in the Earth for Humans Movement.'

'I'm not sure what you're getting at, Jonathan - sorry. Be blunt.'

Jonathan laughed. 'I'm not entirely sure either – I'm not saying that Garen's site is a cover for the Earth for Humans movement; it's diametrically opposed, and it's got a fundamentally different membership – but it shares a similar premise; that alien hybrids will return to earth. But unlike Davies, who has been consistent in his obsession with alien invasions for over three decades, Garen sits down one afternoon and states that one of the central reasons the hybrids will return is to breed with us. I said last night it was weirdly prescient, you care to read the details it's more than that – it's *predictive*.'

'You also said last night he is obsessed with sex; and Jonathan, the web has been full of this shit for years – ever since people stopped believing in the mainstream media. It's just a coincidence!'

Jonathan pressed his lips together, rubbing his buzz cut. 'I'm not so sure – there is something very singular about your boyfriend.'

'You still having him followed?'

Jonathan did not react at first; preoccupied on some pressing matter. 'No; - but I am thinking.' He brought out his tobacco.

'You're smoking way more than you usually do.'

'I am thinking, Jamie, that this trip to the Big Apple might take a day or two to organise, and that we should go down to London and see your toy boy; have a chat.'

'God, and you dare to call me incorrigible! It's not quite normal out there, Jonathan, we can't just take off – do you have petrol vouchers and papers?'

He patted his hoodie pockets suggestively.

'You really think we have time? I'm not sure London is particularly safe now.'

'In and out, quick chat – I can go smoke on the roof if you two need to let off steam: seriously – it's reconnaissance.'

I was intrigued and, yes it would be fun to see Garen. I'd missed the sex. And now of course I was deeply intrigued. 'Ok, but you tell Max and don't give him any details.'

Daniel doubted we would have time, sensing that Sally's comments about the British government was as much a warning as a stray comment and pointing out that UNCSAC could move quickly. Jonathan persuaded him, however, after texting Julian who thought Dena would take about three days at the least to organise transport. We set off in the early afternoon. Jonathan's car had seen better days, but we made good timing and arrived in North London at about four in the afternoon. We'd stopped for petrol once, and Jonathan's vouchers proved up to the job: I found myself wondering where on earth he got them, and how many he had. To someone who had spent some time in London before the virus, I was at first pleasantly surprised to find it cleaned up and to see pedestrians and not a few cars moving about, but a lot of shops and buildings had been gutted with fire and as we approached central London it seemed eerily deserted; except for an enormous number of cats. Things got slightly more officious once we got into Whitehall. There were numerous roadblocks, mostly regular British soldiers, but closer into the West End they were manned by Blue Jackets. It was the first time I had gotten a close look at them: all men, the youngest were in their early twenties but the majority were middle aged and not especially fit or disciplined. At a checkpoint outside Charring Cross, just at the entrance to the Strand, I was asked to prove I lived on Marchmont Street and to state the purposes of my visit.

'When were you last in residence, Dr Relph?' The man was unshaven, and he wore a gun in a holster on the top of his left leg.

'About a year or so – I've been working in the US. The place has been rented to a friend.'

'Uhm, well this looks in order, but you better get this title deed form updated with the tenants name on, or you could lose your apartment, mate. And a word of advice.' He leaned in, smelling of sweat and beer. 'The embankment has flooded near the old fleet river, so don't risk driving down to the Thames and keep this side of Bloomsbury. Marchmont Street should be ok, and you can go into the west end by the British Museum, but don't go down the Kings Way too far from the centre: lot of gangs are operating there and there's a lot of territorial scuffles going on. Watch yourselves; there's been outbreaks of cholera over in Blackfriars.'

He waved us through.

'Still think this is a good idea?' I was spooked as we turned off the Strand; great sheets of water were lapping around the top of Fleet street and down to the river; some houses had collapsed; there was a heavy yeasty smell of mud and raw sewerage.

'It's fine – we leave tomorrow first thing and we'll be back before you can think of something else to complain about!'

We parked up in Russell Square – an impossibility of course in the old days – and crossed Southampton Row, passing the tube station on our right. It was closed, the entrance sealed with a massive steel shutter; the pavements strewn with rubbish and debris. We saw no one. When we reached my apartment – a first floor flat above a restaurant –the locks on the entry door had been changed. Jonathan rang the doorbell, somewhat aggressively. I texted Garen.

There was the sound of someone coming down the stairs inside.

'Hello? Anyone home?'

A silence: heavy with calculation, and then a woman's voice said 'Who is it? What do you want?'

'It's Jamie Relph, I own this place – Garen is my partner.'

Jonathan frowned at the description while the woman appeared to consider the information carefully. There was the sound of locks being withdrawn and the door opened just enough for me to catch sight of a youngish woman, blonde haired, peering out. We looked at each other, and I saw her look across to Jonathan, who was smoking with one foot on the railings down to the basement. Her expression relaxed immediately.

'Jamie – sorry – of course, come in! Garen has told me all about you – is this Jonathan?'

Jonathan seemed put out by her casual identification, stubbing the cigarette out under his trainer.

'Yes, it is – and who are you?'

The door opened. The hallway and the stairs were littered with bin bags and stray mail. There was a heavy smell of weed and sour rubbish.

'Sorry about the mess here – we're going to move it later.' The woman said apologetically. My sense of outrage was less than my concern over the use of the term 'we'.

'My name is Bridget Carter – it's a pleasure to meet you both. You must have come for the gathering?'

'No, we've just dropped in see how Garen is misusing his boyfriend's generosity.' Jonathan, irritated, pushed in and I followed, shaking her hand rather brusquely. She looked embarrassed.

We clattered up the stairs. The locks had also been changed on the entry to my flat and there seemed to be a rather large collection of them.

Jonathan made a shrug. 'Expecting trouble, Bridget?'

'Sorry?'

'The locks.'

'Oh, yeah – well it's been a bit wild here recently, the regular army patrols pull out about 6 and the Blue Jackets take over – they like to help themselves to stuff, and they've been particularly interested in our movement. I'll get you keys, Jamie – it must look like a squat, it isn't, really.'

I felt somewhat appeased. Inside the flat the air was thick with incense and in the living room there were several single mattresses neatly stacked up against the wall.

'Is Garen here by any chance?' Jonathan's mood lifted slightly at the prospect of replenishing his weed supply – huge plastic bags of the stuff were stacked in jars on the table. 'Dealing huh?'

'No. It's for visualising.' Bridget said firmly. Her voice was middle class, 'posh' as Jonathan would say (as he did about mine); she was neatly turned out and pretty in a sort of non-descript English way. 'Garen is out preaching. He'll be back with the others.'

'I see. Well Jonathan and I are going to be staying here for the night, so we can wait.'

'Sure – does he know you're coming?'

'Evidently not,' quipped Jonathan, sitting down heavily on a chair. Dust exploded into the air, picked out in the low sunlight streaming through the bay window. 'Mind if I help myself to some blow?'

'Help yourself. It's so exciting to finally meet you guys!' She went into the kitchen and filled a kettle. As she came back into the sitting room, she looked at Jonathan with an odd intensity. 'You don't remember me do you – not that you should.'

'We've met before?' Jonathan looked at her closely for the first time. 'Sorry Bridget, I don't recognise you.'

'It's a long time ago, to be honest I wouldn't have recognised you were it not for Garen.'

Puzzled, Jonathan put down his cigarette papers. 'Where did we meet?'

'At the Radcliffe infirmary – it's where we all met, although we only recently remembered it.'

'Sorry Bridget, I've no idea what you're talking about.'

I looked at the mattresses, glanced at Jonathan and walked to the window. I filled in the dots for him. 'She's one of the children who was abducted in 1993. Are all of you here?'

'Yes! All 23 – and now Max is back!'

I rarely saw Jonathan speechless. In the middle of my own shock, the sight of his jaw opening had a certain grim satisfaction to it.

Chapter Five: The devil and the detail.

I found the trip back to Oxford infinitely more exhausting than the flight down from Scotland. Seeing Max unchanged from the day he left Farndon Road in 2006 had been a deep shock. I had prepared myself, reigned in my emotions as best I could, but the sight of him running towards me had been deeply affecting. Max's vitality had always made me feel old, now of course I was. In two years, I would be 70 – not a particularly great age but thrown into stark relief by Max, contoured with youth and energy, seemingly restored, despite the elegant Seeth plumage. *Was* it Max? The question seemed absurd and yet it haunted me on the way back. His reappearance had closed a deep wound inside, a grief that I had found impossible to deal with, and yet seeing him filled me with a sense of foreboding. Like Jamie, I had always believed his return would close the circle, restore my world to normality, but Max had never been normal: had he been I would never have adopted him, never have fallen so profoundly in love. Walking with him to the car I had experienced a sense of déjà vu; that he would not be staying, that he would leave me again. I knew, simply and undramatically, that I could not bear to lose him again. Margaret was tearful at the news but also, like her own son, perceptive. She seemed less surprised about the proposed solution to human infertility than I had been. Glad to be in her arms again, profoundly relieved to be in my own home, I had rested for a while before sitting down to email Dena. When I opened my browser, it was to find that she had already contacted me.

Dear Julian.

I hope by the time you read this that you have been reunited with Max; I cannot imagine what it will feel like; you will need time to process it. You know this, obviously! Since your departure, we have been working with the hybrids almost non-stop. The 'Adams' have been model 'patients' and the data we have acquired is both extraordinary and largely unexpected. The general situation up here however is not so good. Several hours after your departure, a Scottish brigade arrived and there was an ugly stand-off over jurisdiction. This is probably just the beginning, although I must hand it to Sinclair that no one starting shooting. My first impressions of him were not favourable. I have had dealings with his kind for years, pompous, slightly superior, at times just downright condescending. Confronted with a diplomatic squabble however he proved that the British military are still professional enough to be pragmatic. After a walk through the woods with his Scottish counterpart - Brady McAllister, who looks about twenty-five tops, they agreed on a joint command structure. So far so good, but I have been around the bloc too many times to expect this to last. As a foreigner, the Union looks as dead as a dodo to me but the British government – wherever it is these days – will never allow the Scots to control the hybrids. We need to think of an exit strategy at some stage. Since no one has yet formally recognised Edinburgh's unilateral declaration of independence in 2020, the British hold all the cards, legally and constitutionally at least. And the longer this goes on, the more demonstrators we have on the perimeter of the lab. Anyway, I am digressing; it comes with the job.

Deborah and Vincent want to release a report on the hybrids as soon as possible and I concur, but I would be deeply appreciative of your input before we go public. As I think you will see almost immediately, we must tread very carefully if indeed the Malaq wish to 'return' to Earth. The hybrids are an isomorphic species in which males and females appear identical and are indeed possibly interchangeable. The hybrid has both male and female genitalia, but only one is sexually active at a time. They are not therefore, as we first imagined, hermaphrodites since they cannot fertilise their own eggs and the change to male or female appears to be controlled be hormonal or possibly environmental stimuli. We can also rule out at this stage any cloning, the remarkable degree of similarity between our three guests is a species characteristic – and there are very small difference between them. The interchangeability of sex looks to me like a 'throwback' to reptilian DNA: you yourself once observed this ability in frogs, but only in conditions of environmental stress and it cannot be ruled out that sex changes in hybrids is conditioned by the proximity of other hybrids. We know, for instance, that some reptiles in same sex populations change sex to facilitate reproduction.

Another surprise is that the hybrids have retained the egg laying reproductive trope of their Raptor ancestors: 'designated' females do not lactate, and the hybrids have no navels. The Malaq are not reptilian however but warm blooded. Eggs are laid not through a cloaca as in modern birds and surviving monotremes, but through an additional opening between the anus and the sheathed genitalia. Hybrids also have a gizzard, evidence perhaps of the link that occurred later on Earth between raptors and birds, although given the size of their digestive tract there is no reason why this feature should have been retained: in eating, the hybrids seem to prefer dairy products but they will eat meat and seem actually to enjoy it. What makes all of this surreal is that the hybrids are a new life form and as yet, none have obviously sexually reproduced. This means that they are of no help in explaining how this reproductive trope works in social groupings or how they themselves culturally configure sex and gender. Are they monogamous? Do they care for their young or is this a collective process? Since in theory a Malaq can be both 'mother' and 'father' to its offspring, how does this work in practice and what sort of broad social interactions will it structure? What, if anything, does this say about how the Malaq will view human dimorphism? It also poses issues that, however unpalatable, will need to be addressed. How quickly do they reproduce? Passive scans of the three hybrids show that they all contain multiple egg sacs, and since we have no idea as to their longevity and presuming that males can switch to female and lay, we are looking at a species with a huge capacity to expand in number.

*There are other bewildering differences which I can only touch on
here. The musculature is powerful and is enhanced by a fine
cartouche of exoskeletal mottling. Jamie observed this of course in
Max in the final hours of his journey in 2006. This patterning is
clearly therapod in origin, but the neck facias also contained a
symbiont, bioluminescent bacteria not unlike that found in the esca
of terrestrial fish. It glows when the Malaq is alarmed or excited –
Adam demonstrated this when he was first placed into an MRI
scanning chamber. Their eyes are luminescent with a third eyelid,
and the pupil is vertical. They have excellent visual acuity and a
well-developed sense of smell. Their epidermal construction is
devoid of any hair follicles, but they do grow a thick down on their
scalps which is either white or grey. While this has all the
appearance of hair, it is in fact more closely related to lichen.
Curiously, just below the 'hair' line, situated close to the left and
right temple of the scalp is a boss of cartilage just below the skin.
Exotically, it is probably a redundant carry over from either horns
or antlers. Their internal organs show a high rate of redundancy;
with multiple systems undertaking the same function. The brain
structure is surprisingly human, although their cranial capacity is
1500 cubic centimeters, considerably larger than ours. In structure,
their brains show far greater connectivity than modern homo
sapiens, and an enhanced series of nodes around the pituitary and
the hippocampus indicate either enhanced memory or learning
abilities. I can find nothing that approximates to the tagging we
found on the children but as you yourself witnessed, the three Malaq
(or the pod) have a demonstrable telepathic link, although this
appears to have weakened.*

*What I really need your help on – and Margaret's – is their genome.
Most of what I am about to say comes from Deborah who seems as
bewildered as I do. The coding is incredibly compressed, rather like
avian DNA. When you and Margaret modelled the genomes*

extracted from Max's chromosome 22 you stated (if I recall correctly) that the genome of the hybrids was 52. The genome of the present hybrids is in fact 46 – the same as humans. Deborah cannot account for the variation, other than suggesting it might have been a clinical or computational error in your original observations. Furthermore, the coding shows troubling mutagenic properties which worries her. Referring to their mode of reproduction, viable offspring could show a large degree of mutation over time. Is this an evolutionary advantage or a basic flaw in the genetic engineering of the Malaq? At this stage we are trying to clear up the data.

By now Max will have presumably clarified Adam's rather enigmatic comment about returning 'home'. You will not like what I am about to say; I don't that's for sure; but someone will say it: if indeed the Malaq wish to settle on earth they have the capacity to breed very quickly. Even before the fertility crisis this would have raised issues – resources, land, etc. Given the present rise of eugenic anxieties caused by the pandemic, and if the latest WHO projections on the collapse of human reproductive rates are accurate, their arrival will cause immense hostility. It isn't rocket science to calculate that we could be displaced as the dominant species in around 75 years. An eventual cure to the present spread of infertility amongst humans would slow this, but time is not on our side. We would not so much cohabit the planet as hand it over to them.

Sorry to end on such a gloomy note. This could be the saving of us all, I know, and I have waited for this moment my entire life, but I have some misgivings that are hard to express and once all this gets out you can imagine how such physiological differences will fuel possible hatred and violence, or worst perhaps, uncritical adoration – the hybrids are very striking in their appearance and in their behaviour, they are powerful; not just physically, but gentle, composed. I wish I felt more confident about where this is going. Please get back to me on the genome, Julian. I have attached as much of the raw data to this email as I could load. And tell me about Max as soon as you feel able.

Best wishes always

Dena.

My Dear Dena.

*I returned from Leicestershire this afternoon, drained physically as well as mentally. I took a nap before sitting down to email you, only to find yours – now I feel as if I had been given several shots of ephedrine. As a geneticist what you have described is staggering and frankly completely inexplicable. The Malaq appear almost chimera like, and as I now know, this is clearly as much the outcome of the experiment's gene splicing as much as any 'natural' evolutionary schema. Much of what you say could have been logically inferred from our understanding of Margaret's data: you are right incidentally, the chromosome count when we sampled Max in 2005 was 52. That it has somehow been reduced to 46 is not surprising given what I must tell you. The plan to return the Malaq to Earth is premised on a deal thought up by the experiment and endorsed by Max. This will come as a shock, it shocked me. In exchange for land to settle, the Malaq will share technologies and also **breed with us**. The experiment has concluded that there is no cure for human infertility, and neither Jamie nor Sally contradicted him. Given that finding a suitable planet to settle the hybrids on has proven problematic – Max is here to negotiate this bizarre, almost unimaginable solution. That they are so physiologically different to us is therefore bewildering to me. You should also be aware that Max is looking to settle thirty million (30,000,000) hybrids.*

Max has not aged, something which must be to do with time dilation and being on board a ship travelling at or close to the speed of light, but it added to a surreal encounter. He is, as far as I can tell, the same young man who left me, but he has retained some Seeth decorative features which I had not expected. I also must confess

Dena, eternally grateful as I am to see him again, that something doesn't quite add up. It's hard to put my finger on it, and although I only had the briefest of chats with Jamie, I suspect he has similar concerns.

First and foremost is the nature of the experiment. As we had long supposed, the experiment is an AI built by the Seeth once they realised that their new settlement was killing them with radiation – Max never once mentioned he knew where this planet was incidentally, and never mentioned Tau Ceti. Max's relationship with the experiment is surprisingly intimate, they clearly converse a great deal and are working together but it is not clear to me who is actually in control. As Margaret postulated in 2006, the experiment realised that it needed Max to assist in understanding a new variant of the Seeth which is now closely related to humans, but the decision to send down the 18 hybrids before Max had liaised with UNCSAC seems to be on the experiment alone. Max described it as 'impatient' and promised it would not happen again, implying he has some influence on its decisions. The arrangements are very byzantine: Max can communicate with the experiment and the hybrids, but the hybrids cannot communicate with the experiment – making Max in effect the middleman, although he doesn't see it that way himself. Dan also described how he saw Max talking with what he believed was the experiment – a bizarre facsimile of Max: it sounded quite frightening. I did not have time to ask Max if a meeting with the experiment is possible – I suggest you might have a go; I suspect the answer will be no.

Sally came over from Nottingham; I invited her and was surprised she came. I haven't seen her since my marriage to Margaret. She was on good form, occupying a position of some importance (as always) but she was cagey: the British government seems chaotic and faction ridden, and I think it highly likely that they might try and get their hands on Max as well as the three hybrids. She suggested that we – that is you and UNCSAC – get Max and all the hybrids we can account for – over to New York as soon as possible. Jamie and

Jonathan also agreed to go, Max seemed quite insistent – sorry to complicate your already complex business. I think this is the best exit strategy we have. Whether this is because Sally believes the government here is finished is unclear, but if you could somehow organise this it would be a great help and soon – something smells wrong here in the UK. So far – oddly perhaps – there has been no official interference with Max's arrival despite the fact that the ship which returned Max (and either is the experiment or houses it) is stuck in plain sight over the wood and Daniel's farm is constantly being overflown by RAF fighter planes.

One last thing you should know – although it will come as no surprise. Sally confirmed that Davies is in effect in the US administration. She also confirmed that the British government have just 'invited' the Blue Jackets – an arm of the Earth for Humans Movement – to assist the police and army here in what is being called reconstruction. Is this also the case in the US? Clearly Davies has never dropped his obsession with alien invasions so tediously voiced by his late colleague James DeSilva, so this will add considerably to our difficulties. All the official announcements here have so far have confined themselves to the hybrid landings; we have had no official statement as to whether we are following the US in a compulsory donative scheme on harvesting viable egg and sperm: again I am not sure whether this is because the government is preoccupied with the Malaq or that they cannot agree a policy to deal with the infertility crisis.

God knows where this imbroglio will lead us, Dena. I will try and get over to New York as quickly as I can, but I have missed Margaret terribly and frankly have not felt well these last few weeks – nothing serious I think – just constant exhaustion. You know what a fussy traveller I am – I need a few creature comforts (such as they are these days) before I am back on my feet.

I'll go print off the data and download it to Margaret's lab here – they have their own power, so we're not shackled to the vagaries of the national grid. One final thought. Can you remember the meeting of the 1993 committee, the late one prompted by the arrival of the Japanese report? The one where DeSilva threw his spectacular fit of hysterics? Do you remember DeMarr suggesting that what we were seeing in Max was an attempt to improve the human genome through 'selective breeding': it's in the minutes, I checked them earlier. Uncanny given what is being suggested? I wished DeMarr were here – I'm sure he would see more than me.

Yours ever Julian.

I sent the email and sat back in my chair heavily, looking at my screensaver – a photograph of my marriage to Margaret, with Jamie, blonde and very handsome, standing just to my side. I went downstairs and found Margaret asleep in the drawing room; she had been working exhaustively at the Institute for Molecular Biology, going through the WHO data and liaising with Sally – and irony in the circumstances, but they worked well together and seemed to get on. The University had been closed for nearly three years, but the government – however peripatetic – somehow managed to get the labs up and working. I hesitated to wake her, but she must have sensed me lurking in the doorway, because she shook her head and sat up, drawing a cardigan about her.

'Julian! Sorry – that was supposed to be one of my powernaps. How's Dena?'

I slumped down next to my wife, holding out my mobile and showing her the emails. Margaret yawned, fished out a pair of glasses from the depths of the sofa and read them briskly. As she went through Dena's detailing of the hybrids she sat up; I could see the luminous text on each lens of her spectacles. After a few minutes of scrolling up and down she handed back the phone.

'We should go over the data together – it will be like old times, darling!'

'Margaret you've been at the institute all morning – I can have a provisional dig around, and we can then go over it here tomorrow. It's important but we have time; Dena's got more than enough to be getting on with.'

But Margaret was standing, clearly motivated. 'The sooner we can help her the better; Dena is right about releasing a detailed report on the hybrids as soon as possible. Given what it contains, any delay runs the risk of it leaking out first – and everything seems to leak these days – then we will have a panic on our hands. And we need to get this out before anyone mentions hybridising with the hybrids!'

Although I had retired several years ago, I had retained an emeritus status at the University and I still had access to the labs; I rarely visited them. Margaret of course virtually lived there. The institute had moved since the heady days of 2005, when we had used DeMarr's mysterious gift of Davie's stolen software, and the equipment had been significantly upgraded; sixteen years is a long time in research design, despite the dramatic halt caused by the pandemic. Since the development of a cure for HN71, Oxford and other institutions had been co-opted into examining the collapse of human fertility. I was surprised therefore to find the place largely deserted.

'Shouldn't this place be humming with researchers?'

'Well most of the technicians died in 2020, and we haven't really trained up enough yet – it's not so much the computing or the energy, it's having skilled people to problem solve. We lost a lot of very capable individuals, many of them were irreplaceable.'

'Of course – stupid of me, sorry darling.'

'It can be quite eerie here sometimes!' Margaret switched on a series of computers and uploaded Dena's files – several were audio clips, recorded usefully by Deborah Ewing. 'Civilisations collapse not because people become stupid or forget, but because they lose information and the ability to interpret it. Of course, we believed we were immune from this with all our glorious digital archives!'

I thought of Dena's comments about the NASA probes sent to Tau Ceti and the distinct possibility that they would beam back their data to a dead planet, or one dominated by hybrids.

'Jamie is convinced the infertility issue is a syndrome and that it is terminal. He didn't say much, but I suspect he agrees with the experiment's predictions.'

Margaret looked up at me thoughtfully. 'Yes – I think Sally does as well, but that's not what people want to hear.'

'Did you read the bit in Dena's email about the possible timeline for the emergence of the hybrids as the dominant species?'

'I did.' Margaret's voice was distracted as spools of data began to fill various screens. 'So we'd better get to work.'

I fell silent, turning my attention to a series of print outs emerging next to me.

We spent several hours going over Deborah's findings, cross referencing a lot of the data with records from the 2005 imaging of Max's chromosomes. The similarity to avian DNA was striking, not just in the sheer amount of genetic information in the Malaq genome, but in the way the individual chromosomes were packed up closely into dense swirls of coding. Margaret, in her typical way, worked quickly and methodically, her energy seemingly limitless. Just after midnight she made coffee and we sat, much as we used to, theorising what any of it could mean.

'Thoughts, darling?' She pushed a powerful expresso in my direction. Coffee was incredibly hard to come by. I nursed it like a vintage malt.

'Well we need a lot more data; when the opportunity arises, we should ask the other hybrids for samples, but I think I see the problem.'

Margaret laughed. 'Thank god! I'm not sure I do.'

'Avian DNA has always been notoriously difficult to map; it was suggested in 2011 that the amount of short, stubby chromosomes enabled birds to adapt very quickly to specific environmental niches, and for variations in coding to quickly develop different species. We know that the closest ancestors to raptors are birds so what we have here is not surprising. But the DNA base sequences appear to have bypassed the principle of conservation: the essential stability of the DNA code over time to provide and transmit the basic physiological functions to ensure life.' I had looked up suddenly. 'Sorry darling, I'm not implying you don't know that!'

Margaret laughed and ruffled my hair. 'It's always good to be reminded, go on!'

'I think the problem is intentional, and – if I'm not mistaken – I think it involves our old friends; the Seeth amino acid bases.'

Margaret stood behind me, her head close to mine, working through a schematic drawn up from Dena of one of the Adam's genotypes.

'Well, well. I think you're right!'

One of the first breakthroughs in 1993 was the identification that three of the basic amino acids present in human DNA were being replaced by three distinct and unknown bases derived from the Seeth genes. While DeMarr and James DeSilva knew what they were looking for, the rest of the committee had been clueless. Deborah's provisional sketches showed that the mutagenic properties of the hybrid DNA – its susceptibility to quite sudden change were closely related to the Seeth amino acids. During normal cell replication, in which millions of cells are replaced by simple division. the position of these bases should obviously remain the same – in the hybrids, just hours after they had gained consciousness, three base sequences had shifted.

'I don't get this – at this rate of mutation they should have been dead on the table within hours?'

'Not necessarily, Margaret; we can't see immediately what proteins are being produced by the change in coding – and don't forget, that's exactly what we said about Max!' I had flicked forward to a later sketch, showing another change. 'I think there's a pattern here.' I pushed a stack of printouts away. 'You were the first person to suggest that the changes to Max's 22 were not random, not evidence of retroviral activity or mutation, but systematic. I think this is was we are seeing here. It's as if the process we saw in Max is still continuing in the hybrids.'

Margaret leaned against the desk next to me. 'I don't understand Julian – you're saying that the hybrids are still changing?'

'Yes; evolving, still adapting – it's incredible! They are becoming more human.'

It was late, we were both excited, perhaps even afraid. Stripped of all the science and the jargon, the hybrids were in effect a work in progress. I was convinced of this, despite the obvious need for more sampling and observation. The most obvious explanation was that the experiment had designed the hybrids to breed with humans from the beginning; the mutations had in effect reduced the genetic mismatch between the two species. But Max's account of the experiment's agreement to 'solve' human infertility and hybrid homelessness implied it was contingent, a sudden idea. Could the experiment have tweaked the hybrid genome so quickly? Later, curled up with Margaret, I had thought of Bradebarker; the morning that Jonathan's mother had telephoned him to say that she and her husband could not accept Jonathan back into their care. When pressed as to why, Mrs Price had said that she did not believe the boy found in the wood was Jonathan, but an imposter. She also confessed to being haunted by nightmares in which her son changed shape, often into animals, and that she believed – however irrationally – that these were warnings. Bradebarker recounted this to me, chain smoking outside the John Radcliffe infirmary. He had been intrigued. Dreaming in situations of anxiety was not unusual, but the actual form taken by the images in the dreams were not aliens and spaceships, something he could reasonably account for, but images of shapeshifting, shamanic tropes that were very terrestrial. I too, of course, had dreamed of Max in the company of wolves or lizards; and Jamie had even dreamed of running with Max into the wood, a premonition, with wolves on either side. I dozed, my mind wheeling and circling over the past. Was this because the Seeth communicated through dreams? Were these residues, echoes, of a now lost Seeth ability – or a precursor, a forerunner of some entirely new life form? And deep in those echoes, in the images of shape shifting and colour, were three distinct base sequences.

Chapter Six: Garen Lane.

As dusk fell, more of Jonathan's long-lost companions drifted back to my apartment. Not that he recalled any or recognised them, for they were all now in their early thirties, brought together it would appear by Garen who, it turned out, was an abductee who had been found with Bridget. We had retreated to my bedroom – littered with bongs – to collect our thoughts. My tasteful artwork had been replaced by Garen's rather bizarre taste in erotica: naked men, masked, their thick penises dripping pre-cum.

'This is the weirdest piece of shit yet.' Jonathan had been unnerved, a rare occurrence, and was smoking an enormous spliff. He had gone around looking at the photos tutting loudly like an old maid.

'Do you recall any of them, their names?'

'No. Max and I were the last to be found, and we were kept in separate bays – I mean we socialised, but they were younger than me. I wonder how long ago Garen identified them?' His eyes were glassy. I had gone to rebuke his excess but thought better of it.

'It could be some sort of scam – I mean – this looks and feels like the Adams Family, they might all be experiencing some sort of collective delusion. Presumably, Julian would know their names, or Margaret?'

'Yeah – although it was a long time ago.' He inhaled deeply. 'Of course, thanks to DeSilva, they were screened for years afterwards, but I assumed separately. I don't think they're faking it; not consciously at least'

'I thought that of all the 24, only you and Max were modified in anyway?'

'All the kids had tags, but they broke down very quickly, Julian thought it was some sort of immune response. It's possible there was some sort of change – your scar for instance, you said it lit up when Max returned. We need to talk to boss man – wherever he is!'

'If we leave first thing we could call in at Oxford – see Julian – I'd like to see mother before we go to the US'.

'Sure; if we have time.' Jonathan made the qualification sound ominous.

People started to cook food – my stomach rumbled appreciatively – and at about seven there was some commotion and I heard Garen's voice whoop in delight. The bedroom door opened and Garen ran in and threw his thick arms about me dramatically. I hardly recognised him. He had shaved his head, which I was disturbed to find made him look insanely sexy and he was wearing a sort of kaftan over a black T-shirt and jeans. We kissed deeply, his firm shapely lips smothering mine. Jonathan coughed politely.

'Jono! Man – it's so good to see you both – and at the beginning of great things! Max is back! Have you heard!'

'Yes, we've just come from seeing him.' Somewhat reluctantly I disengaged Garen's hands, which were cupping my buttocks suggestively. 'How did you know?'

'It's all over the internet – come on – you've got to see this!'

In the living room a sheet had been spread on the floor and bowls and dishes of food were being placed by Bridget and two men, both with identical haircuts to Garen. We were led out of my apartment and up the stairs – clearly Garen had appropriated the whole building. When I asked about the occupant on the second floor – a miserable Greek who had frequently complained about Garen's music – I was told that he had died of the virus. It had been particularly bad in central London.

'I take it you've been vaccinated?'

Garen turned on a giant TV bracketed to the wall and leaned down to fit up some cables snaking over the floor. I noticed several DVDs with rather suggestive titles littered about.

'Sure – we all have – no one's been infected for over a year. Watch this, guys!'

Garen, slack with a sort of adoration I had not seen before, played the stream that had been broadcast from Scotland as the hybrids had emerged from stasis. Brought up on fake news, doctored videos and hysterical accounts of alien autopsies, my first reaction was that it was staged – despite the UNCSAC timestamp in the bottom and clear recognition of the hybrid's Seeth physiology. As the realisation dawned that I was seeing something real, I felt numb. The beauty of the hybrids was obvious if not obscure; there was something troubling in their form, something almost too perfect, too removed from human experience.

'Are there any females?' asked Jonathan curiously.

'You're looking at both male and female!' Garen caressed the screen.

'I don't see any females, Garen.' Said Jonathan slowly,

'They're both; man! They come with both bits!'

'Sorry to be crude, Garen, but I can't see any breasts.'

'That's because they lay eggs, Jonathan.' I said quietly. Given that Max's plan was to encourage breeding between the hybrids and humans, their physiology was obviously, distressingly problematic. The whole idea suddenly seemed insane.

Jonathan then asked if they were hermaphrodites, but Garen said no – emphatically. They selected their sexual identity as and when appropriate.

'How the fuck do you know that?' Jonathan asked; he's paused the screen on a frame of the hybrid's bulge and was looking at it with a drugged, bemused expression on his face. He fast forwarded an image of solid pectorals, the nipples subliminal, a blush of shade.

'I have inside information, dudes.'

Since Julian had ran into his mates demonstrating outside the lab, it was not hard to imagine that Garen had some contacts with the technicians or even some of the soldiers. After watching the clip several times, we went back down to my apartment to find a communal meal in full swing. Jonathan and I sat down and joined in various conversations; about the state of London (generally bad) about how and when Garen had contacted the others and finally on the news of the infertility crisis. There was excited, rather prurient conjecture as to how you had sex with the hybrids. Bridget seemed disturbingly keen to get pregnant as soon as possible. Garen was fascinated by whether a pregnant male was possible, or whether it would have to be a female. Since there was no evidence of mammalian glands or penises, the distinction struck me as rather pointless. All I could think of as I sat listening to the group was how in God's name Max's plan was going to work.

After the food had been cleared away, Garen vanished for a bit and I spoke with a guy called Paul, who claimed he had been abducted near Liverpool in 1993. He described his experiences with obvious conviction, but the fact that he too was gay struck me as more than a coincidence. Of the 24 abductions in 1993, the pairings were mostly boy-girl; Jonathan and Max were the only boys to be found together, along with a pair of girls. Of all the people crammed into my living room, most were gay or bisexual. I asked others about their experiences which were freely shared. None could remember how they were taken, but only recall being returned. Several had clear recollections of the John Radcliffe infirmary, one girl even claimed to recall my stepfather talking to her. Meanwhile Jonathan, socialising with an ease that frankly surprised me, managed to get all their names and the places they were found in without making it seem obvious. As we approached the mandatory lights out, Garen reappeared and after cleaning up and offering 'prayers' for the safe delivery of the hybrids, cleared the floor and turned into a dormitory. Somewhat too obvious for my liking, he then took my arm and pulled me into the bedroom.

We had sex, rushed and incoherent, but perfectly executed. Garen's body was landscaped with tattoos, some new and Seeth inspired. Afterwards he smoked an enormous number of cigarettes, pulling them out of yellow Camel packs with long, greasy fingers. I noticed that the health warnings were printed in French. A thick smog lay just above our heads.

'You ok, baby?'

'Yes, I'm fine Garen, I'm a bit exhausted and well – this is a lot to take in.'

'Yeah, but man it's a whole new beginning! The combination of two races into one.'

I lay thinking of the image of the hybrids in the live feed. I asked him when he first realised that he had been an abductee, and then, more cautiously, when he had decided to contact the others. The answers seemed candid, post-coital; Garen had been 19 when he read something about the 1993 abductions. It hadn't taken him long to figure out that the dates – March to June – coincided with his own experience of a serious childhood illness. He recalled visiting a clinic until he was about ten, once a year, assuming they were screening to see if he was still in remission, but it had seemed odd, the doctors unhelpful and silent; the whole process stinking of secrecy. He'd then scoured various websites and blogs, piecing together stories and testimonials like his, and gradually he had found the other children: by then mostly successful adults, but all with the same strange gap in their early lives. The inspiration for forming what he called a vigilante came after he was visited by Max.

My eyes narrowed slightly; I had been drifting asleep.

'Max?'

'Yeah – the emissary of the experiment – he came to me and told me of his plans; said I was to prepare the way, like sort of John the Baptist – you know, spread the word.'

I lifted my head up sharply, suspecting Garen was joking. But his face had a blank expression that shocked me. Evidently, as far as he was concerned, Max really had appeared, and he had really been chosen.

'When was this visitation?'

'Two – three years ago – I can't remember exactly. I was ill – down with some bug – everyone was convinced it was the virus, even me. Then this beautiful, naked man appeared, eyes like a cat but luminous, Jamie, like stars!'

'That's pretty awesome.' I said, my voice flat. I would have been in the US at the time, or worst still, in London. Had it not been for the bizarre intensity of Garen's description I would have dismissed this as a weed fuelled fantasy; but something wasn't right. Before I had met Max and heard about his mission, Garen's little sex-fest obsession with aliens was ludicrous; but as Jonathan has recently pointed out: it was exactly what Max and the experiment had proposed. Garen had said a lot more, random disjointed comments on angels and old testament apocrypha but I couldn't really focus on it. He'd clearly given this matter a great deal of thought.

I said very little, in part so not to disturb his own account. We lay surrounded by candles and I had started to feel slightly claustrophobic and sketchy. Just before he fell asleep, Garen sat up and said

'Have you been tested?'

The question caught me by surprise. 'For HN71? Of course.'

'No, for fertility.'

'I haven't yet – I'm waiting for the government to work out its policy.'

'You'll be waiting for ever – I have; I had it tested yesterday – jacked off into a jam jar.'

'And?'

'No baby batter. All deficient in some internal structure or something.'

Unfairly I had assumed it to be some underhand, back street job but the diagnosis seemed accurate. I turned around to face him in the deep amber of gutted candles.

'Does it bother you? I never thought of you as the parenting kind?'

'Nah, not really. It's kind of weird though, given that I dodged the virus. And I was sort of excited about knocking up some alien – but there it is.'

I felt myself growing suddenly irritated, unusually, since I rarely listened to Garen's views; certainly not enough to invest an emotional response to them.

'Isn't this all a bit creepy? Aliens sent from God – it's just too neat, too simple?' The idea that Max had appeared was not impossible; but that he would have in effect engineered my boyfriend as a leader of a sect was difficult to believe; and this visitation had occurred long before the discovery of infertility. 'I mean you are thinking of your God, why even link this to angels and the old testament? Why not a Hindu deity or a Muslim Sufi? And why announce to you that the plan was to breed with them?'

Garen sat up, hugging his knees, his back to me, curved up into broad shoulders, rigid now with his own irritation. He was pissed off and suddenly petulant. 'I hate it when you do this – cast me as some muscle Mary without a brain: get outside your smug little scientific comfort zone, look around!'

'Garen I just don't know this side of you – it's just a bit too weird.'

'Well you never knew me, you never guessed I was an abductee; and you've never shown much interest in my work either; Mr I am a great scientist! You're such a fucking hypocrite; now because I am acting on my insights, because I have been shown the plan, you think I'm some pervert.'

'Well you could have told me about your abduction when we first met, I wasn't aware I had to guess – and you clearly knew about my association with Max – I've looked at the website, some of those images of Max are mine, taken by Jonathan. I certainly didn't give them to you. And why didn't you invite me to join the group yourself?'

Stung, Garen stood up and pulled on a T-shirt. 'So, I'm stealing from you now?' He bent down, his abdominals folding in thick grooves as he leaned to stand into his jeans. 'Are you with us Jamie? There's nothing stopping you and Jonathan joining us and being on the side of the angel, for once! We are here to protect the hybrids, to renew ourselves – or are you going to cling to the fucking wreckage of the old world! Something big is happening!'

'Who are you protecting them from?'

Garen looked stunningly incredulous. 'The government, man! The Blue Jacket fascists! You know that they've just made a pact with the Earth for Humans movement, we'll soon have ministers in the government from that xenophobic little outfit – and they're all homophobes, incidentally. You think these fascists are going to allow the hybrids to stay? You think they're going to just sit back as a new race emerges?'

'I did know about the pact; and I am as opposed to them as you are, but when we get to the sex bit, it's going to have to be more organised, assessed, even if compatible how this is going to work will require careful consideration. The hybrids look entirely different to us in that regard. Not everyone is wired like you.'

I should not have used the tone of voice I did; and I should have said *we* not you. I could hear myself; superior and condescending; implicitly saying that inter-breeding was too explosive an issue to be left to what I considered a fringe group and a guy with a dick fixation. His comments on the blue jackets caused me to think suddenly of Sally, standing in Daniel's sitting room playing nervously with her necklace; anxious about something other than the arrival of her adopted son. But the damage was done. Garen snarled out an uncharacteristic expletive and left, slamming the door behind. Startled voices consoled him. I waited, my heart beating fast with anger and frustration and then, dressing quickly, I went to find Jonathan. As I walked through my living room, Bridget grabbed my arm and said plaintively, 'guys don't fight!'. As I left, I saw Garen spooned up on Paul, who lay seemingly comatose underneath him. I eventually found Jonathan upstairs, looking through the recordings that Garen had made of the Dena's press conference after the live streaming of the hybrids. I slumped down next to him, smelling of smoke and sex.

'We need to go first thing. Forget Oxford.'

Jonathan looked up from his phone. 'What happened?'

'Garen has just, in utter seriousness, compared himself to John the Baptist; there is something really sinister going on here. I've left him ball deep in one of his disciples; and he claims that Max appeared in person and instructed him to start his movement two years ago.'

'Really? That sounds improbable – but it would explain a lot.'

'What does that mean?' It was a dishonest as well as rhetorical question: I knew exactly.

'Well before the power went, and while you were engaging in your sex for answers scam, I did a little digging around of my own.'

He passed me his phone. The Wi-Fi was down but Jonathan had taken a screen shot of a list of names, lifted from some Home Office file. I didn't ask how or why; it was evidently one of Jonathan's skill sets, like forging papers and vanishing for weeks on end. I scrolled down. The room seemed hot and airless; a dead man's flat, the windows still sealed.

'What the fuck!'

Jonathan had managed to acquire a list of the children from a classified copy of a home office report closed in 1995. The names were entirely different, except Garen's, who had indeed been taken from a cancer ward.

'I don't understand – there could be a mistake? Might they have changed the children's names, for security reasons or something?'

'No.' Jonathan took the phone back and switched it off. We sat in the dark, stuffy room. There was the sound of music from downstairs. 'Given the publicity around the abductions, the parents were given an option – none took it, although I remember Julian telling me that he had considered it for Max.'

'But they're so convincing, they clearly believe they are the abductees!'

Jonathan yawned. 'Garen has clearly done a number on them, that's for sure: cult psychology 101, why is either a mystery or not. He could just be a sad little bastard who wants to be a leader, and he managed to be at the right place at the right time when the world went to shit. The game changed and he seized the opportunity to live out his fantasies. The mystery version is that the website, the reconfigured man, contains information that we know to be uncannily accurate and this site has been running since the pandemic, long before the hybrids returned and any suggestion of inter-breeding made: why, because he was recruited. He might well be John the Baptist.'

'You really believe Max, or the experiment, contacted Garen and told him to prepare the way for interspecies sex before the onset of infertility was even identified?'

'Well it would account for the prophecy bit – and don't pretend you've not been thinking of this.'

'But doesn't that mean Max has just lied to us.'

'Not necessarily. It does mean that he might know less about the experiment than he imagines.'

I sat incredulously, looking down at the floor. If Garen had been abducted, he would have been known to the experiment; his story became suddenly much more credible. I did not believe in prophecy.

'But Garen said Max appeared, not the experiment?'

'And Daniel implied they look much the same.' Jonathan said quietly.

'Do you think the experiment created the infertility crisis?' My voice was scarcely a whisper; afraid as I was to hear myself asking whether the experiment was genocidal.

'Possibly, or it could have simply had seen the signs; the Seeth died from sterility too. One thing's for sure.' Jonathan stretched out on the sofa, fidgeting into a comfortable position. 'We need to get Max on his own; soon!'

I tried to sleep but found it initially impossible. Eventually I must have gone off because I was awoken at about 3 am by the power coming on suddenly. I sat up blinking, disorientated, convinced it was morning but as I checked my phone the lights failed again. There then came the distinct sound of gunfire, somewhere towards Russell Square. Jonathan jumped awake, the rattle of automatic weapons echoing off the buildings in Marchmont Street. We both stood between the windows, Jonathan leaning down peering through the blinds, but everything was in total darkness. The shooting appeared to recede and stop around 4.30 am. For a long time, Jonathan stood motionless.

'We've got about four hours until sunup, we should leave and head back to Dan's.'

Outside, their red light diffused by smoke, several flares bloomed in the sky and drifted lazily over the rooftops. There was a deep boom and the floor vibrated, followed by another, fading slowly.

'Artillery.' Said Jonathan, as if to himself. 'This sounds serious.'

'No shit!'

Someone came running up the stairs, and Bridget appeared darkly in the open doorway. 'You guys ok?'

'Sure. This happen every night?'

'No – get away from the windows, come into the stairwell.'

We followed, stumbling over various objects scattered on the floor. On the landing, Bridget pulled out a torch and angled it low. She had a gun over her shoulder.

'Woah, what is that!'

She looked bemused, following my gaze to her side. 'It's a colt AR 15, semi-automatic, not much use out there at the moment. You guys leaving?'

'Yeah – we need to get back to Leicestershire.'

'It might not be that easy – there's been a coup.'

'A what?' I sounded vaguely hysterical.

'An illegal seizure of power.' She answered pedantically.

Jonathan, seemingly calm although his face was hidden in darkness, asked if it was the Blue Jackets.

'It is – one of our people got word out from Nottingham that the PM has been arrested along with several members of the cabinet. The shelling is from the Army, still loyal, and still packing a lot of fire power, but our alien hating friends seem well prepared. Most of the fighting is down by Whitehall and Charring Cross. Going to Leicestershire is mad; they want to capture Max. Going to him is not such a good idea.'

'We're going, coup or not.' Said Jonathan. Bridget looked at him intently for a moment, calculating something.

'Ok – have it your own way - you'll have to go via the West Way; you can't get back into north London. Keep moving – some nasty gangs out there – they'll take your car and probably sell you on to traffickers if they test you and find you're fertile. Keep off the M25 and the M40.'

'How the fuck do we get to the M1 then?'

'You'll have to figure that out.'

I stood rigidly, the soft pop and rumble of shelling still audible. Bridget turned, hesitating. I could sense her looking at me now, with the odd intuitive stare she had used on Jonathan. I was close to telling her that Garen was a big fat fraud; that she had never been abducted, that he had insinuated her fantasy into his own experience, but it would have made no difference. If I had shown her Jonathan's list, she would have said it was fake, and given that it was possible, I had no other evidence. Perhaps she knew it was all lies but felt that Garen was worth following; that in the coming chaos people like Garen always managed to survive. She turned suddenly and ran downstairs.

'What about Sally? She knew something was up – you think she's ok?' I did not recognise my own voice.

'She's ok, she's more than capable of handling herself.'

'And what about Max? What if they take him?'

'Jamie, Max has a fucking great ship suspended over his head, he can look after himself as well. We, on the other hand, are in deep shit so we need to concentrate on the problem in hand. We need to get a message through to Dena.'

'How the fuck do we contact her? There's no Wi Fi and no power. We can't drive to Scotland!'

We went back into the dead Greek's apartment. From outside came the panoramic sound of explosions and gunfire, ratcheted up to a grand scale. Oddly when the pandemic broke, I never entertained the idea that I would die; squatting up against the wall, watching the night sky flash and blink, I was now far less sure.

'Give me your phone, Jamie.'

Jonathan's face lit up as he switched it on; although his face was tense in concentration he still looked remarkably together. I was intrigued to see he knew my access code. He swung the phone about watching for a signal. He put it down on the floor and started fishing about in his hoodie, back jean pockets, and finally pulled out a small piece of bubble wrap. I was about to suggest that this was not the best time to get high but as he spilled out the contents, I saw it contained several sim cards. A large bang – much closer – made us both instinctively duck. Plaster dust fell from the ceiling. Jonathan opened up the back of my phone and messed about reconfiguring my network.

'Won't that give me a new number?' I had no idea what he was doing, but a brief glance at me advised silence. On about the third or fourth sim card a secretive smile spread from the corner of his lips. His long nicotine stained fingers flashed over the keypad. He then shimmed over to the window.

'Yeah. That's still pretty shit – we need to get on the roof.'

'I don't think there's access.'

'Sure there is – come on.' Further protests were clearly pointless. Out in the hallway a third flight of stairs led to a small landing. In the ceiling above our heads was a square wooden hatch that led to the attic.

'Make a step.'

'A what?'

Jonathan took my hands and placed them together, and standing, placed his foot in my cupped palms.

'It's just like the gym except more useful.' I lifted him, squatting with my back straight. He pushed the hatch open, pulling his head back sharply as dust and grit showered down onto his shoulders. Groping for a hold, he suddenly heaved himself up. 'Stay there.'

'Jonathan – just don't get shot.'

I heard him moving slowly above my head and then gradually, cautiously, towards the front of the house. After an ominous silence there came a sudden sound of tearing and the sharp break of ceramic tiles. More silence, a distant sound of jets, the sharp metallic rattle of automatics. Finally, I heard Jonathan drop back down onto the rafters and in the waving, bobbing light of my phone, saw his legs poking down towards the landing.

'Did you just make a hole in the roof?'

'Yeah – it's cool, it will take a few weeks to leak anything into Garen's little ashram. Besides, they clearly use the attic for storage. It's stuffed with weapons.'

'Jesus!'

'Exactly. Yes – eureka!'

The sim card had connected long enough to download a WhatsApp message to retrieve a message sent to my original number five hours ago. It was a set of coordinates from Dena.

'See – we are surrounded by capable women, Jamie.'

I ignored the jibe, looking at the message. 51.5759 N, 04212 W. 'Where is that?'

'Somewhere near Hillingdon.'

'How do you *know* that!'

He tapped his nose. He handed me back my phone and we went back downstairs. 'We need maps – you think this dude had any?'

'I have no idea – we only exchanged complaints.'

Jonathan was rooting through various bookshelves, pulling out draws in a nearby desk. He went into a bedroom, converted – presumably by Garen – into an improvised dungeon with slings and other unidentifiable implements. On a bedside table the dead Greek beamed out a smile from a bygone age; a woman smiled shyly next to him. Jonathan carefully moved through piles of books and papers from under the bed.

'Ah, a classic!' he pulled out a 1997 A-Z of London. We sat gingerly on the bed. Jonathan leafed through the A4 book using his phone as a torch.

'But that won't have GPS coordinates surely – it's almost pre-internet!'

'Jamie!'

Jonathan scanned several pages, turning the maps around. Suddenly he seemed to find what he wanted. He nodded to himself.

'Ruislip. It's an airbase; RAF probably but most likely leased before the pandemic.'

It was the first bit of good news for some time.

'It's relatively close, about 18 miles up the A40 but we can't risk taking the car though – we'll have to walk.'

'Jonathan that's mad – we'd be walking through a war zone. We could at least drive to Wembley?'

'You heard from Bridget said – even before this, the whole place occupied by gangs; anyone in a car would attract their attention. Wait – yes – if we could get to Paddington, we could walk the railway line, it virtually dissects the airbase; we'd be less conspicuous and off the roads.' He looked up at me. 'You've got your passport on you?'

'Sure.'

'Does it have any ID linking you with UNCSAC?'

I unzipped my back pocket and took out a battered magenta coloured passport; issued before the UK left the EU; valid for one more year. I flicked through the pages; nothing except a CDC transit visa to a facility in Baltimore issued a year ago. I passed it over.

'That'll have to do. If things go south, we should try and attach ourselves to a British military unit, they might be persuaded you're genuine. We should leave now; on foot the darkness will give us some cover.'

What belongings we had brought with us we left; most of it still in the car. As we passed by the closed door of my apartment it was silent. Once on the street, we headed towards Marylebone, zig zagging through deserted side streets as much as we could. Behind us, back towards the Thames and Holborn, the sky was red with fires, but there was no sound of any fighting. We saw no one until, confused in the darkness, we hit Regents Park. Turning to the east, we passed close to Baker Street and saw what appeared to be a downed plane smouldering and sparking, one wing pressed up onto the steps of the Planetarium. A group of people were trying to put the fires out, presumably to salvage the wreckage. As we crouched behind a bollard, several people ran past us.

Suddenly, in a bloom of debris and dust, the front of a building collapsed behind, cloaking us in thick dust. It scattered the scavengers, and covering our faces as best we could, we ran towards Paddington. Gunfire and shouts erupted behind us. The main entrance to the station was barricaded off, but with effort, we managed to crawl under a metal grill and enter through a ventilation shaft. Once inside, the station was eerily silent; the main forecourt littered with long abandoned luggage; overturned shopping trollies and broken glass. At the end of last year some trains had started running west again but the effort had petered out. People were still anxious over exposure despite the vaccine, and crews had refused to go through the suburbs without protection.

We walked down a long, rubble strewn platform and after Jonathan doubled checked that the power was out, dropped down to the rail lines. To the east the sky was turning a faint silvery grey and it was bitterly cold; our faces were powdered in plaster and I felt suddenly incredibly hungry. It was a surreal experience; the blind backs of houses and offices to either side, filling out in the dawn, mysteriously long tunnels which I could not recall ever being there, snaking metal lines beneath our feet. Jonathan, having torn the necessary pages from the A-Z, stopped several times to get his bearings: I was utterly lost with no sense of direction.

Eventually, around 8.30 am, we approached Morning Crescent station, a relief in that we had managed to keep heading east despite the vines of tracks and junctions. In the dull metallic light we could see foxes walking – almost strolling – alongside us – and already the main lines were vanishing under a thick canopy of weeds. The air was thick with birdsong; soon, perhaps, this would all be unrecognisable, re-colonised by a natural world that outlived us. I started to relax when suddenly Jonathan dropped like a stone, pulling me down with him. For one terrible moment I thought he had been shot.

'Three o'clock, on the platform.'

I lifted my head up as much as I could, face down with the metallic sleepers ribbing my chest. Squinting, I saw two men armed with rifles, pulling a third towards a makeshift scaffold. The victim's face was covered in a sack and was screaming horribly. One of the men lifted them by the waist while the other fitted a makeshift noose around their neck.

'For fucks sake Jonathan, we should do something!'

'Like what? We're not armed and if they see us, we might well be next.'

Horrified, I studied the armed men, camo jackets and boots, improvised by the look of it and no sign of any insignia. I felt sick to the stomach. As I turned my head to avoid the final brutality there was a soft, fleshly plop and glancing back I saw the executioner's head drop suddenly, half his forehead missing. He fell onto his knees, still holding his victim in what seemed a bizarre embrace and then fell forward. The other man dropped to the platform, pawing at his rifle but as he aimed somewhere ahead us, he was killed with deadly accuracy. Jonathan rolled off the track and lay in the gravel, looking east. Four or five men were walking, bent down, coming straight for us. They had clearly seen us.

'Ok, ok – Jamie – let me do the talking.'

'We're dead.

Jonathan stood; his arms raised; pale winter sunshine spilled over the buildings opposite into my eyes. The men stood as well, their weapons still pointing at us. I lifted myself up by my arms and joined Jonathan. As the men approached, we could see they were in uniform, well equipped, the fifth guy already talking into a radio.

'When I say, get your passport out – but not until I say ok, they might think you're pulling out a gun. You got that Jamie?'

'Yes, I've got it.'

Coming out of the sun, the soldier loomed up slowly, pausing about ten or twelve feet from us; the automatic now thankfully lowered slightly. Behind the radio operator more men began to appear, fanning out into the abandoned station to our right.

'We're unarmed. My name is Jonathan Price, and this is Dr James Relph. We're trying to get to Ruislip on UNCSAC business.'

Jonathan sounded calm, precise.

'Is that so.' The soldier spat suddenly, wiping his mouth with his right sleeve.

'We have documentation to prove it.' Jonathan added; a stretch I thought but stood mute as instructed all the same.

Two other soldiers flanked the first, their eyes hidden by sunglasses.

'Jonathan Price and James Relph, you say? James as in Jamie?'

I thought the tone sarcastic, a prelude to our arbitrary arrest or something even worse, but suddenly the man breathed out deeply, puffing up his cheeks. He turned to look at the guy with the radio, squatting down near a signal. 'We've got them – fuck knows how - radio in we're coming home, they can call back the other units.'

I saw Jonathan frown momentarily; clearly (and disturbingly) surprised that our luck had held.

'You know who we are?'

'Never met either of you, just following orders, lads. We need to double back quick to Ruislip before we lose the window to fly you guys out.'

Stunned, I was suddenly afraid I might burst into tears but luckily there wasn't time. We headed back the way they had come, clambering up a bank onto a side road and jogging to an intersection where several army vehicles were parked up under guard. We clambered in, and once the rest of the platoon had joined us, we drove off at speed. Our saviour was a 31-year-old platoon sergeant called Wallace, known affectionately to his men as the duchess. Dena had learned via Julian that we were heading for London; found out my address and alerted the base: she had even guessed we would go on foot.

'You guys must be important; you've tied down at least three platoons – but all's well that ends well.'

I thanked him profusely. Jonathan asked about the attempted execution on the platform.

'This whole section of town, down as far as Parliament hill, is controlled by a white supremacist group; the intended victim was a black woman; unfortunately, this shit is happening everywhere; different groups, different vendettas.'

I asked how it was that the Blue Jackets could even mount a coup; 'Given what I had seen so far they all appear to be fat overweight bouncers. Is this serious?'

Wallace hesitated, spitting again over the tailboard. 'Pretty serious – they've got some serious firepower from somewhere, probably acquired illegally, but they're also getting some logistical support from somewhere.' He lowered his voice, slipping a white tab of chewing gum into his mouth. 'The outcome depends on whether the grand old British army stays together on this or not.'

Jonathan looked up thoughtfully. 'On our way here, near Baker Street, there was a downed drone. It was hard to see the specifics, but it looked like a Northrop Grumman.'

Wallace, his stubbled jaws working mechanically, shifted his eyes to Jonathan and then back out to the road. 'You sure about that? Manned?'

'Couldn't see, I suspect it was being used for unmanned intelligence gathering.'

Wallace spat again. 'No shit. Interesting. You might have a chat with our commanding officer before we evac you to Edinburgh.'

Someone called out from the top of an armoured carrier in front us; Wallace stood and went up front to see what was up. The soldiers sitting to either side of us watched us curiously.

'You saved our lives Jonathan, I'm pretty useless at this.'

'Nah, you saved mine – you're the asset – I'm just the bodyguard.' He smiled and I fought down a very powerful urge to hug him.

My admiration for Jonathan was matched only by my awe over Dena. Despite presiding over the most significant event in human history she had managed to work out our location and send help. A mixed British and NATO force were holding the base at Ruislip, which as Jonathan had rightly guessed, had been mothballed for years. Struggling to cope with the sudden inrush of military hardware, the base commander looked evidently relieved when Wallace handed us over. Wallace took him to one side and after a brief, minimalist chat, the commander talked quickly with Jonathan about the drone. We were then fed with brisk efficiency and put onto a monster plane – another A30 Atlas – which had required the temporary annexation of the main runway to the high street to enable it to land and take off. As we lumbered over outer London, pitching to head west then north, the city angled lazily below us. Everything seemed normal except for plumes of smoke over Whitehall and Vauxhall and the absence of any obvious traffic. We both looked out of the window; I thought Jonathan looked tired or thoughtful. As we levelled off, I asked him about the obvious interest Wallace and his commander had shown over the drone.

'It's an advanced tactical drone, still technically in the testing phase, so it shouldn't have been there.'

'One of ours?'

Jonathan pulled a face, a quizzical look with a down turned mouth. 'It's American. It's not even been deployed with the US air force let alone shared with NATO. Kind of weird, huh?'

We arrived over Edinburgh around 12.30 pm. On the final approach there was some excitement; what few service people were aboard crowded to portside, shielding their eyes as they looked up. The plane circled and thundered down towards thick cloud, the disks of sun streaming through the windows sliding around like searchlights. Having come full circle, we saw the cause of the sudden chatter – the experiment hung motionless above us. It seemed enormous, and while still high, we were close enough to see that it was tetrahedron in shape, with the point downwards; the wide flat surfaces covered in what appeared to be an intricate design of swirls and lines. Shreds of grey cloud flickered and then quickly engulfed us.

Jonathan's face relaxed, his lips curving in a faint smile. 'Looks like Max beat us to it.'

PART TWO: Terra Nullius.

Chapter Seven. Samuel Davies.

Samuel Davies was born south of the Missouri in 1944, at the dawn of an American century that would peter out, revive, and then collapse without warning. His parents were small time professionals; his father was a criminal lawyer and his mother a schoolteacher. Both were southern Baptists, passionate believers in the word of God, but they were also upwardly mobile and ambitious for their only child. The Davies' witnessed the gradual expansion of an American middle class; the migration of Afro-Americans into the suburbs and the anxieties of the civil rights movement that proved problematic to their interpretation of privilege. Samuel was too educated to openly express his racism, but it burned deep into him, along with his father's eventual suicide over debt and a not so secret gambling vice. Strangely perhaps, his inclination to eugenics, and his fear for a white based American society survived his gradual emergence as a famous geneticist. For Samuel was a gifted child; outwardly reclusive but painfully observant. He developed an early interest in Math and was able to ride the first wave of computer research into the late 1960s. Scholarships took him away from the back waters of his ancestral home and, like many lower middle class white Americans, he was keen to affect a social sophistication that was demanding and often un-nerving. He secretly despised the east coast WASP as a fake, a copy of the American idea of European manners even as he sought to emulate them and he particularly disliked east coast women, who he saw as the antithesis of his hard working, no nonsense mother. Such prejudicial views notwithstanding, Davies grew into a seemingly urbane, bowtie wearing academic with a weakness for expensive cigars; but it remained a self-conscious disguise, something he knew to be fraudulent.

Graduating *summa cum laude* from the University of Maryland, he developed a variety of interests that led to a graduate career not just in Math and computer programming, but in genetic research and virology. And Davies, like his soon to be colleague and friend James DeSilva, always seemed to have the knack of being in the right place at the right time. In 1973, Davies attended a meeting of SETI, and was lucky enough to sit next to Frank Drake, who had in 1961 published his famous equation on the probable number of advanced civilisations in the Universe and the likelihood that they could communicate with each other. Dismissive of its status as an equation, especially given the highly speculative nature of calculating the variables, Davies was excited by the enthusiasm of SETI and its clear conviction that, given the vastness of space, humanity could not be alone. He developed a secret interest in aliens, and although seemingly too clever to take Roswell seriously, his curiosity took him to the usual places, the short anthropoid 'Greys' so beloved of science fiction; stories of reptiles living deep in the earth able to take on the shape and appearance of humans. Such fantasies amused him but invidiously fed his imagination, even the conviction, that he would one day be able to confirm the existence of extra-terrestrial life.

In the mid-1970s, Davies was a tenured professor of biochemistry, comfortable in Maryland and with a growing reputation in the rapidly emerging field of gene mapping. The outbreak of the HIV-AIDs pandemic brought a whole array of scientists to the US, and it was at a conference on viral shredding that he met DeSilva. Seemingly years from a cure, Davies oversaw a research team looking into the evolution of the virus, in particular the probability that the original source derived from an African simian population with its first human victim dated to the 1930s. Little was known at the time about the ability of viral agents to jump from one species to another and the evidence as it emerged was intriguing as well as deeply controversial.

Davies had no sympathy for what was popularly termed the 'gay plague'; he thought homosexual men were perverse and undermining of family values, although as he remained unmarried, this was an abstract position, like many he was to take in his life. Data acquired from the Congo indicated that simian HIV was endemic in chimpanzee colonies, although the virus was inert and expressed no pathology. Beginning the collaborative research on the retrovirus that was to culminate in its successful identification and modelling decades later, Davies worked closely with DeSilva and it was while going over the field studies that they both encountered three novel base sequences in a DNA sample taken from a dead ape. Seemingly unrelated to the simian HIV variant, Davies was curious about its origins but the technological limits to genetic research prevented him from appreciating its importance.

Had DeSilva been an American, Davies would have disliked him. The son of a first-generation Sri Lankan immigrant to the UK, DeSilva represented exactly the sort of invasive takeover of white privilege that so angered him. Given he was foreign however, Davies took to him and they worked well together. DeSilva was a snob, anxious that he would fail in meeting his families expectations, and as he grew older, profoundly dismissive of immigrants arriving in Britain. Like Davies, DeSilva was a confirmed bachelor whose attitudes to women were deeply if not explicitly misogynist.

By the late 1980s Davies was tired of the politics surrounding HIV and turned his attention back to computer programming. Identifying the need to increase the computational tools required to deal with the mapping of complete genomes, Davies set up a private company that worked on gene sequencing, designing the algorithms himself and becoming very rich in the process, establishing with some personal satisfaction the Davies Foundation. His polymath skills brought him to the attention of the US defence community who were interested in bioweapons research, and it was at a conference funded by the Rockefeller Foundation that Davies came across an interesting story told by a rather corpulent, bizarre European by the name of Louis DeMarr.

On first impressions, DeMarr was absurd; flamboyant, openly demonstrative, air kissing his way through the delegates; his smooth boyish face obscured by a huge hat. Yet he was evidently clever and wealthy, a graduate student of Julian Grey, a stuffy Oxford don who was widely respected for his work on human genetic disorders. One evening, treating himself to a cognac, Davies had sat close to a large table where DeMarr was holding court. The conversation was at first random, derogatory comments on some of the papers given earlier, but gradually it turned to aliens.

DeMarr had recently returned from a trip to West Texas where he had discovered a rash of what ranchers called cattle mutilations. He had been taken to a freshly killed steer that had not just been dissected with clinical precision, but was completely desiccated, it's internal organs packed up in its own hide. However sceptical DeMarr was over the more lurid details – no markings on the ground, no previous ill health in the animal - he bought the remains and took them off to examine. The rancher – suffering a significant loss of his herd free ranging close to the New Mexico state line, was convinced that aliens were responsible; he had even claimed to see lights and flashes in the sky the night before the mutilations occurred.

DeMarr's audience had laughed politely, but he then added that, while scrutinising what was left of the poor animal, he had discovered evidence of genetic modification; possibly an attempt at protein synthesis very similar to that being tried by his British counterparts using nitrogen-15, a tell-tale non-radioactive isotope that was present in the carcass. The conversation lingered over possible natural causes, the possibility of satanic cults or vendettas against ranchers until ending around midnight. Davies, draining his glass, retired thoughtfully to his room.

Davies was now a man with considerable connections, many directly to the government. Applying himself with some enthusiasm, he discovered that cattle mutilations had already been the subject of two federal enquiries: one by the FBI and another by The Federal Bureau of Alcohol, Tobacco and Firearms. The 1979 FBI report had been headed up by an agent known as Rommel, who had dismissed the various outlandish theories as the work of self-seeking publicists. He had concluded his investigation by claiming that natural predatory activity was the main cause.

The ATF report however indicated the possibility of a covert government program aimed at investigating emerging cattle diseases, stating that laboratory simulations of dead cattle revealed that normal necropsy could in no way produce the precise scarring found on many mutilation cases. Through various contacts with a gaggle of right-wing Republican senators, Davies was able to acquire several carcases and, working alongside DeSilva – who had a morbid fascination with anything unusual – he confirmed DeMarr's alleged findings. He also found a great deal more: tissue samples from the discoloured, brittle hide revealed that chromosomal alterations had taken place in which specific phrases of genetic material had been altered – more specifically – that three generic bases that controlled the coding had been substituted for new ones, identical to those found in the Congo ape sample.

In 1983, fascinated by his findings, he and DeSilva offered to fund a broad investigation into the mutilation phenomena, premised on all possible explanations, and co-opted an old program previously run by the State Department and SETI but mothballed in the 1970s: Operation Wildfire.

In 1984 Davies was entering his forties; he was a solitary man without friends, considered unknowable by those who worked under him, and seemingly dedicated to his profession. His views, whenever he expressed them, were out of fashion, cranky opinions on mixed race marriages, the increasing use of Spanish, the absurd concept of gay men as a 'community'; but his profound isolation from American popular culture merely enhanced his work ethos. For just under ten years, as the scientific world progressed to more ambitious projects such as the decision to map the human genome, Davies dug away discretely and usually at night in his lab.

By the early 1990s he had successfully isolated the trinity of new base sequences and in his gut, he had no doubt that what he was looking at was alien. These novel bases – which formed the spine for the DNA molecule – systematically substituted the terrestrial bases of adenine, cytosine and thymine through every stage of replication – although for what purpose remained unknown. In the cow, most of the activity was concentrated on chromosome 24 in a bovine genome of 60. Returning to the Congo sample, the activity was seemingly isolated to chromosome 22 in a simian genome of 48: it was as if something was looking for a key, a specific genetic expression, testing various life forms for a fit. In 1991 he classified the information and continued to speculate and theorise until, in March 1993, extraordinary news arrived from England.

At first the reports seemed incredible; 24 children abducted from various medical facilities across the country and then found in pairs, in most cases miles from where they were taken. The commonalities were their age and the fact that they were all suffering from cancer.

Given the provincialism of US reporting, it took several days for Davies to realise that the British were setting up an investigation, headed by Julian Grey, his wife, and Louis DeMarr. It was the membership of the committee that alerted Davies to the fact that something was amiss, and that public speculation over terrorists was both wrong and probably a cover. James DeSilva, having run into criticism for his later statements on HIV, was working in semi-retirement in London; chain smoking himself to death with a misanthropic bitterness; it did not take much effort to contact him. DeSilva reported back that all the children had been genetically altered. It was a moment of simple revelation to Davies; the burning conviction that there was a pattern, a purpose, behind everything he had studied in apes and cattle and now, insidiously, in children. These were in effect experiments.

It took considerably more effort to get the US federal government interested enough to insist that it be represented on the British committee. Attempts to nominate himself ran into an implicit ban from the recently elected President; a vapid Democrat called Bill Clinton and an apparent veto from DeMarr. Given the decision to keep the committee small, Davies' only success was to get DeSilva on it; two other Americans, a scientifically illiterate African American code breaker called Dena Small, and an overpaid shrink from Boston, had no connections with Davies or his foundation. Outraged at such a missed opportunity, Davies skulked in Maryland, having provided DeSilva with a simple schematic of the three amino acids.

James DeSilva did not disappoint at first; he kept a running commentary on the committee's work and provided information that eventually got the US to up the pressure on London, trying to persuade them that they did not have the necessary facilities in Oxford to conduct a thorough investigation. On two occasions the Americans almost succeeded in shifting the committee to Maryland, only to find that the move was frustrated by the British Foreign Office. But DeSilva failed spectacularly in trusting DeMarr with the schematic, the result being that Davies was effectively duped for years over the extent of the genetic and physiological changes to the children, and the identity of one boy in particular: Max Lennox.

It was only in the late 1990s, when his own research work took him to England – the use of his software programme to assist in the cloning of the first mammal - that Davies discovered what the committee had actually found in Max, and to confirm that, for some inexplicable reason, Max had been adopted by Julian and Sally Grey. Ironically given the degree of his duplicity, Davies' host in England was none other than Louis DeMarr; as fat and as capable as ever, working either with the Greys or on his own mysterious agenda. It was on a visit to Oxford that Davies also heard rumours of some sort of artefact or device being found in Leicestershire with the last two children, Max and an older boy called Jonathan Price. DeMarr had poured scorn on the story; another stupendous lie it turned out, since he was already in possession of it. Davies never challenged DeMarr to a direct explanation; it seemed too precipitous, better to keep him close and on friendly terms, but such inaction frustrated him.

Unable to influence the British as effectively as he could the Americans; Clinton notwithstanding, Davies concluded that Max was some form of host, and redoubled his efforts to get the US to alert the British to some sort of extra-terrestrial viral agency, but to no obvious effect and as the years went by the immediacy of his warnings diminished. No more abductions took place, and the screening of the children revealed no anomalies; Max had seemingly disappeared into a normal life, shielded by the watchful eyes of his adopted parents. But in early January 2005, Davies' luck changed.

Louis DeMarr turned up in Maryland a changed man, contrite and confessional. He revealed to Davies the enormity of the changes that were taking hold of Max's chromosome 21, convinced it was a preliminary stage to the entire re-writing of the boy's genome. He also revealed that Julian Grey was desperately looking for the device, an object that DeMarr had discarded and handed over to the British government for safe keeping. DeMarr was now adamant that it was intimately linked to Max's fate; a possible communication device for the host to inform the aliens that their experiment had finally worked. Pallid and sweaty, DeMarr had suggested a trade: his data on Max in exchange for a copy of Davies' software, software that he desperately required for his own research.

Davies had sat bemused but deeply suspicious; unable to work out DeMarr's motives or indeed to comprehend the extent to which he had been kept in the dark for so long. Davies knew that Louis had fallen out with the Greys, and that he was now very much working on his own – but on what he remained clueless. Despite his palpable mistrust, Davies struck a deal, and obtained the necessary evidence to finally get the US State Department and the CIA to back channel with London to prepare for what looked like an existential threat to humanity; an alien engineered virus capable of over-writing the human genome; a biological invasion that had been planned for decades, possibly centuries.

DeMarr left Maryland but did not return to the UK immediately; hanging about in Boise in Montana and travelling to Wyoming; and only later did Davies realise that DeMarr had somehow managed to steal a lot of important equipment and squirrel it back to his London lab. Yet instinctively Davies knew that Louis DeMarr was dying; a triumph of sorts, although secretly Davies admired him.

Davies was excited; it was a sensation he experienced so rarely that he initially took it as signs of illness. DeSilva – forgiven for his failure to measure up against DeMarr's considerable cunning – wormed his way into the British government, armed now with tangible evidence that sometime soon, the aliens would return to take Max, the youth's mission complete. Attempts to get his hands on the device finally succeeded, and prepared to use it as a bargaining chip, Davies laid his plans carefully, aware of his past mistakes and determined to obtain Max. For a while the net closed elegantly and smoothly. DeSilva terrified the British authorities so much that they implemented long dead civil defence plans; and when a sudden illness hospitalised Max, Davies grabbed the opportunity to meet with Sally Grey, now the UK's senior medical advisor. He even managed to obtain his own samples of Max's serum. After thirty years of waiting, Davies was seemingly victorious.

But things went badly awry. Max eluded him, discharged from the hospital and, like DeMarr, Sally Grey proved to be a traitor, hiding information and warning her clearly estranged husband that the 'Americans' were up to no good. In the summer of 2006, Davies played his hand too early; guessing that Max would try and return to the same place he was found in 1993 he forced the British to detain Julian Grey and hand him over to DeSilva who had both the device and Jonathan Price.

Max's re-abduction astounded the world; there was no obvious invasion but a departure, ablaze with extra-terrestrial power and glory, and the device revealed itself not so much as a communications array but as some sophisticated genetic storage technology. As Sally stuck the knife in and twisted it about with clinical alacrity, his plan imploded. The British government collapsed amid cries of a cover-up, and Davies found his powerful friends and colleagues in Washington did not return his calls or even acknowledge they had ever supported him. By the summer of 2006 the whole international community had weighed in, demanding a full enquiry and the establishment of a global forum to coordinate future responses to alien contact: and of course, by now the aliens had a name; Seeth. Davies refused to attend an elaborate de-briefing, concerned the British might seek to detain him, and for a while he was even placed under house arrest. Exposed to a startled and uneasy public, Davies found his life and work scrutinised. There was some innuendo over his life as a bachelor; his association with right wing think tanks and some of his earlier, unguarded statements on race. He even had the indignity of receiving his first death threat.

Isolated as he was, Davies had no influence on the formation of UNCSAC, a classic bureaucratic response to the unique experience of alien contact. He witnessed the absurdity of Dena Small becoming its first director, apparently after both the Grey's had refused. The official account of the Seeth; that they were a sentient species which had evolved on Earth and returned to repair a damaged genome, was to Davies ridiculous; if it were true, whole swathes of terrestrial fauna would contain the three base sequences he had identified and paleobiologists would have found them in species pre-dating the emergence of the Seeth. Yet the fossil record was utterly blank.

By his early 60s, too young to retire despite his ruined reputation, Davies grew convinced that the SETI inspired pacifism of UNCSAC would be no use when the Seeth returned, armed with the hybrids hatched in Max. Whatever their origins, the Seeth were patient in their assault upon Earth, able to play a long game. By 2011, Davies decided to use his considerable wealth and ability – not to say the vast amount of time he now had at his disposal – to start a blog. From the blog emerged the beginnings of a society, even an organisation, eventually called Earth for Humans, initially envisaged as a platform to counter the liberalism of SETI and the innate stupidity of people who believed that the Seeth were not just benign but actually well meaning. But as Davies was gradually rehabilitated, it became much more. It provided him with a platform to release his own research, documenting in thoroughly, and to warn that alien experimentation had long been visited on Earth with one obvious purpose: to invade or control.

Times had moved finally in Davies' favour. The emergence of President Maitland as a populist Republican, a man with enough will to take on liberalism and the pettiness of America's liberal elites, brought Davies' views back into favour. The world was one of increasing anxiety, implicit trade wars, anti-immigrant and less tolerant of the assertion of difference. His blog became a source of general interest, discreetly supported by his own foundation and Maitland's Fox News allies, and he acquired followers that ranged from concerned scientists, retired public servants and even politicians.

In early 2018, he was persuaded to help organise a public protest over continued funding of UNCSAC and supported the policy of withdrawing from any further international collaboration. It brought out a vast coalition of anti-abortionists, anti-gay, anti-immigrant activists as well as various political militias linked to the gun lobbies. Its success encouraged the formation of an active membership, and Davies was enthusiastically organising this when UNCSAC announced a startling discovery in the Antarctic; a vast structure long buried in the ice; the central shaft full of reptilian bodies. Several weeks later the first cases of a mysterious virus were reported in Hong Kong. There was no obvious connection, but Davies realised that as he approached his 70s, it was his final opportunity to complete a crusade he now conceived of as a mission; so a connection was made.

Attributing his comments to an un-named source, Davies cited a member of the US research team sent to the Antarctic as saying that the reptilian graveyard was the result of an ancient viral epidemic. During the resulting outcry, President Maitland re-tweeted all of Davies' comments, and as the pandemic spread, arranged to meet Davies in person at a popular resort in Florida in 2019. Outwardly different; one educated, urbane, somewhat awkward in the spotlight, the other raucous, pithy if not articulate and dramatically unconventional, they shared a common egocentrism; an indestructible belief in their own truth; a fanaticism that came from their own doubts.

In an interview that lasted several hours, Davies convinced the President of the need to side-line UNCSAC and to set up their own dedicated organisation, controlling information and centralising research. Maitland had initially objected on the grounds that the pandemic was his top priority, laying waste American cities and collapsing the international order, but Davies, connecting the horror of the viral outbreak with the Seeth's insidious plans, and seeing his last chance squarely before him, made a rash and at the time absurd prediction: the Seeth would return very soon, genetically armed with a hybrid species which would be, via Max, partly human; and however shocking the current fatality rates were, the virus was a tactic not a strategy. As they shook hands, Davies also reminded the President that the world they were entering would be so scarred and broken, so thrown in upon itself, that the old political dispensations would not hold; it would be a brave new world to be shaped as they desired. Maitland, deeply impressed, and much to the anger of his own staffers, agreed to every aspect of Davies plan.

Davies set to work with a cold resolution. The epidemic hit worse than he had anticipated, but he left it alone, watching anxiously as it spread and killed; afraid it would sniff him out and strike him down before his work was complete. By the time a vaccine was in mass production, the America he knew had gone and he did not mourn it. The soft, aimless lives of his species had reverted to an instinct to survive; and his 'movement'; a term he used only to himself, flourished in spurts of violence and sudden activism.

When the news of the infertility crisis emerged, he was darkly satisfied. It was, in his focused imaginings, a novel but effective strategy. Cripple the world with a virus so elusive and adaptable that it would decimate the global population before it was effectively cured, then reveal the undisclosed damage that would hand over dominion to the Seeth. He was so impressed with this that he forgot that it was a lie he had himself invented. His survival, typically, merely reinforced his belief in his own indispensability. Maitland, on the other hand, had proved less effective than he had hoped. Despite his earlier disregard for the conventions of presidential power, he had proved less adaptive than Davies had hoped for, still crippled by a populist's desire to please and unable to comprehend that democratic, electoral politics was dead. While the President starved UNCSAC of funds, diverting them to FEMA and the CDC, he did not withdraw from the 2007 convention, nor did he effectively fire Dena Small. As states withdrew their embassy staff and closed down their foreign consulates, however, Davies comforted himself with the fact that she and the UN had been side-lined.

Chapter Eight: The Faraday Cage.

For some unknown reason, Davies had dreamed of DeMarr the night after he had successfully located the hybrids in Arizona. His old nemesis had been sitting in a chair opposite his bed, eating cake and flicking the crumbs off his waistcoat with an agitated expression. Davies, startled, had asked him what he wanted – aware in that curiously indirect way that he was, he *must*, be dreaming. Louis had not answered, but merely looked up from his fastidious flicking, staring not at Davies but slightly above his head, his expression one of surprise or fear. Unsettled, Davies had turned around to see what DeMarr was so interested in. Standing above him (however impossible such a thing was, given the dimensions of his bedroom) was a tall, muscular youth, his body covered in mysterious markings, alive and writhing like snakes. His raven black hair hazed over a powerful forehead and the young man's eyes were luminous and judgemental. It was a terrifying sight and Davies – intuitively aware that he was looking at Max – awoke screaming. It was 5.32 am on the 25 January 2022.

Three days had passed since the hybrids had landed in the South West of the US. Despite the continuing chaos in government – with Maitland moving about from city to city and with many states still reeling from the news of the fertility crisis, Davies had been able to move fast, securing the cylinders containing the three alien hybrids and recovering much of the ship. However delayed, the arrivals sealed Davies' reputation with the President, and he was rewarded for his hasty prophecy by being made under secretary of state in Homeland; a strangely cautious move since the secretary and over half of the staffers were long dead and most of the department had been absorbed by Defence. Davies had waited too long to quibble, and once he had secured his patients he went to work quickly and efficiently, isolated in a secure purpose-built facility on the outskirts of Phoenix, Arizona.

He had recognised the composition of the cylinders immediately, derivative of the device he had once examined, and he had also anticipated the possibility that the aliens would exhibit some telepathic or kinetic abilities. Aware that others like them had landed planet wide and having himself advised the President to deny all knowledge of their arrival on US territory, Davies was anxious to isolate them as soon as possible. His solution had been to go with the classics: he constructed a series of Faraday cages, one for each hybrid, with an outer wall built of depleted plutonium metal casings surrounding the whole complex. Research staff had been kept to an absolute minimum.

Despite his single-minded determination to save the planet for humans, Davies was misanthropic, perhaps even bitter. His emotional repertoire, never great, had diminished over the years but he was impressed, almost moved, by the emergence of each hybrid from their powdery cuticle; their form perfect, a Vitruvian symmetry to their faces and bodies that commanded attention. But they were also an abomination; a circus freak of a being without discernible genitalia and containing a menagerie of different species as if thrown together randomly. Emerging in isolation from each other, they were clearly disorientated; the electromagnetic fields generated by the faraday cages clearly caused them some discomfort. If they sensed anything amiss with their surroundings however, they did not show it and were from the start oddly cooperative.

The first hybrid to emerge could speak perfect, if not exactly vernacular, English and Davies had sat by the side of its cot, discussing the Seeth casually. In this first, bewildering interview, Davies learned of the hybrids desire to 'return' to Earth, believing it would seem in the UNCSAC narrative that they had indeed originated on Earth some 65 million years ago. Davies also learned that the experiment was sentient, masterminding through Max the genetic design and propagation of the hybrids which called themselves Malaq. Davies had asked why the Malaq had unleashed a virus that had not only killed a large number of humans but rendered the survivors impotent.

The answer, not surprisingly, was not just a puzzled denial but an offer to 'save humans', the old colonial sleight of hand, as patently malicious as saying 'we come in peace.' Davies left the hybrid to rest, pausing to look once more at the extraordinary sight that lay before him. Yet as he prepared to undertake comprehensive tissue samples, Davies was interrupted by a summons to New York. Despite his strenuous objections, and an attempt to impress the presidential aide that he was at a critical stage of his work, he was informed that transport was already on its way to fetch him. The blocking of all communications by the faraday equipment – an intentional side effect to allow Davies to concentrate completely on his work – had not shielded him from the tedious necessity of meeting with the President.

Maitland and what were left of the cabinet was housed in a hotel just off Fifth avenue in New York City. Congress had last met in the autumn of 2018 and was even now agitating to be recalled but attempts to return to Washington DC were complicated by extensive flooding and an outbreak of typhoid. Davies had arrived in the remains of JFK Airport and had been driven along deserted roads to Manhattan, and although still seething with rage he was attentive enough to see that something was seriously amiss.

Maitland was in the bridal suite, and the cabinet meeting took place incongruously in a long white panelled gallery decorated with rococo cupids scaling the doors and ceiling. Elegant 19th century furniture had been pushed aside and replaced with stacks of technology and monitors, hastily cabled through to generators in the hallway.

'Sorry to winkle you out of your bunker, Sam, but we have a situation here.' Maitland sounded tense, his slab like face sweaty and lined. Davies noted distastefully that his shoulders were thick with dandruff.

'I was about to begin the first scans but I'm sure you didn't bring me here on a whim.'

Apart from himself and Maitland, there were about twelve others in the room, crammed around a dining table: the President's handsome if not hapless son-in-law, the secretaries for State and Defence and two generals, the newly appointed directors of the CIA and FBI, a clutch of air force officials and representatives from the New York Mayors office. In an adjoining room, several aides and staffers crowded back awaiting instructions. Maitland looked slowly about the room; his lips pursed in their customary pout. Before he could speak, the Secretary for State asked Davies if he could confirm the story that the hybrids were seeking to return to Earth. Still irritated, Davies said yes, he had been told this from the hybrid itself.

'How many are we talking about, Sam?'

'I'm afraid I had not progressed that far Mr President before I was called away.'

'Ok I get you're pissed, but I'll tell you how many – 30 million.'

Davies blinked owl like; calculating the probabilities – the number was much larger than he had expected – but it would not do to look blind-sided.

'I see. And where did you get this information from?'

'Dena Small's office has released a provisional report. You should watch the news, Sam.' said the President sharply, coating his lower lip in spittle. He wiped it away with a napkin. Davies thought instinctively of his dream.

'Due to the nature of our facility in Arizona, and the need to isolate the hybrids from being able to communicate with the other fifteen known to be here, I have not been able to keep up with events; perhaps someone could fill me in?'

The secretary of state for Defence, an old golfing ally of the President and someone who had disliked Davies from the start, pushed a laminated folder in his direction.

'You can read it later, in your own good time Davies. Suffice it to say that Dena Small managed, god knows how, to get a first contact team to Scotland and has broadcast her findings on the hybrids to everyone capable of holding a smartphone; even worse –'

'That bitch has managed to get her hands on Max, and two members of the British government who survived the coup, the one we arranged.' Maitland exploded; his clenched palms banging the desk with sudden violence. 'Max is now on his way here to address the UN with all fifteen hybrids to make some sort of proposal.'

Politics, at least in its conventional format, did not interest Davies but the news was a shock, indeed an anxiety. The inclusive reference to his involvement in a coup made no sense, but Davies' mind quickly processed what he was hearing, assessing the mood in the room which was one of anger but also barely supressed panic. He resisted his instinct to remind the President that he had urged Dena to be removed from office almost two years ago.

'I see. But the UN has almost no diplomatic representatives; and surely we can stop anyone arriving?' The practicalities of a cordon were beyond Davies' concerns.

The secretary for state, flicking through a wad of documents, looked up with obvious irritation. 'Perhaps you are unfamiliar Davies with the ramifications of the 1944 San Francisco Treaty, but the UN building in New York is designated as international territory; accordingly it has its own security force, its own fire brigade and I believe –' she had looked across the table to a man sitting opposite, 'its own postal service.'

Again, the old way of thinking, the old mantras from a world that was lost. 'Embedded in US sovereign territory nonetheless if I am not mistaken.' Davies parried gently.

Maitland pressed his large fleshy palms together, prayer like, his beady eyes turning to the secretary of Defence. 'Could we do that? Seal off the lower east side without actually violating the UN's diplomatic status?'

The New York delegation – several young men and one woman – all protested together, a gaggle of noise that resulted in Maitland thumping the desk for order. 'Can I just remind the New York posse that under an early Presidential decree I made Manhattan Federal territory, and that you are here as a courtesy!'

'We could do it.' The secretary for Defence replied as the noise abated, 'but there are complications. We know that several hundred diplomats are already on their way here, and while we could detain them at both JFK and New Jersey, it would cause a stink. Of more concern is the ship.'

'Ship?' Davies asked. He was nursing the summary handed to him on his lap, running his hand over the binding thoughtfully.

'Yes, Davies; *a ship.*' The secretary indicated to a technician standing near a huge Greek vase full of silk roses, who dutifully flicked his hands over a keyboard. Instantly one of the monitors showed either a live feed or a recording of a massive triangular wedge of metal gleaming over the New York skyline. Davies felt a deep chill, but also a profound rush of excitement. He ensured, however, that his expression remained one of placid disinterest. He stared at the image of the vast structure and felt something close to awe.

'We are assuming this is where the hybrid pods came from; and it was earlier located over the British isles, but since Max left Scotland it has repositioned itself here in a geostationary orbit. It measures approximately a quarter of a mile by one mile in length; it's tetrahydric in shape but detailed observations appear to confirm that it can change its geometry. We have no idea of its capabilities, but it is fair to assume it would intervene in some way if we attempted to frustrate Max's arrival. It also controls the smaller unmanned escort ships or drone – which appear, incidentally, to be self-replicating.'

Davies rose slowly and walked towards the screen. *Escort ships?* After almost forty years of his life, Davies studied what he held to be his personal adversary; the emblematic symbol of an alien plan of domination. His thoughts ran back to the discovery of the ape carcass; the animal mutilations; the sudden revelation that he had waited all his life for this moment.

'What is it Sam?' The President sounded bemused. Davies hardly heard him, until slowly he became aware that everyone in the room was watching him intently. He turned away from the screen as if he had seen a ghost.

'Nothing – it is just the first time I have seen my theories so categorically vindicated. If that is indeed where the hybrids are coming from, it must be the place where they have been in effect engineered; the source of the intelligence behind this insidious invasion.'

'Yes, our thoughts entirely.'

'Apart from the status of the UN buildings and the extremely large ship, there is another complication.' The Director of the CIA said, as Davies seemed almost to stumble back to his chair. 'It is widely suspected that we have the missing hybrids; and their continued detention could precipitate a confrontation whether we seek to quarantine the UN or not.' His voice was heavy with southern intonation.

'I trust no one is suggesting that we release them!' Davies said quietly, glancing again at the screen. 'I am on the brink of a major discovery.'

'Sam, no one is suggesting anything of the sort – yet.' Maitland said quietly, 'But it also seems to be the case that we left a few too many grubby fingerprints over the supplies sent to our British friends.' The President glared at the CIA director. Again, Davies felt the cost of his recent complete isolation, his utter ignorance over what had been going on.

'Mr President, you should forget the UN, the key intelligence is on that ship: You should take it out. It is an ark of hybrids, and I would imagine, a sufficiently large target.'

There was a gaunt silence. Davies was clearly serious.

'Can we nuke it?' added Maitland casually, turning his solid frame in the direction of the monitor and then back to the Defence Secretary.

'We could try, if push comes to shove, but I wouldn't advise starting a shooting war. It clearly commands the smaller ships – perhaps if we take it out, they simply drop from the sky or we get the shit kicked out of us. My gut instinct is on the latter.'

'And perhaps you may have noticed it is about 3,000 feet over New York.' Said another representative from the City. 'I presume you don't wish to incinerate your newly acquired federal territory so soon?'

Maitland glared with deep malice, his eyes narrowing. 'We're discussing contingencies; and cut the tone, I don't care for it.'

Davies struggled to regain his calm. He looked up and stared about the room.

'Gentleman, ladies. At the risk of speaking out of turn may I just remind you that we are clearly and irrefutably facing an invasion. We are confronting the very entity that masterminded decades, possibly centuries, of covert experiments on this planet to produce a hybrid form that could successfully colonise it; and once that had been created, infected us with a virus and has now rendered a majority of the survivors infertile. That ship has long eluded us; taking specimens to experiment on, masterminding the abduction of children in 1993, never seen, never even imagined. It is not fanciful to even theorise it dates back to the Antarctic structure, and yet now

– here it is in plain sight. Listening to some of you, it strikes me that you have yet to comprehend the gravity of what we are facing; the threat here is not a moribund, dead internationalism represented by the UN, or the diplomatic niceties that governed the old ways, but the survival of our species. I have in my lab three genetically engineered hominids of incredible power and ability. 30 million of them would finish us off in your lifetimes! And they are there.' He pointed emphatically at the monitors, 'all racked together in their biomorphic casings. Once on the planet, they may well prove unstoppable.'

His voice fell heavily and decisively about the room. After a stunned silence several people all talked at once, affirming, contradicting, seeking for clarification. The New York representatives stood up as if to leave, but Maitland, standing himself, his big bulk pushing back his chair, shouted for quiet.

'Just sit down; goddamn it. Everybody just take a breath – the only person who walks out of these meetings is me, you got that! What is it Jeannine?'

'With all due respect to Professor Davies, we have no evidence that the virus is linked either to the Seeth or indeed the onset of infertility: on the contrary we have significant data that implies that the virus was a novel mutation reported long before the outbreak and before the hybrids arrived. As for an invasion – again this is pure speculation, and I for one I am not prepared to start a fight over a hunch. My advice, and the advice of the entire state department is that we allow the UN to convene the general assembly and see what this Max guy has to say. Dena mentioned a proposal: let's see what it is. We also recommend that you announce we are holding the hybrids.'

'Recall Congress!' someone shouted.

The room erupted in further noise and agitation; Davies watching each face in turn; some in avid agreement, including some of the military brass, some clearly opposed; too many seemingly undecided, puzzled, incapable of acting decisively.

'The Mayor agrees with the state department on this; we are living through extraordinary times, but conventions have to be observed; if you wish to go hard ball on the Seeth you should convene Congress, even if it means cramming them into the New York Public library! Besides, the UN Security Council is already in session. The Seeth have sent a representative to discuss the matter, in good faith seemingly.'

'The matter! The matter is obvious – it is the terms of surrender!' snapped Davies savagely.

'I'm inclined to agree with Davies on this; but if you're seriously suggesting that this object could be over 70 million years old, we need to assess its capabilities before we do anything. It might be wise to allow the UN to proceed while we investigate our options. Besides, the security council is missing two of its permanent members, and the General Assembly might not even muster a quorum.'

'It won't if you detain the delegates as they arrive!' An officer from the Mayor's office, the only other woman in the room, stabbed back angrily.

Maitland sat down, mastering himself with difficulty. Although the room was far from warm, he looked feverish, possibly even unwell. There was a momentary silence, and in the background, displayed in all its bizarre majesty, the ship hung glistening in the chill winter sunlight over the East River. The President turned to look at the Director of the FBI, a youngish man who had so far remained silent, seemingly doodling over his paperwork.

'Malcolm? How's the state of my mighty Union?'

'Excuse me, Mr President?'

'The mood, for God's sake, how is the mood out there – what the fuck have you been doing since I appointed you!'

'Ah.' He put down his pen calmly. 'Agitated, much like this room. The bureau is still seeking to recruit field officers to replace those killed by the virus, and we have no effective National Guard to speak of. FEMA is still operational, although since the vaccine we have been winding down most of its operations. We have a serious law and order issue. Many of the populated areas are ruled by militias, a majority of them recruited by or loyal to the Earth for Humans Movement, but there has been widespread interest in Dena Small's streaming, and some groups are clearly pro-settlement, especially if it means getting our hands on technology. We've been monitoring activity from a particular outfit calling itself The Reconfigured Man, with help from our friends in the CIA naturally; it has a wide following and despite looking like a freakshow, they worry me.'

'In what way?'

'Well they're well organised and funded. Three days ago, we raided a compound just outside San Diego and they were armed to the teeth. If we decide here and now to squeeze Max's balls, they might give us trouble, and if we reveal that we have the hybrids in an underground bunker they'll definitely go apeshit.'

'On the subject of militias, Mr President.'

'Not now, General, not now; I am intimately acquainted with your view.'

Maitland circled the room; Davies watched him carefully, trying to interpret the body language. The iconoclast President, the President who had effectively dispensed with the entire White House press corps and reduced daily briefings to strings of tweets from his personal Twitter Account, who had attended pro-abortion rallies and belittled the Supreme Court, appeared oddly broken. Despite his academic reserve and a sudden sense of his own vulnerability,

Davies said quietly, 'this crisis presents us with an opportunity, however dangerous, that will not come again. It also presents us with an existential challenge to our entire species. If we drop the ball on this, it's over. We are running out of time.'

The New York delegation had not resumed their seats and were looking at Davies with concentrated malice. Maitland's back was turned to him, seemingly absorbed by the images of the ship. Slowly, his head lifting, the President turned to face the room.

'Ok. This is how we play it. We place a cordon around the lower east side but – BUT – we allow the delegates to arrive and for the UN to entertain this alien freakshow; but I want them to know that we could have stopped them had we wanted to, so rough them up, not literally, intimidate is a better word. I want a lot of hardware on show as well.'

'And what if the hybrids want to visit New York?' someone asked from the gaggle of city representatives.

'I'll shoot them. Secondly – we keep the hybrids and deny everything for now. Davies, get back to the lab: you have twelve hours to give me a full assessment of their abilities, Sam; you hear me, even if it means dissecting one. Thirdly.' He glared at the clutch of generals. 'Having given you every goddamn toy and dollar you ever asked for, you get me some assessment of this ship and any vulnerability you think it might have. You got that? And then I want a plan on my desk first thing tomorrow telling me how, if we must, we blow the fucking thing up! And the FBI can get off its bony ass and send me a report on this Reconfigured Man outfit, again, 8 am tomorrow bright and early.'

Maitland glowered, wedging his hands in his trouser pocket. Aides poured in with slips of paper and cell phones, swarming about him. Davies sat, still playing with the binding of the report, watching as the New York delegation stormed off. He was then aware that he was being scrutinised, in an unpleasant, direct way, by Jeannine Maxwell. He clearly had no friends in the state department. As the room cleared, the President, waving aside various interruptions, beckoned Davies to join him. They stood in the bay window, looking over the green, bare treed oasis of central park.

'That was quite a speech, you should have run for office! But listen, don't dissect anything just yet, Sam; that was a figure of speech.'

Davies, disappointed, nodded.

'And one last thing – I'm sending Junior with you.'

Davies looked back towards the dining table at the President's son-in-law. 'Absolutely not.'

'Excuse me?'

'I have all the personnel I require; I do not want the added responsibility of providing security for Ryan or risking a security breach.'

Maitland's mouth creased in a smile, but his eyes were venomous; Davies had not seen this particular look before. The President leaned in confidentially. 'Listen to me you son of a bitch; he goes, and he reports to me; he'll keep out the way – he's good at that – we clear? I can't have you incommunicado now, so deal with it.'

Maitland turned. Davies heard him ordering one of his aides to get the new British PM on the phone or on-line. Placing the report he had yet to read into his slim briefcase, Davies walked down into the lobby. Ryan Kruger was already standing with the driver that was to take them to the airport. They shook hands cordially. Davies understood Ryan was coming to Arizona to report back on him as much as on the hybrids. He was more curious than alarmed as to why. Once on board, Davies sat opposite Ryan, despite the accommodating spaciousness of the private jet. He thought he would look tetchy if he sat across the aisle, at his own walnut laminated table. He skimmed through the report while studying the President's recently widowed son-in-law. Raven haired, well groomed, there was something too pretty about the young man, too manicured.

Davies always considered such men as closet homosexuals, secretive in their habits. Ryan had been a college quarterback and clearly worked out, but it was also rumoured that he was extraordinarily stupid, a mannikin, with his deep blue eyes and masculine jawline; a typical product of millennial in-breeding. Davies turned his concentration to the report.

He had clearly chosen the wrong 72 hours to sequester himself in his lab, whatever the urgency of his work. Dena had excelled herself, able to acquire several transport planes and a team of technicians – Davies suspected covert help from the department of State. The British coup – utilising the Blue Jackets – struck Davies with a disturbing sense of déjà vu, bringing into play his old adversary Sally Grey. For the first time in many years, he had an imminent sense of failure. Closing his eyes, he saw the ship, suspended in its alien majesty. If Maitland could not act, someone had to. Thinking of what lay inside; of the skill and ability required to engineer the hybrids, he felt an old, cold excitement.

Chapter Nine: Heading for Babel.

The evacuation of UNCSAC people from Edinburgh had been surprisingly smooth, given the circumstances. The arrival of several hundred senior ministers. civil servants and former MPs from the British government – including Max's mother – was an irony not lost on the Scottish administration. We sat on the plane while it was loaded; the temptation to get off and find Max or Sally mitigated by the press of people and the chaos at the base. We met Dena, profuse in our thanks; she looked exhausted but determined. 'Well it gets tougher from herein boys' was all she would say after hugs of relief.

In the end only a few other people boarded, Sally, the ex PM who had managed to escape, and then a surreal cohort of fifteen rather bemused, angelic looking youths in an assortment of clothing, each holding a bag decorated with a large UN logo and a water bottle. Sally stopped by as we were strapping in, looking as cool and immaculate as ever. We talked about Max and Julian, and then she left for her seat, leaving me staring at the hybrids to the point that Jonathan reached over and pretended to close my mouth. Each face was remarkably similar but also different, different markings, different eye colour; and each was a gentle, reassorted facsimile of Max.

'If you need the bathroom to relieve any pressure, we have about ten minutes to take off.'

'I'm fine, Jonathan, thank you. I can cope; I think.'

'So there like both boys and girls? How does it work, exactly? If I was, well hypothetically, to sleep with one, where would I start?'

Dena, sitting behind us, propped up on an array of massive kit bags, started laughing and leaned forward putting her head between our seats.

'We're not entirely sure, Jonathan; and I don't think they are either. But they're very sociable, capable of communicating in a multitude of languages, and quite tactile. You should both introduce yourselves – it's a long flight, but don't try anything too intimate, yet!'

Jonathan laughed and then, unable to smoke, pulled at the lining of the seat in front of him. Despite the illuminated seat belt sign he suddenly climbed over me and went and sat with the hybrids. I asked Dena where Max was and she said he had vanished just before we departed, assuring her he would be in New York when we arrived to deal with any nonsense from the Americans.

'You think they'll be trouble?'

'You bet. Maitland was instrumental to the coup working here, although it's far from certain who is going to win. Before he left Leicestershire, Max confirmed that the US have the hybrids in a facility in Arizona, under the careful eye of my old buddy, Sam Davies! Max nor the experiment can communicate with them, and Maitland will be seriously compromised when it gets out.'

'Are they in any danger from Davies?'

'Definitely; he's a skilled sociopath: this is what he has been hoping for all his life, but I'm leaving that to Max for now.' Her face became thoughtful. 'I wouldn't be in his shoes at the moment. After all we've been through, human hospitality is not what it once was.'

'I'm not sure it was ever much, Dena. But what do we have to lose? 30 million sounds a lot, but god knows there'll be enough space around here soon enough.'

Dena shrugged, but her expression was equivocal; doubt etched about her eyes and mouth.

'I have no idea, Jamie; I hope you're right but two species cohabiting the same world, one significantly more capable than the other, I don't think it bodes well for us. Not that I think we have a god given right to survive. But how sex plays out in a world riven with fear and hostility, well that's another matter entirely. In some bizarre way this is just what Davies needed to spin a tale of body snatching and dominion and alas, it will make immediate sense to billions of people.'

I agreed, sensing both the enormity of Max's mission but still deeply troubled by Garen's account of his vision. Something else was evidently on Dena's mind however, because she unstrapped herself and came and sat next to me in Jonathan's seat.

'We need to talk.' The tone of her voice alarmed me. I watched Jonathan – who was having his buzz cut stroked by several hybrids – and then looked at Dena sharply. The aircraft, which had been taxing to the end of the runway, turned and stopped; its engines revving.

'Does Max seem the same to you? I never met him until his arrival in Scotland, but you – you were like his best friend?'

There was a jolt and a sudden sensation of speed. It took several minutes for the nose to lift and the giant fuselage to clear the ground. A locker banged and several objects fell into the gangway.

'Well, apart from the age thing, he seems much as I remember him – more demonstrative, perhaps, less of what we used to call 'Max time', perhaps a tad naïve, why?'

'While we were tracking you guys down, I had a series of email exchanges with Julian. Some of what Max said at Daniel's didn't seem to make sense to him nor your mother.'

'Such as?'

'Max gave us what is, in effect, the UNCSAC narrative: that the Seeth were a sentient therapod species forced to evacuate the planet to escape extinction. But we haven't believed that narrative for some time, not since the Antarctic discovery. It is possible, well it's highly probable apparently, that the hybrids might well be part alien; I mean the whole deal – extra-terrestrials – a part of their genome, perhaps the most significant – never came from Earth at all.'

'What?'

My mouth was dry; my tongue glued to various parts of my gums. I was afraid she was going to ask about the timing of the breeding proposal and was not convinced I could hide my own doubts from her, but her statement was even more startling,

'Dena, how is that possible? What did you find in Antarctica that changed your minds?'

Dena sighed and rested her head back. We were punching through the clouds and the interior of the plane was suddenly filled with warm, golden brilliance.

'There were always anomalies, Jamie; mostly to do with the base sequences found in Max's chromosome 22. Julian was never entirely satisfied that they were terrestrial and despite my best efforts we've never located then elsewhere.' She leaned in, her anxiety infectious. 'And as for the fossilised remains of the therapods we discovered in the Antarctic structure, we *were* able to isolate some of their mitochondrial DNA, and later at the bottom of the pit, we managed to get a reasonable somatic DNA sample. And the simple fact is that there was no trace of the three bases on either sample; they were regular raptors.' She smiled weakly.

I was distracted by the hybrids who, as Jonathan spoke to them, frequently turned to look at me, smiling, their eyes flashing. 'So, you're saying that they couldn't have built the structure?'

'I am, Jamie. And I am also saying that it is possible that – whatever accounts for the number of raptors found in the central shaft – it might well be that they were being experimented on, much in the way that apes and cattle were experimented on. There is a striking similarity between Max's ship and the structure itself; especially the decorative cartouches. Moreover, NASA managed to use a satellite to estimate the age of the ship Max calls the experiment: its nearly 2 billion years old.'

I felt a chill touch my neck and face, and then a sudden anger; at the absurdity of such a conjecture, at the delay in even suggesting it; but also, at the sneaking possibility that it might be true, more evidence that Max had lied or was being lied to.

'I presume you want me to do something?'

Dena nodded, pulling her coat tight around her. 'Talk with Jonathan, and then if we get time, talk with Max; he clearly loves and respects both of you, and Julian tells me you were one of the few people who could get Max to open up.'

'That was a long time ago, Dena; and it met with limited success even then. If anyone can get Max to open up its Jonathan. I'll talk to him – but – how many people know about this?'

'Almost no one knows about the raptor data from the Antarctic platform; the debates on the origins of the three amino acid bases has gone on for years, admittedly in academic journals, but nonetheless in public. Look I'm not asking you guys to interrogate Max, or presume he is hiding something, I guess I want you to warn him that, given the extensive scrutiny he is about to come under, if there is any truth to what I have said, he needs to put it out there first. If it comes from Davies or the Americans, we have no deal, and this gets messy.'

'Thanks Dena, and here I was looking forward to flirting with eighteen perfectly formed hybrids.'

She smiled, evidently relieved to have cleared her conscience. 'You can flirt with Max instead; I hear you were good at that.' Dena leaned closer. 'He is the most beautiful guy I have ever seen, incidentally.'

The flight seemed endless and given that we were in a transport plane hastily reconfigured for passengers, incredibly uncomfortable. After a while Jonathan returned but seeing Dena fast asleep next to me, climbed in behind. He looked oddly elated. There had, apparently, been an interesting discussion of sexual anatomy and Jonathan looked smugly satisfied with himself. After a few moments of rolling an imaginary spliff, Jonathan sensed that something was wrong.

I gave him a brief synopsis of Dena's request to talk with Max, conscious of her snoring fitfully next to me. Jonathan did not seem particularly surprised but doubted we could corner Max anytime soon. He asked me if I had talked about it with Sally. I'd had tried, but she was surrounded by a gaggle of civil servants and appeared deep in some conspiracy or other. At this stage Jonathan pulled out a battered blue baseball cap, wedged it over his face and fell asleep. Alone, I was tempted to go and introduce myself to the hybrids but felt an irrational paranoia that they would read mind or something; sensing my unease over Max, or my lurid interest in what they looked like naked.

Several hours passed. I tried reading a copy of Verne's collected novels, squirrelled away from the dead Greek's flat before the fighting, but gave up. Climbing over Dena – who was clearly catching up on a week of sleep – I walked down the massive interior of the Atlas, which looked not unlike a parking lot. A batch of soldiers were playing cards at the far end and smoking discretely. I wandered up to the hybrids who were, like Dena, out cold, their heads resting on each other's shoulders, a pastiche of seemingly male faces relaxed and dreaming. Sally was also a sleep, her jacket rolled up into a pillow and wedged between her seat and the bulkhead. I paused at a porthole, looking down through a thin canopy of clouds at what appeared to be ocean. I was suddenly aware of an object creeping into view, about 50 or so feet from the wing. As it slipped alongside, I saw it was a fighter jet, either escorting or intimidating us. Crossing over to the portside I saw another. As I leaned into the glass to try and identify any markings, the captain asked us all to fasten our seatbelts and secure any lose luggage. He also asked Dena to join him in the cockpit. Anxiously, but with some reluctance, I went over to her and shook her awake. For a moment she clearly had no idea where she was, and then, hearing her name announced again, rubbed her face with incredible vigour and headed towards the front of the plane. Jonathan yawned, coughing and swearing.

`What's up?' He asked, swivelling his cap around his head.

'We have friendlies or hostiles – of course I have no idea which.'

'That's why I'm here, Jamie.'

He bound off to investigate. I saw Sally also heading up to the flight deck. After a while Dena returned, a silver beaker of coffee in her hand.

'Good news or bad?'

'Bad, probably. We're being buzzed by US F-35s. They are 'advising' us to change our course away from American airspace. I've just told them we're a UN chartered plane heading for New York. It didn't seem to make much difference.'

Dena did not seem unduly alarmed. Jonathan returned, having clearly been denied access to the cockpit.

'VIPs only it would seem. God, I need a smoke!'

'For fuck's sake Jonathan, there's a bunch of guys down at the back smoking away merrily; just go get your fix.'

He pretended to be outraged. 'I'm just too law abiding, Jamie, it never occurred to me to just light up.'

'Yeah, sure it didn't.' I turned back to Dena as he jogged away. 'Can we contact Max?'

Dena drank her coffee. 'No, but I'm hoping that Max can contact us.'

We were then joined by Sally, looking alarmingly refreshed and wilful. She crouched down next to us all.

'I've just got off the radio from the British Consulate in New York; it's pretty chaotic. Maitland has blockaded the lower east side of Manhattan and is detaining delegates trying to get to the UN building. The Mayor of New York has declared it an open city however and there are about a quarter of a million protestors trying to push back several thousand US Marines. There are also counter demonstrations – so the military have their hands full. US air traffic control want us to proceed to Toronto, but we don't have enough fuel. As an encouraging side note, apart from Maitland, no one has yet recognised the new British government.'

'There's a surprise. Well.' Dena drained her coffee. 'We just have to keep going. You ok with that?'

Sally stood, straightening her dress with a long, elegant hand. 'Whatever you say, Dena; we certainly can't turn back now.'

Dena left to speak with the captain again. I sat as more jets appeared around us, below and above. Several came in close, so close that looking down you could see the pilots and even the flashings on their arm badges. A bloom of smoke, a cartoon cut out of an explosion, puffed up just above us; moments later we heard it, buffeting the huge transport plane. The soldiers were cramming the windows. Jonathan reappeared.

'They're bluffing, right?'

Jonathan shrugged. Another ink blob of smoke momentarily obscured our view and then someone behind us shouted, an incoherent noise partly drowned out by a slap of turbulence. We craned our necks to look under the first massive propeller. A slim, wedge like object had appeared behind the jet to starboard, luminous in brilliant sunlight. Another appeared on the opposite side of the plane. Side on it was hard to decern any shape, but then they suddenly closed rapidly, V shaped and apparently solid, with no obvious signs of propulsion or pilot. Both jets dropped behind and below us before suddenly disengaging, peeling back and disappearing. The new escort – presumably dispatched by Max – pulsed out great flashes of blue light repeatedly and remained in position, following us in over the eastern seaboard, and as we banked towards a distant JFK, I caught sight of a whole string of them behind us, a line of flashing darts beaded out and curving up toward the top of the atmosphere. I sank back into my seat, relieved, but the power implicit in such a display was troubling. I wondered if it had been wise; if this was not the beginning of something; a harbinger of violence. As I buckled in, I noticed that the hybrids were all seemingly still fast asleep.

The landing was not without event. On the final approach to the only runway that could take a plane of our size, several attempts were made to block it with firefighters and emergency vehicles. The pilot aborted just in time, and as we pulled away at the last minute, we could see that about fifty to a hundred people in a massive scrum, some dragging the drivers out of the cabins, others being assaulted by a group of people waving signs saying 'NO ALIENS'. Luckily by the time of our second attempt, the runway was clear, and the fighting had moved off towards a series of hangers.

Later, while waiting for transport to the city, the pilot confessed we had landed on fumes. In contrast to my recent visit, JFK was heaving with activity, mostly police and security, and on the main turnpike, rows of military vehicles and personnel. Of particular interest was the activity of the Seeth escort ships, which were stationary and inert, hanging at about 500 feet above the ground but flashing in unison. I counted something like sixty or so. After an hour they all moved off, a great thicket of dazzling metal, heading towards Manhattan. In the distance, the outlines of the experiment hanging over New York struck me as vaguely gratuitous; heavy with symbolism.

Once on the tarmac, Jonathan and I walked about the rear of the transport, momentarily abandoned as Dena and the rescued Brits were escorted towards the terminal building. It was cold after the fug of the plane and in the end, raw and hungry, we decided to stick with the hybrids, especially since they seemed to like Jonathan, and it was unlikely they'd be left behind. We were put into a bus and I found myself crushed up against a rather beautiful hybrid calling himself

Adam; confusingly so since several others were also called the same name.

At first, I was tongue tied over the nuances of gender so absent in the English language. The obvious approach was to use the plural, but it seemed stupid, especially since it might imply I was talking to them all at once. Sensing my difficulties, Adam smiled with such effect that I fell silent and, with infinite tact said I could address him as a 'he' since that would make it easier. He had powerful, sapphire eyes that glinted and shone as he spoke. His skin was incredibly clear, almost translucent except where the speckled banding appeared at the top of his forehead and down the side of his neck. I asked him if he knew what was happening and he said yes. He had inherited not just Max's looks but also his minimalist habit of speaking. As we approached the somewhat dilapidated arrivals building, a large crowd of pro-hybrid demonstrators crowded around the bus, banging its side enthusiastically. Most of them were young, chanting and clapping, some in tears. One guy had fake hybrid markings on his face (in the wrong place, I noticed), and I realised, not without a spike of anxiety, that these were members of the Reconfigured Man movement. The bus slowed and kangarooed its way through the mob. Adam fell against me, and instinctively I took hold of his arms.

'You're famous, see.' I joked, nodding towards the banners and flags. My arm lingered, despite my best intentions.

'Or infamous.' Adam said, watching me carefully. He then touched the side of my face, a gesture so like Max that I was startled. 'We know you, Jamie. There is no need to be anxious. You were the companion of the *Qua Quendi*; the one you call Max.'

'Yes, I was, I am.'

It took us several hours to get out of the airport. While it was clear that Maitland had been bluffing over the threat of force, he clearly wanted to cause as much delay and confusion as possible. We were joined by about thirty of forty delegates trying to get to the general assembly meeting, some had been in the arrivals lounge for three days and had survived by raiding the vending machines. The most helpful in organising the chaos were the NYPD, who were clearly working closely with the Mayor's office. After a long and somewhat heated conversation between Dena and the President, overheard by about five hundred people since it involved both shouting into a radio, the US marines blocking the exits to the airport stood down. Everywhere I looked I invariably saw Dena, cajoling, encouraging, arguing. She even had time to push us into a taxi.

'If I were thirty years older, Jamie, I'd marry that woman.' Jonathan said appreciatively. We drove into Manhattan on highway 27 before cutting up to Brooklyn Heights and crossing the East River, the roads surprisingly full of people, clustered around banners and signs either welcoming us or demanding we leave. We were eventually put into a hotel just off East Houston Street, not far from the River Park which was, appropriately enough, under water, as was much of battery park and the area immediately around the 9/11 memorial. After food we climbed up onto the roof where we could now see the experiment sitting possessively over the UN building, much lower than it had been so far, huge and silent, surrounded by swarms of drones, insect like in comparison. More of the escort ships were clustered over various parts of the city, points down and no longer flashing. I was moody, depressed at not seeing Max and having an opportunity to confront him. I was also depressed at having been separated from the hybrids.

'Patience Jamie, our boy is going to be busy and besides, he needs us, lie or no lie.'

'Do you think he knows what he's doing?' My tone was one of anxiety and worry.

Jonathan slapped my back laddishly. 'Let's hope so.'

Wherever Max was, he was certainly busy. The protocols for getting him to attend a general assembly were bizarre, complicated by the fact that the American ambassador used every possible clause of the charter to frustrate an address; partly because the General Secretary had died and been replaced by someone who was both terrified and incompetent. There was also the sheer difficulty of moving about a city that had been badly hit by the virus and subject to several tidal surges over the last few years. We learned later that Max had asked the Mayor's office to prioritise what it needed repairing; and having identified the power grid and the need to clear lower Manhattan of flood water, Max set to work; partly to impress I guess, partly to get on with his job.

Twelve hours after our arrival, New York was aglow with electricity and the anti-alien protesters had thought it prudent to abandon their outrage and enjoy the spectacle. From the roof of our hotel, a place we sat out on whenever we could - the sight was emotional, a restoration of sorts, a promise. The power appeared to be directed down from the experiment. We also noticed that the smaller escort ships were replicating like amoeba, splitting off from tip to stern, and several hundred were swarming over the tip of the peninsula below Wall Street seemingly fabricating something on the ground. The internet was up, and we both spent several hours communicating with Julian, Daniel and Margaret.

The coup was still on going and the situation seemed extremely volatile, but I was relieved to hear that Julian sounded better, more like his old self. He asked after Max; anxious to know what was going on. I texted him saying that Max was planning to appear on every possible cable outlet he could find, a spectacular celebrity, but my mood was still glum; despite the sense of momentum, I could not shake my fears that the experiment was linked to the events of the last few years; an irony, since if it turned out to be so, Davies was largely vindicated.

'I wish you'd fucking cheer up, Jamie. There's a gym in the basement, you could go and work up some enthusiasm.'

'Sorry. It's just well – what are we restoring? Can we go back to things as they were – do we want to? Even before the pandemic we were fucked; we just didn't know it. Every time Max shows them something amazing, he'll just stoke up their greed, their desire to take whatever's on offer and sneak it back to their own state. Worst still, he'll look like Cortez on the shores of the New World. Even if Max can talk, they'll just talk back, offers, counter offers – babble, babble. It's worse than all those environmental conferences, all those pointless, empty commitments even as water gathered about our ankles. And God forbid we find out from Max that the experiment *caused* all this.'

Jonathan was burning the sides of what appeared to be a massive wedge of hash; I had no idea how he had managed to track it down. 'Jesus, I never realised you were such a misanthropist! We can change – perhaps Max and his buddy up there will set things on a new course; a new system, if the hybrids stay things can't go back to normal; no one believed in democracy even before the outbreak, it was all broken – I never understood a system which gave someone like Garen the right to vote.'

'So a benign dictatorship – that's just what we need! What if they – if *we* – refuse to allow them to settle? Do they just go? I know Max gave his word, but what if the experiment ignores him?' I thought suddenly, impulsively, of Adam. 'Which would confirm everything our little fascist cabal the Blue Jackets have been saying all along? Jonathan – you've set fire to your sleeve.'

'Oh shit – yeah. I hate hash, but there's no weed for love or money.' He slapped his smouldering arm out indifferently before scowling at me. 'I can't believe Max is subservient to the experiment, it looks weird and the whole 'I'm going to speak with the experiment' is creepy but what kept us both going for the last sixteen years was the hope that Max would come back. He's back, and not as an accomplice to mass murder – or not necessarily. You're spooked by Garen; I get it – so am I – but let's just wait! You've been going over the data on infertility – have you seen any evidence of a plan? Something obviously alien or unaccounted for? The Seeth were never very subtle; unique base sequences, tags, flashing eyes. If the experiment is behind the virus, you'll soon know.'

Jonathan's loyalties to Max were momentarily greater than mine; but then he had been taken too, he had spoken with the experiment for years through his tag. I felt sick with doubt and indecision.

'Ok, you're right. But even if Max is now the poster boy for a new faith, how will it work. In the end we will just divide into tribes like we always do, those for, those against, and whoever loses will refuse to be reconciled; it's a basic flaw in our human DNA.'

'Not for much longer, if Max gets his way.'

The next day we were moved opposite the UN building itself, into a series of office blocks which had been requisitioned and turned into hostels. We were back with the hybrids, who had been the subject of obvious fascination and interest as well as various threats. I found I was looking for and yet also avoiding Adam, a difficult job given our proximity. I spent most of the morning watching various interviews given by Max; indiscriminate in his use of outlets, including a particularly amusing appearance on Fox News. The anchor, some preppy right-wing guy with a quiff hairdo – kept bombarding Max with hostile questions, mostly about the ships, which kept sliding off harmlessly every time Max smiled. He was wearing a white, open collared shirt that hugged his physique and showed a tantalising boss of muscle just below his throat, and the hair was designer chaos personified. Max was genuinely confused and kept asking calmly whether the anchor was asking him a question or answering it for him; the result being that the interviewer ended up on a massive, incoherent rant while Max sat frowning, beautifully bemused and unassuming. Other channels showed Maitland, hair slicked back, face oddly powdered, calling on the American people to stand firm in the face of threats to their fundamental rights and security, but also indicating that he was – indeed he had always been – willing to cooperate with the UN.

Around 2pm there was some sort of diplomatic breakthrough in the logjam as to how and when Max would address the UN itself. The US Ambassador had agreed finally to participate in the Security Council meeting, and the British Ambassador – appointed before the coup, was found under house arrest in his apartment up on 44th E Street. As a sign of goodwill, the Americans released him, and he was able to take the British seat. There priority for the council was to fast track their recommendation for a new General Secretary which turned out to be none other than Dena Small. Surprisingly the US abstained from the security council vote but refrained from using its veto. The General Assembly ratified her position almost immediately and set aside the next few days for Max to address them. Jonathan noted that we were doomed to know famous people. I caught sight of Adam, dressed in a T shirt and jeans sunning himself like a giant, lithe cat, his head tilted upward, his eyes closed meditatively. I was summoning up the courage to go and speak with him when I was summoned to meet Dena. I found her, not in the General Secretary's office, but the old annex of UNCSAC.

'Do I bow?'

'No, and if you try, I'll hit you with a spoon.'

I was anxious she wanted an update on Max who I had been avoiding, but instead she invited me to join a special committee being set up to oversee work detailing the extent of the global fertility crisis. I accepted immediately and then annoyed her by calling her Ma'am.

'Don't you start – I'm not sure what's worse – Ma'am or Madam General Secretary' but she then turned to me with an obvious sense of urgency. 'Maitland is one slippery son of a bitch; this sudden 'let's all talk' is more worrying than being shot at while trying to land.'

'Have they confirmed that they're holding the remaining three hybrids?'

'No – but Max will put that right. Regarding this committee, Jamie, you're going to have to hit the ground running; the severity of the crisis has been effectively under wraps since last year, and the last thing we want is for Maitland to make a connection between it and the arrival of the hybrids.'

'I suspect that's why he's suddenly interested in talking: but there *is* a connection, Dena – Max said as much.' I spoke cautiously, anxious to see if Dena had any doubts herself and was somehow testing me.

'The connection is between the hybrids and a solution to infertility, not to the cause: blame is going to be Maitland's pitch – so you need to expose the real cause why we can't have babies without the hybrids offering us intimate assistance. The good news, however, is that things are not too rosy in his administration: I've had the Secretary for State on the phone saying that Congress is going to convene itself; they're trying to nominate minority and majority leaders – since the previous occupants are all dead. Incidentally, what do you know of a group calling itself the Reconfigured Man?'

I sucked in my cheeks and looked into the middle distance.

'More than I would like to since my ex-boyfriend seems to have started it.'

'Garen Lane?'

Her tone disturbed me, as if Garen was a sort of celebrity or well-known public figure.

'What do *you* know about them, Dena?'

'Not much, except they have been incredibly helpful and organised. I couldn't really make head or tail of their website, but they seem to have got on board the breeding idea quickly. : have you looked at it?'

'Yeah – it didn't make much sense to me either. Very gay in a sort of bisexual way, and to be honest a bit too explicit even for me. It was

Garen I went to see in London with Jonathan; you know he was an abductee, one of the children taken in 1993?'

Dena's face froze dramatically. 'I didn't know that – the name was familiar, but I couldn't place it' she said eventually. 'And the others – are many abductees?'

'No. They think they are, Garen has convinced them, but it's all fake; Dena; Garen managed to convince them to convince themselves; and although it's definitely on board the sex part of Max's agenda, I worry that they are a bit too weird for main stream opinion – whatever that is these days.'

The palms of my hands were sweaty. I slipped them into my pockets.

Dena looked momentarily inscrutable but seemed genuinely thrown by my reply. 'Well I would never have guessed that. And yes, the weirdness is unfortunate but the fact remains they're the best organised outfit here after the Earth for Humans movement, and they seem to have effectively infiltrated much of the civil service in the federal and state governments here – I was thinking of ways in which we could deepen our cooperation with them, but now I'm not too sure. Is Max connected with them?'

She asked it innocently enough.

'I doubt it – why?'

'He was talking with some of them earlier; they all looked very familiar. I wondered if he'd met any in England before he left. You ok?'

'Yeah, sure – just thinking.' I thought it best to change the subject. 'Do you have any idea what Max is going to say over the next few days? How this offer is going to work? Isn't he going to run it past you – to make sure it's feasible, practicable?'

Dena sat down heavily. 'That's the plan; I'll try and see him later – but he's become a bit of a rock star; do people still say that?'

'I think they do.'

Chapter Ten: Davies and the Angel.

Bored by Ryan's banality, Davies read through the report several times; and each time his mood darkened. Dena's summary of the physiology of the hybrids could hardly be accurate, but Davies knew Victor Lall and had indeed recruited him some years ago to keep tabs on UNCSAC. He was a competent biochemist and unlikely to be wrong. Deborah Ewing was an unknown, but she seemed well trained. The similarities between hybrid and avian DNA were interesting, suggesting a possible line of research when he got back to his lab, but the wider political sections struck Davies as singularly ill advised.

Why Maitland had become embroiled in the British situation made no sense to him, and he was disturbed to read again those familiar names from the past: Sally Grey and Jonathan Price in particular. Sally seemed to have some powerful if vague position in the now defunct British government. Jamie Relph, he knew about, thanks to his championing of the infertility syndrome explanation for the current crisis, but he was something of an unknown entity. As to the experiment itself, its transformation from an activity to a thing was not unexpected, but it added even greater urgency to concentrating on the ship. Whatever was on board, whatever was controlling events, implied beyond doubt that that Max was a puppet of some higher, dangerous power. And why did the experiment not reveal itself to discuss matters with the UN; why use Max at all? He put the report down and beckoned the steward, asking curtly for a glass of cognac.

As they were curving down towards Phoenix, Ryan stirred and yawning, flashed his perfect, well insured teeth before straightening his cuffs. They landed on a small airfield near Tempe and then drove south at speed in the direction of Tucson. By early evening Davies was back in the facility and was pondering his next move. To remain in contact with Maitland, he had been forced to agree with Ryan's insistence that one of the numerous outhouses on the surface be used as a communications centre. The Faraday shielding left most of these unaffected, and it gave the boy something to do. Davies vetoed the suggestion that guards should be called for their protection, dismissive of Ryan's claim that the location of the lab was already widely known.

The hybrids were resting, and Davies resumed the blood work he had started before his frankly wasted journey to New York. Already he could see that most of Dena's information was correct. The mutability of the hybrid genome was promising; opening up numerous avenues to destroy them by removing or splicing sections of the coding; but later over dinner, it struck him as too easy a weakness to be there by accident. The pressing need was to gain information on the nature of the experiment and its identity. Ryan joined him for his meal; an irritant but given his position, a necessity. He had just got off the phone with his father-in-law, and Davies was forced to listen politely to the absurdities taking place in New York. It was clear now that Maitland was a spent force; no longer capable of seeing the bigger picture, and no longer prepared to act ruthlessly and decisively. Others would, of course but Davies felt too exhausted and too old to wait for another patron. They ate in silence to the clip and tap of cutlery on china until suddenly Ryan asked if he could see the hybrids. No doubt that was part of his brief as well.

'In good time.'

'I'm not sure we have much time.'

Davies glanced up, noting with distaste the smooth firm jawline chewing opposite him.

'If you are referring to the UN, I can assure you we have all the time in the world. If that organisation has perfected anything it is the ability to procrastinate.' Davies smiled, wondering if Ryan understand the word. 'I doubt they will get around to hearing from Max Grey for at least a fortnight. It will debate procedures for the first week, I guarantee it.'

'I was thinking more of the hybrids.'

For Davies, meals were not social occasions, but the comment intrigued him.

'I have already told you that they are adequately protected.'

'But what about the other fifteen hybrids – I read somewhere that they are telepathic. Isn't it just a matter of time until they come looking for their missing companions?'

Davies smiled weakly. 'You should not believe everything you read, Mr. Kruger, especially if I suspect rightly, you read this on the internet. I have made a profession of disseminating false information; I find it useful. This facility is shielded against all forms of electro-magnetic radiation, which is why you have to go to the surface to talk with your father-in-law.'

Ryan leaned back in his chair. 'So what do you intend to do with your – patients?'

Davies reached for a napkin and dabbed his dry lips. 'With all due respect, Mr Kruger, that is a little beyond your pay grade. But since you asked, I intend to prove once and for all that the 'returning home' story is a lie and that the hybrids are alien, in least in part; obviously their hybridisation with Max has produced distinct humanoid elements but in essence, they are not from Earth, they are not refugees, and the simple fact is that once this ruse is exposed; they will use force.'

'Ok, that fits. I read some of your work, published around the time of the 1993 abductions. You believed then that it was an invasion. Is that still what you think, Sam?'

Davies watched Ryan carefully. The use of his first named irritated him considerably.

'It is. I believe that the appropriation of certain human characteristics is a deliberate strategy to assist them in adapting to live here.'

'How human are they?'

'Too human, in my opinion.'

'I don't understand.'

'Of course you don't. Mr Kruger. Let me put it another way. In a few years' time, there will be no human on this planet under the age of five. Despite our public announcements, and our glib reassurances to the contrary, we have been unable to identify the causes of infertility. Worse still, and this even you may not know, the policy of harvesting viable gamete cells is problematic, to the point of being fruitless; no pun intended. The hybrids, on the other hand, are extremely fertile and because of their peculiar sexual physiology, which I am sure you know about, they are capable of being male or female. It is not rocket science to predict our extinction. It is a mathematical certainty.'

'But in truth, you don't really believe that the hybrids are the cause of the infertility, do you?'

'What I think is irrelevant, what other people think is important.'

Ryan cleared his plate and deterred from further questioning, excused himself. Once alone, Davies sighed heavily and pouring himself a coffee from a nearby table took an elevator down to the main cells where the hybrids were eating, still physically isolated from each other. Since their emergence from their cylinders they had altered colour slightly, their skin darkening, their eyes taking on an intense luminosity.

They all looked up as Davies entered, their expressions were of curiosity as opposed to hostility. He had spoken with them all, especially the 'lead' hybrid, the first to emerge. There seemed an implicit hierarchy, at least to start with. He looked at each hybrid in turn, sucking in his cheeks. There was only so much he could get from further scans and tests. Maitland's retraction of his permission for a dissection was unfortunate; but the fact that it had been offered at all would have to suffice. It would be an unpleasant business, but Davies had no moral or ethical qualms; it was a necessity to safeguard humanity. He pondered the irony of his current position. Ensuring the survival of his species meant furthering the proliferation of people like Ryan, anaemic narcissists without an original thought in their pretty little heads. He wandered back into the lab, looking over various schematics. An egg laying reproductive system was truly bizarre; but eggs can be laid sterile, or at worst destroyed but if the experiment survived it would surely just resume its work, the slow millennial cutting and pasting of genetic material. A dissection was the only viable option followed by the destruction of the ship.

Davies worked for two days, planning how to prep one of the hybrids for surgery with the minimum amount of fuss. He was not sure he could trust the few technicians to assist him, but he would require some initial help. It would be difficult enough without an anaesthetist. He would also have to keep Ryan occupied; although he could secure the lab and the operating room from the residential part of the facility, Ryan would grow suspicious; and he had a habit of just turning up unexpectedly. Davies pondered Maitland's response to the eventual news of an autopsy but considered it irrelevant: Maitland operated by suggestion and innuendo, enough to direct people in the right direction, enough to deny everything if things went wrong. Despite the Faraday shielding, he was worried about the impact a dead hybrid would have on the others, and the remote possibility they might sense something was amiss. On the third day back from New York, he was ready to act. The news from Ryan was not encouraging; despite being politically moribund long before the pandemic finally put it out of its misery, Congress was agitating for a recall and despite numerous vacancies left by the virus, the Supreme Court was in session in Philadelphia. If push came to shove, Maitland would collapse like a punctured balloon. Davies chose the 'lead' hybrid, informing it that it would have no food prior to a cursory medical examination. He briefed one of the assistants, keeping the details vague and retired early.

The design of the lab had been completed during the epidemic, double air seals between the three levels, all with separate air vents; a separate prep room and operating facilities further isolated by metal doors. It was as robust as a level four biolab. Davies took breakfast early, primarily to avoid Ryan and then scrubbed up. He went to the observation gallery, a long corridor that looked through glass walls into each individual cell. The lead hybrid, seated at a low table, was dressed in army surplus clothing; the powerful body and short blush of the moss like substance on its scalp gave it a strangely dangerous look. Davies opened the door, heard the snap of air as the pressure equalised with the cell itself, and walked inside carrying an operating gown over the crook of his left arm.

'Good morning, Professor Davies.' The voice was soft, without any discernible accent, clearly implanted before the hybrids were placed in their casing. At first Davies had assumed that the experiment had cleverly transmitted to each set of hybrids the necessary language skills to match the designated landing site: Arabic, English, Thai – but he had discovered that they could all speak over 4,000 languages as well as write them in numerous scripts. They were also familiar with key aspects of Earth's rather complex and tragic histories, again indicative of careful and skilful planning.

'Good morning. How are you feeling today? Satisfactory?'

'Perfectly, thank you.'

Davies looked about the spartan room, a bed, a table, two chairs, an alcove leading into a separate bathroom. He had talked with the hybrid before, questioning it about its physiology, its understanding of where it was, trying to decern some reflective purpose. It had proved pointless. However incomprehensible, it did not even know what it was. Davies pulled up the second chair, and pinching his trousers up neatly at the knees, sat down. The hybrid watched him carefully with its pelagic, swirling eyes.

'I wish to carry out a medical procedure. I assure you that it will be quite brief and not in the least painful. But before we begin, I would like to ask you a few more questions, if you don't mind.'

'Not at all. It occurs to me, incidentally, that I have not taken a name – there are hybrids in New York; they have names. I would like one.'

Davies felt disconcerted by this request, unexpected as it was. Having been kept in isolation, it was troubling that the hybrid had received news from outside the facility.

'How do you know of the hybrids in New York?' Davies asked, keeping his voice quiet and measured.

'One of your assistants told me; he said there were quite a few.'

Irritated, Davies looked down at his square, neat hands resting on his lap. 'Well I don't think there is any need for a name.'

The hybrid frowned and then, moving the table aside, grew suddenly obdurate. 'I would like a name. I have already given the matter some thought.'

Davies ground his teeth together, anxious not to convey any irritation or unease. The hybrids had quickly become adept at interpreting human emotion. 'Very well. May I suggest, in the circumstances, that we call you Nemo?'

The hybrid, understanding the reference completely, laughed. 'I would prefer, Professor Davies, to be somebody as opposed to nobody.'

'We don't have much time. I would like you to change into this before we take you to the medical bay.' Davies laid the gown over the bed next to the hybrid who looked at it briefly before saying with sudden resolution.

'I would like to be called Gabriel.'

Davies looked up sharply, his eyes hooded; the hybrid pronounced the name with the emphasis on the first syllable. During his first encounter with the hybrids he had considered them as exotic animals, potentially dangerous given their size and power, but once it was clear they could communicate he had looked upon them as automatons; cleverly designed but speaking on behalf of their programmer. He kept that image now in the forefront of his mind. With the monitor scans of the ship still disturbingly fresh in his mind, he was doubly convinced that they were in effect drones, machines of flesh and blood but machines, nonetheless.

It was easy to be taken in by their casual, sculptured physiques and their minimalist talk; it held a certain charm, but they were not individual, they were part of some monstrous collective. He did not enjoy the prospect of killing the hybrid; he did not consider himself a sadist. The procedure was a necessity, and difficult enough without anthropomorphising the thing with a name.

'A curious choice. You are thinking of the archangel?'

'I am. I thought you might approve.'

'Does that make me God?'

'On the contrary. But it seems you are troubled by God, Professor; either your own or someone else's. How can I help you?'

The tone in the voice was new; potentially sarcastic if not ironic. Again, Davies felt a creeping concern, either the Faraday shielding was not working, or the hybrids had been interacting a great deal with the technicians; the most probable explanation given the whole naming fiasco. Instinctively, Davies reached down and felt the floor; the Faraday device could be felt as a soft, persistent vibration. All seemed well with the integrity of the isolation unit.

'I have no interest in God, Gabriel. But I am rather pressed for time. Would you please change so we can begin your examination? The sooner it is done, the sooner you can eat something – you must be hungry.'

'I am perfectly fine. What exactly have you in store for me today?' The tone was almost jovial, potentially knowing. Davies' irritation grew and he found himself glancing at his watch, a nervous habit.

'Nothing unusual; just a few more scans and samples; your physiology intrigues me, and we need to find out more about the differences between us, between our species.'

The hybrid stood as Davies spoke, and undressed quickly, holding out the gown with a look of some curiosity. Initially it put it on back to front, and Davies stood and helped – standing on his toes because of the hybrid's height. The gown was the wrong shape, snaring on the broad grooved trapezium and the curious ribbing that ran from the neck to the top of the front deltoids. The musculature struck Davies as absurd; clearly a redundant feature, but he was annoyed to find himself looking at it with admiration, the tapered waist and the powerful glutes framed by powerful thighs, the bizarre and perverse bulge that presumably sheathed its male genitalia. Standing to face Davies, the hybrid looked not unlike a Greco-Roman statue except for the absence of a navel and the slightly forward posture; a product of the spinal alignment with the pelvic girdle, which unlike humans, was set back slightly, making the hybrid use its upper body to balance upright.

'There. Perfect.' Said Davies, casting his eyes down and placing his hands in the pockets of his lab coat. 'If you would just come with me, we can get you on a trolly.'

'No assistants today?' asked the hybrid casually, looking up through the glass and into the gallery.

'Yes; they are waiting in the prep room.'

Davies put his hand on the door handle into the airlock. The hybrid was standing motionless.

'Come along.' He tried to sound breezy; the avuncular tone of a family doctor. The hybrid followed, but with an expression that Davies found hard to gauge. They walked into the elevator and descended to the basement. In the prep room, Davies saw the technician working on a series of gas cylinders.

'Thank you, Peters.' Davies guided the hybrid to the gurney and watched as it adjusted the pillow at the base of its neck; a perfect imitation of a human gesture.

'An arm, your right arm, if you please.'

A thick, contoured arm reached out, veins thickly bunched at the back of the elbow. Davies swabbed them and then extracted samples of blood. He felt more relaxed now, back in control. He placed the self-sealing phials of blood on a rack behind him, and then took the hybrid's right hand in his, turning it palm down. A lattice of veins showed just below the knuckles.

'This may prick a little.'

As he was about to insert the tubing for the anaesthetic, the hybrid leaned up slightly and said loudly 'Peters, I have chosen the name Gabriel. What do you think?'

'That's perfect for you! You realise that people will call you Gabs!'

Davies felt his face scowling; glancing back at the technician his expression was scathing. 'Peters, please concentrate on your work.' Davies looked down at the hybrid's hand; long well-formed fingers and a strange clay like texture to the skin. He found himself thinking of a cave he had visited in Norway many years ago; its name escaped him. At low tide it was possible to enter the main chamber and see a startlingly piece of art, a pastiche of hennaed imprints made by a Neolithic people holding their palms down against the rock and blowing red powder over the back of their hands. The cave floor was even littered with tools used to apply the pigment, scattered about as if just abandoned. Davies had found it impossible not to place his own hand up against those of a long dead tribe, contemplating the symbolism as he did so; a greeting or a warning.

Davies shivered and looked up keenly. The hybrid was watching him carefully with his glowing, disconcerting eyes. He was also aware that Peters was standing beside him, holding out a clipboard.

'Peters please connect the mix so I can complete the preparations!' His tone was sharp, but Peters remained preoccupied. 'What is it!'

'Can I have a word, Professor?'

'Yes?'

Peters moved back to his station, implying with a gesture of the head that Davies should follow. They walked several feet away from the hybrid who lay with its arm still dutifully extended.

'What is wrong – we need to complete this procedure quickly!'

'Professor this mix is way too high. It also contains an anti-coagulant – that must be a mistake?'

Angered, Davies glared at the technician and repeated his instructions for the anaesthetic to be attached to the drip.

'But this concoction will kill him.'

'Nonsense; I calibrated it myself. Just do your job man, for God's sake.'

Peters remained looking at the clipboard with an intensity Davies had not seen before. It occurred to him suddenly that, however placid the technician had become, Peters might refuse to carry out the procedure. He was also aware that the hybrid was watching them with keen attention.

'Sorry Professor, I'm just a little confused as to what we are doing today.'

Davies turned away from the hybrid and put his hand across the technician's back, an expansive gesture that he hoped would disguise his growing anger and – oddly – sense of panic.

'What *you* are doing today Peters, is following a direct instruction from me to carry out your job. If, for some reason, you are incapable of doing that, I want you to leave now and we can discuss the implications of your insubordination later.'

To Davies' surprise, Peters grew more defiant.

'Killing the patient is generally considered unethical, Professor; you were an MD once, I don't need to tell you about the Hippocratic oath?'

'The oath refers to human patients, Peters; to people who were born and not genetically manufactured in a lab. Again, I ask you to do your job or leave the prep room.'

Peters looked back over Davies' shoulder, came to some sudden resolution, and placing the clipboard down on his desk, turned and walked briskly out of the facility. For a few seconds Davies felt stunned and stood stiffly as the elevator door close. He had personally selected Peters; two felonies for lab thefts from the CDC and a record of minor offences; yet underneath he was some lily livered liberal with a conscience. The betrayal stung him. Pulling himself together, Davies wheeled the pre-mixed gas cylinder towards the gurney himself, his back to the hybrid as he pulled it across the tiled floor. When he turned, the hybrid was standing over him, his angelic face incredibly close to his. Davies moved his head back in obvious surprise.

'Please return to the trolly.'

'So that you can proceed with my dissection? I think not, Professor.'

Davies had considered using constraints from the onset but had decided against them in the first instance; it would have shown that the procedure was unusual and probably have led to complications. He felt adrenaline spiking his heart rate. Denial seemed irrelevant now. Davies moved away, catching his legs on the wheels of the gas cylinder, and stumbled backwards. With extraordinary reflexive speed the hybrid came forward and caught his arms, holding him upright.

'Careful – you might injure yourself.' The tone of sarcasm was obvious. 'What is it you are so curious about, Professor – perhaps we could discuss it?'

Davies could feel the hybrid's powerful grip on his arms. 'I think we have discussed things long enough, enough for me to know what you are and why you are here.'

The hybrid frowned, then with almost no visible effort lifted Davies up like a doll and placed him on the trolly. 'The invasion myth, I suppose?'

Davies laughed humourlessly. 'You are not returning to Earth; you were never here. I have seen the experiment with my own eyes as well as your robust genome. I have no idea where you originate but I am not intimidated by you or your technology.'

'Are we not, as you said earlier, human enough? One of my progenitors was the Qua Quendi, the one you call Max. Another was a therapod that evolved on Earth – must you concern yourself with a few alien anomalies?'

'Yes, because those anomalies disguise your real intentions. A wolf in sheep's clothing if ever I saw one.'

The hybrid smiled, looking at Davies keenly. 'So you are pondering our creator? "What immortal hand or eye did frame thy fearful symmetry?" – I take it you are familiar with William Blake?'

'I am not here to play games, *Gabriel*.' He spat out the name, feeling spittle on his lips. 'I will stop you, and if you kill me someone else will.'

'I have no intention of killing anyone, Samuel. But I am curious about you. Do you still believe in God?'

'What is this sudden interest in God? I never believed in God.'

'I thought you did once. Your parents were Baptists, no?'

Davies ground his teeth. The question, like the Blake quote, un-nerved him but that was presumably the intention. His eyes were scanning the wall near Peters deserted workstation. Two alarm switches lay next to a row of electric points and USB boxes at about shoulder height.

'Yes, for all the good it did them.' He tried to calm himself.

'I see. It was your dislike of immigration to the suburbs that began your hatred of black Americans, the splits in the Church, the economic distress?'

'What are you talking about?' Davies snapped back. The hybrid was standing behind him now, arms crossed; it would be impossible to get to the alarm unless it moved. It was best to indulge this sudden invitation to reminisce.

'I'm talking about prejudices; which puzzle me in a man who is so evidently clever. Knowing as you do that the human genome is the same for your entire species, you continue to hold a deep dislike of non-white humans, a curious phrase given that many of you are not white. You also have a particular horror of 'race mixing' – again, a peculiar misnomer since there is only one species, one race. When you were injured in the 1970s, from a rock fall if I am not mistaken, you required an infusion of blood before your wound was repaired. You did not inquire whose blood it was, and nor did the medics who administered it: all that mattered was that the blood proteins were the same as yours. And yet in your earlier works on eugenics you denounced 'blood mixing' – miscegenation – as an act of betrayal. You even worked on a program to forcibly sterilise repeat offenders on the grounds that crime or social standing was a genetic condition, many of them conveniently Afro Americans or Hispanics.'

Davies felt a sudden almost visceral doubt. The accident had occurred just after he had left the cave with the handprints, something he had just recalled vividly. Almost no one knew about the visit let alone the accident that almost killed him.

'How do you know this?'

'I am familiar with the works of Jean-Baptist Lamarck; as well as the eugenic movement is helped spawn in the early part of the 19th century. I am also familiar with its revival in the 1970s under Wilson and the socio-biology movement.'

'How do you know about *me*, you pedantic creature – I have no interest in discussing, let alone defending my research to a data base.'

'Oh.' Adam laughed. 'That bit was easy. Your parents called you Samuel after the last great judge of the Hebrew faith; your father wanted to call you Saul, but your mother objected; she thought it was too Jewish. Your life has been eminently successful, but you have never been happy. You have been driven by the revelation of alien DNA.'

'Exactly. I've been waiting for this moment all of my life. You may imagine you can manipulate the UN; it doesn't matter; that's not where power lies.'

'Power.' Said Gabriel vaguely, thoughtfully. 'I presume you think it lies in your Earth for Humans movement? Or in people's innate fear of difference? Let us assume for the moment that we are not granted permission to settle here. What happens to you, Samuel? Your species is dying; through no fault or action of ours. Your accusation that we sterilised you is a lie; one you know and accept even as you keep repeating it. You have poisoned your world, deep to its roots, a slow insidious act of suicide. You know that HN71 was just the most potent of many new and lethal viruses that adapted their blind instinct to survive into cities choked with people; cohabiting with wildlife forced to share your space because you had shredded and destroyed their natural habitat. You know there is no link between the virus and sterility, as much as you know that no matter how hard you try to engineer a solution, the end result cannot be averted. Too many variables, so little time.'

'So I presume you are telling me, in this rather picturesque way, that you have arrived to settle and wait for our end and then manage the planet for yourselves? I admit I know the truth, but the truth is of no use to us, and you under-estimate human ingenuity. The solution to our current inability to breed is, I admit, sadly missing, but it will be found I can assure you.'

'It is standing in front of you.'

Davies was half listening, half calculating the chances of getting to the alarm. He was evidently no match for the hybrid, and even if guards arrived, he would be inside the prep room inches away from a large predator while they would need to open the door to either restrain or kill it. There was also, given Peters behaviour, the distinct possibility that no one would come at all. Amid the preoccupation with his own survival, he heard the hybrid's comment without immediately comprehending it. He heard it again, echoing in his head. Preoccupied as he was, he felt a palpable shock as if he had been stabbed. Seconds later he felt close to laughing.

'If you are implying what I think you are, your rather perverse physiology would make it impossible to breed with humans; you are indeed a different species, and the results would be more perverse than you are.' His voice slowly trailed away. He seemed to be having problems concentrating. Amid his desire to slam his hand on the alarm, the intrigue of Gabriel's gnomic comment, his mind suddenly returned briefly to the curious schematics littering his office desk. He felt silenced by a sudden doubt, the emphatic similarity between the hybrids DNA, its configuration, and the composition of avian DNA; the simple undeniable fact that the hybrid genome would, in all likelihood, now produce fertile offspring when crossed with a human.

'I see we are beginning to understand one another.'

'It will never happen. I will see to it. If that is the price we must pay to survive, it is too high. What you are suggesting is disgusting; humans do not breed with animals!'

Gabriel said nothing, holding Davies gaze with his glowing eyes. He then turned and walking towards the wall, stabbed the alarm with two elegant fingers. Davies saw a blue strobe light set in the ceiling flash silently. He felt bewilderment as well as relief, and within minutes he heard the elevator ping and saw through the glass panelling the doors slide open. He was surprised however to see Ryan step out, followed by a blonde haired man and then, to his utter incredulousness, he saw Max – the Qua Quendi, following behind.

Chapter Eleven: The Seventh Seal.

I was glad of Dena's offer; it made me feel less like a spare wheel and it gave me an opportunity to look for something alien in the syndrome that I might have not noticed before. Part of my work was going to be an attempt to sort out prophecy from causality. I was given a small space in her cluttered office. UNCSAC had all the relevant data sets from the World Health Organisation, and the CDC had already started overseeing 'donations', mostly from the military. The provisional results were bad; even from individuals who had been screened for healthy lifestyles, the live sperm count was zero and the spermatozoa oddly deformed.

In many women ovulation had slowed considerably but seemed less final and was responding to hormonal therapies. How long this creeping malady had been spreading through the male population was impossible to guess, since no extensive sampling had been done before the pandemic. It could well be that the HN71virus had indirectly accelerated a process already present, but my feeling was that the two were entirely unconnected. The HN71 was, without doubt, a simple if not powerful coronavirus: I could find no signs of genetic tampering. The species jump from bats – well documented and vital for the eventual vaccine – seemed a perfectly normal process. There were no Seeth footprints in the viral genome or indeed in the larger syndrome of infertility: it seemed more like a cascade effect; a slow proliferation of faults over time.

I drew up some research ideas, suggestions to try and help frame the bewildering information into something that could be meaningfully applied in the field, something suggestive of an eventual cure. I had about ten colleagues, most had not yet arrived, and the imminent meeting of the General Assembly distracted everyone. Instinctively I felt that Max's relaying of the experiment's verdict was accurate: there was no cure.

The day after my 'appointment' someone tried to assassinate two hybrids on the upper east side; no one was injured, but tensions were high. I had gone immediately to see if Adam was alright, forgetting of course that I was avoiding him as well. He had been with the other hybrids, sitting and lying in their dorm as if nothing had happened. Disconcertingly he was naked, and my eyes had inevitably dropped below his thick lower abs to the sinuous curves of his bulge. I had noticed it had darkened, and I fancied that I saw the thick phallic outline of an emerging masculinity.

Luckily, he was preoccupied with asking questions about New York. He invited me to eat with the others, which I did along with several other people; the hybrids were clearly at ease with humans and human curiosity. I also sensed that their rather intimidating sense of collective solidarity – the feeling that in speaking to one you were speaking to them all, was breaking down and that they were becoming more individualised. The meal was fun; the hybrids ate everything randomly and appeared to like everything; especially milk. There was a strange discussion about churches, which I presumed they had just visited. Adam asked me to visit him soon and perhaps go with him on his next excursion. I said I would, although I cautioned him to be careful – a warning underlined by a visible increase in guards around the UN plaza. As I left, he had asked about Jonathan; about my relationship with him, as if he was clarifying boundaries. My reply had been somewhat breathless and probably incoherent.

Falling in love with Adam was easy; in that perfect symmetry was Max; it embarrasses me now to say this so categorically. But there was also someone else; tactile, immensely clever, curious too and with an acquired use of english that made every question a show of innocence. There were difficulties; obviously. While this was not one of my classic 'gay man loves straight man' dilemmas, interpreting the extent of Adam's interests took time and some skill.

Hard as it is to believe, I think he was shy and unclear as to how physical intimacy should or could work between us. He also had a habit, typical to the first born, of hoarding information and then discussing it in clinical detail; a visit to Washington DC, a lecture at the UN on energy generation and sharing. He never bored me; but as a human, I was always concerned that this habit was evasive; in fact, he was showing me intimacy as well. I did contemplate how I would cope when Adam became female; not that it seemed to matter anymore, and since Adam had no idea about it either, it was an irrelevant point of detail that rather excited me. Jonathan shamelessly encouraged me to 'act'; a euphemism that exasperated as well as amused me. One evening he had been especially pushy; back from one of his mysterious trips. Initially I had been annoyed,

'Jonathan, for the love of God; anyone would think you're on commission!'

'I'm just concerned about your wellbeing and the boss's 'project'. Found any smoking gun yet?'

'No – which leaves us with the equally worrying issue of prophecy.'

Max was working on his speech, meeting leaders and organisations; including a recent and rather tetchy visit to the Pope in Rome in which Max had offended the Curia. Air travel was suddenly possible again, although extremely limited, there were complications adapting their engines to the technologies provided by the experiment. Dena too was attending endless committees.

'Nothing wrong with prophecy, Jamie: I predict here and now that you and Adam will be an item by next week.'

'Good try – and that's not prophecy, that's path dependency. I'm just going to get on with it – if he runs away or strangles me in outrage – you'll have your work cut out. Counselling or requiem.'

'I thought you guys were used to this.' Jonathan said quietly, concentrating on potting up tiny seeds of cannabis.

'Meaning?'

'Well, don't you always have to start with 'are you top', can I put this in here, can we do it bareback, do you like me doing this.'

As he spoke, his long fingers poked and nurtured the tiny plants and the effect was so comical – so adorable – that I burst out laughing. And of course, he was right. Later, with Adam halfway through an incredibly detailed description of 19th wilderness art in the New York Metropolitan, I had clamped my hand gently on his mouth and climbed into his lap. He only stopped speaking when my lips were sealed to his, and although I felt a moment's hesitation, he placed a hand on the back of my neck, and sitting up, kissed me back deep and passionately. Afterwards of course all the hybrids knew about it, either because Adam had told them, or more disturbingly, they had shared vicariously in the experience.

Two days after the attempted assassination on the hybrids, I was working late in Dena's 'cave'. With Jonathan's help I had acquired a large amount of the raw data produced by the 1993 committee, hoping that I could, once and for all, rule out any foul play in either the HN71 or the onset of infertility. There had been numerous mass demonstrations across the planet, pro-Malaq, anti-Malaq, it was hard to see the numbers of each exactly. Several states had used the arrival of the hybrids to settle old scores, and there had been a rash of regional conflicts. There had been constant pressure on the UN from Maitland, but always just short of violence. No doubt he was waiting patiently for a first act of political terrorism by the Reconfigured Man, or better still, however unlikely, the Malaq themselves. He was also presumably waiting for Davies. I was concentrating on a batch of printouts when two firm, cold hands slipped themselves over my eyes. Someone who had crept up behind me.

'Guess who?'

It was Max; I could recognise his smell anywhere; cold, airy – the scent of open, liminal spaces.

'The alien boy.'

Max laughed, walking around to perch himself on the desk in front of me. He was wearing his black suit and white open necked shirt and looked like a Mormon. 'So you can tell the difference between me and Adam!' he said winking.

I pulled a face. 'How is the speech coming?' I placed my briefcase rather self-consciously on the desk, hiding the papers and data.

'God – you're as bad as Dena. Slowly.' Max looked at the briefcase and frowned.

'That's probably a good thing given the glacial speed of the UN.'

'What you up to?' Max ran his hands up my arms and suggestively lifted me up out of my chair.

'Nothing much, just going over some theories I've been working on. What are *you* up to, Max Grey?' I smiled, but the feel of his touch and his presence was hard to bear; doubts oddly unsettled my feelings for Max; it had also induced a sort of self-loathing.

'Nothing. I'm spending quality time with my best friend.' He glanced again at the hidden reports, I felt absurd; terrified. 'You've been avoiding me.'

'I have not! It's hard to avoid someone who is never here!' But I spoke too quickly, and long out of the practice of deceiving Max, reproached myself as he smiled beautifully, spotting my anxiety immediately.

'But I hear things are well with Adam.'

'Possibly.'

He slipped his arms around my waist and hugged me with a strange intensity.

'Have you been avoiding me because' Max spoke slowly, his voice resonating through the side of my neck 'you are afraid I am not entirely on the level?'

I moved my head back and looked into Max's eyes; specs of light blue and green eddied and shifted around the black pupils. A curl of hair hung down across his forehead, aligned with the thick bridge of his nose.

'Are you doing the mind reading thing again?'

Max smiled slowly, his eyes narrowing. 'Possibly.'

I pulled a face, placing my hands on his shoulders. I could feel the soft ribbons on the Seeth cartilage under the fabric of the jacket. 'I want to trust Max; god knows I do; but the circumstances are so bizarre; so surreal. It's not how I imagined we would meet again.'

He kissed the top of my forehead. 'It isn't exactly how I imagined it either. So, tell me what's bothering you: you were always particularly good at that!'

We walked away from the desk and sat together on a small sofa that Dena had managed to wedge between her desk and a defunct, foul smelling water cooler. I had a sudden, disorientating sense of déjà vu – Max's bedroom in Farndon Road – Max sitting me down to work out why I was being moody or difficult.

'Well?' Max said softly, playing with the front of my hair.

'Don't hate me.'

He laughed and wrapped a long arm around my neck.

'It's about Garen Lane.'

'Ah. Your boyfriend – I had no idea you two were an item incidentally, the Universe can be incredibly small.'

'So you do know him. Did you appear to him several years ago and ask him to set up the reconfigured man as a movement, to prepare the way for your arrival and the suggestion of inter-breeding?'

Max did not look surprised by the question.

'I didn't, but the experiment did. It can take my form, and often does when we communicate. It wasn't my idea.'

'Do you control the experiment, Max or does it control you?'

'No one controls anyone, Jamie. The experiment is impetuous at times, ironically because I don't think it understands immediacy; it is too old. It has been in existence for so long that it sees time in aeons, not years or decades. If the experiment stood in a valley or on a mountain range, it would not see it as we do, it would see the slow, casual erosion and weathering of rock, the vast uplifts of the planet's crust.' Max's voice was almost dreamy. 'I often think it's like one of the time lapse videos of glaciers or eruptions, where the speed and existence of human life is so fleeting, so ephemeral, that we are a blur of shadow, transparent as ghosts. It acts in deep time and not in the present.'

'How did the experiment know about the infertility crisis before it was even discovered?'

'It didn't cause it; Jamie. The experiment predicted it based on a detailed intimacy with Earth and ironically with the abducted children. We've been poisoning ourselves for decades and remember – it has seen sterility and extinction before; its basic premise is to save life, not destroy it. Years of eating and breathing pollutants had rendered the human species infertile; nothing else, and the real trigger appears – if the experiment's data is accurate – to be incipient radiation from mobile phones and wireless networks.'

I stared at Max's throat, watching his Adams apple rise and fall as he spoke.

'You're telling me that humanity has been cut down by Wi-Fi?'

Do you believe me?'

I looked away. I wanted to, I needed to. 'I do, but the experiment has created a movement which, however helpful, is going to be very divisive; its foreknowledge of your proposal will look like a conspiracy.'

'I know.' Max said quietly. 'But there isn't one. Saving the legacy of two species by making them one is not genocide.'

'Jesus, Max! Why didn't you say anything about the reconfigured man movement at Dan's!'

He was silent for a moment. 'I was afraid it would sound like it sounds. And you didn't ask me.'

'And the Seeth? They didn't come from Earth?'

'No.' Max sighed and pressed my head onto his chest. I could feel his body heat and the slow beating of his heart.

'So, what is the experiment. An alien playing God or just a very capable abacus?'

'I am not entirely sure what it is. I'm not sure it knows either; it was built by a sentient race that confronted its own extinction. They built it to preserve their memory, their culture, and to seek out the conditions for life in the galaxy should any be found. Its basic program – if that's the right word – was to resurrect the species that built it. They were called Seeth – that much is true – but they evolved in a star system far from us both in time and space, when earth was probably a swirl of cooling gas. They were probably the first sentient species to evolve. Does that sound absurd?'

'Nothing sounds absurd any more Max, believe me. Current opinion here is dating the experiment to around 2 billion years, that's half the age of the cosmos. So it *is* alien then, and there was never any connection between Earth and the Seeth?'

He snuggled my head further into his chest. 'There was a connection. Despite Drake and his perfectly logical deduction concerning the amount of sentient life in the universe, it is hard to find. The Illuvatar found many planets, but they were either dead, dying, or in the process of being born. Eventually it wandered to the edge of the galaxy and found a planet teeming with life, but that planet – Earth – suffered a massive extinction event just as the Illuvatar arrived; a contingency that it had failed to predict. A meteorite rich in iron ore had the misfortune to hit a part of the crust rich in sulphates, producing the K-T boundary, suffocating almost

93% of the biosphere in acid and dense, freezing clouds. The Illuvatar rescued a powerful, bipedal therapod which it believed could provide a template to resurrect the Seeth. There was a superficial resemblance between the raptors and the Seeth, I think. Both were warm blooded, both laid eggs, and there was a commonality in their social hierarchy. The difference was, of course, genetic. The Illuvatar was able to hybridise Seeth DNA into the raptors but the alien DNA produced a highly mutable genome that killed most of the hosts. In an attempt to rectify the problem, the experiment waited until the re-emergence of mammalian life in the Eocene period, and began its long, endless search to solve the problem of introducing the basic building blocks of alien life – the three, distinct amino acids that so excited Davies – into terrestrial mammals without killing them or producing fatal congenital illnesses.'

'And the solution was – *you*?'

I felt Max smile. 'Eventually. As hominids evolved, the experiment diversified its search but, as DeMarr was the first to appreciate, followed quickly by Julian, cancer cells provided a way of not only proliferating the alien DNA into a host, but also of stabilising the mutability of the Seeth matrix.'

'But Dena noted that the hybrid genome is still highly mutable? Did the final hybridisation process fail?'

'No; that bit is deliberate; to ensure that the hybrids can evolve quickly to their new home and their new neighbours.'

'In order to breed.' I concluded for him.

Max did not disagree. 'The experiment has run various projections; after the fourth or fifth generational cross – depending of exactly who is sleeping with who – there is too much uncertainty to make any predictions. Malaq could become placental, humans might become egg laying. You can calculate and plan, but the universe is full of random events.'

'And you're going to say this to the General Assembly? The whole story?' I imagined the creeping look of shock and awe on the faces of delegates; the revelation of the sheer otherness of the hybrids, even though they were partly human and seemed destined to become more so, as the surviving humans were destined to become less; merging into a new people, and entirely new beginning; because we had cooked ourselves in our own filth.

'Yes. In the end I persuaded the Illuvatar that if we stuck with the 'returning' story – suggested of course in the first instance by UNCSAC based on the 1993 committee's findings – it would all blow up in our faces. Something that is half true is still a lie.'

'It might still blow up in our faces, Max.' I said softly. 'And Garen's appointment as high priest will get out as well, in the end. He's hardly discrete. Besides, it might not work. Even if the biology is right, Max; we have individual humans and hybrids to think of; this isn't like breeding a new herd of sheep; it's about people's desire, how they visualise and imagine intimacy.' I struggled to speak, to order the cascade of images in my head. 'I confess I fancy Adam; I think he is sexy as hell, but as a gay man I am attracted to his masculinity, despite the fact that 'he' has no defined sex or gender. I am sure women will find the hybrids attractive, there is already 'a sex with aliens' porn site running, but to be honest, I and people like me, we're probably outliers. Heterosexual men will never overcome a sense of revulsion, even horror, even if the hybrid 'female' had breasts – which of course they don't.'

'You once told me that heterosexual men would probably have sex with anything, in the right circumstances?'

'That sounds like something I might have said once, and I was probably referring to you. But Max, in your absence, the world has shifted backwards, all those nasty little racist traits have re-emerged despite the obvious fact we are all the same species; things are really ugly at the moment. People, serious people who should know better, believe in eugenics, on links between ethnic and cultural identities and IQ, and now we are confronted with an actual difference; despite the convergence; and despite the obvious similarities between Malaq and human. Besides, the Malaq might prefer to have sex with each other – there'll be enough to ensure they can do that without risk to their genetic diversity. The Illuvatar is correct about the uncertainty principle; once started, with each throw of the genetic dice, we'll have no idea how it will end.'

'If we do nothing, humans will be extinct and there is the risk that the hybrids will never find a place to survive.'

'Some will choose extinction.'

Max looked momentarily perplexed; his face clouded. 'Surely even the most violent opponents to the hybrids understand that is illogical. Isn't there some basis for a compromise?

'Fanatics don't compromise, Max; that's the problem.'

'The experiment wanted to use Garen as a counter weight to the earth for Humans Movement, it realised that Davies was gaining momentum and had to be checked – the rather esoteric use of religion was not what it planned, nor anything it understands. I must confess I was surprised that Garen thought so much about it.'

'He was brought up a Catholic, Max: go figure.'

Max looked at me searchingly. 'Jamie? Do you believe me, do you believe any of this? I need you to. Check the nature of the syndrome – check my data – anything.'

'That's what I have been doing.' I said, glancing down sheepishly at the briefcase.

'Ah. Good man.'

I believed Max, but it had been hard, and the fact that even I had wavered made me realise that Davies would now be a much greater threat than before, that Max's job was now infinitely more complex.

'Just rein in the experiment, Max; and I would not tell anyone of the link between Garen and the experiment. Ever.'

He nodded. 'We can talk about anything Jamie, and we can talk this over again. Now, however, we need to go somewhere.'

I half hoped, half feared, that we were going to see the experiment and was only mildly disappointed when Max announced we were going to see Davies.

Chapter Twelve: The closing day.

I thought often of Max's analogy about humans and the experiment, the Illuvatar – the image of a time lapse video, the foreground a blur of immediacy, without purpose or form. Or was it possible that the experiment was God? An approximation to it, a high tech version, scanning time and intervening? It foretold the end of humanity based on either an algorithm or divine insight: I was prepared, for now, to see them as the same thing. And certainly the interventions of the experiment were indeed God like, as on the occasion it disarmed fifteen nuclear ICBMs mid trajectory launched under Maitland's orders before his coup collapsed, or enforced five ceasefires on warring states by withholding technology and emitting electromagnetic pulses to knock out tracking and guidance systems. But I am getting ahead of myself; time and solitude distort memory and my recollections. Let me go back to our visit to Davies.

That was the first and only time that Max used, what we used to call back in the Oxford days, Seeth juju. Of course, he didn't use anything, the experiment did all the work, following Max about from low orbit like a lost puppy. Many years later, when I had time to muse such things, I wondered if the experiment had not fallen in love with Max – like everyone else – and took his form and teleported him about because it enabled it to *be* Max – if just for a moment. We were folded up like origami figures and unfolded outside an elevator. Next to me was a butch looking guy with a pretty face, and next to him was a fattish guy in a white coat sweating profusely. Max leaned in between us all and opened the elevator door as if we were on a shopping trip in Macey's. Once in the basement we were confronted with the sight of an elderly man – his face curiously devoid of detail as if rendered from plastic – sitting crossly on an operating table, a tall hybrid standing behind, arms folded. This was the first time I had seen Davies; long described to me by my mother and step-father; clearly the black beast of the genetics world. How close he had come to sticking the knife into Gabriel – a disturbingly apt name, incidentally – was clear from the array of instruments that were waiting in a sterilisation tray. Even Garen would have been impressed by the extent of the collection.

The dark-haired hunk turned out to be the President's son-in-law who had joined the Reconfigured Man group. Max, ignoring Davies' demands to be released immediately, placed his hands on the hybrid's face and kissed him. There followed what appeared to be a silent conversation, presumably about what to do with Davies. Ryan Kruger, the straight man in gay clothing, asked me if I knew what was going on and how I had materialised outside the elevator. The answer to both was in the negative.

While we awaited the outcome of the mind meld, Davies spat out a long denunciation against Ryan; suspecting that he was the instrument of Maitland's betrayal, when the simple fact was that Ryan had double crossed both. I thought affectionately of Louis DeMarr. The decision was made to simply leave Davies in the lab, watched over by the two remaining hybrids, who Adam released. Max wanted him silenced until he had announced the deal to the UN – breeding and all, and not before. At the time I thought this was madness, but in the end, it helped mitigate the prolonged crisis that followed. Davies did the most damage of any human to the settlement program, he rallied every reactionary force he could, and condoned violent resistance until the cause was irredeemably lost. He stood trial in 2030 but was so old and demented by this stage that a joint tribunal released him into palliative care. Maitland was arrested after his attempt to nuke the experiment. He remained in a federal penitentiary until there were not enough wardens to look after him. The Malaq released him in 2031.

On leaving Davies locked in his own operating theatre, we winked back to Dena's office with Adam. I remember that Ryan was particularly impressed by this mode of transport: he vomited over his shirt. Dena made the most of Maitland's duplicity – summoning the American ambassador to the UN to explain the hybrid's detention, and then holding a press conference. Maitland began his slippery decent amid denials and threats to attack any alien settlements placed on US territory.

In March 2022 Max gave his speech to the General Assembly after two delays due to bomb threats. I, Dena and Jonathan had read through various drafts of the speech and thought it was as good as it was going to get. It was choreographed to follow the preliminary report of my committee on infertility, which made grim reading: 98% of infertility in men, 48% in women with the possibility that this could be reduced by relatively cheap and conventional means. Max's pitch was to allude to interbreeding rather than spell it out, and he agreed to propose clinical trials as a way of assessing whether there were any pre or post-natal risks in birthing human-hybrid children. It would also give us time to assess the social and cultural implications of mixed unions. The offer of technologies was made carefully and sensitively; carbon scrubbing, restoration of power using a form of plasma fusion, synthetic food production; all conditional on the immediate elimination of carbon-based fuels. After his speech I had imagined there would be applause or outrage but instead, there was a horrible, gaunt silence the likes of which I had never heard before nor wish to hear again.

That the plan worked was a miracle. There were several years in which it looked like it would fail. Socially conservative movements were a huge obstacle, and there was huge resistance from organised oil producers to resist the introduction of clean technologies. But the economic collapse had dramatically weakened the demand for oil; and although the industry lobbied long and hard against the ban it failed in the end to stop the legislation. Countries that held out on religious grounds could do so but were denied technology. When there was any doubt over the viability of a new gizmo, the experiment engineered dramatic displays of what was possible.

And in return? Max requested that 30 million hybrids be allowed to settle on Earth, in designated zones to be chosen by terrestrial authorities but administered by the UN. The territories would allow humans to settle alongside Malaq on a voluntary basis. They would not be internment camps or even reservations, but places of interaction between the two related species to build on their commonality. A vast majority of the first volunteers were under 30, mostly women, and aligned with the Reconfigured Man.

As the movement proliferated, it evolved its own bizarre theology with the experiment as God and the Malaq as 'watcher Angels' – references that incensed orthodox Catholics and Protestants alike. The fact that the Malaq were part alien galvanised the Earth for Humans Movement and spread the old racial trope that the hybrids were here to rape 'our' women. Many people, and not just the Blue Jackets, still believed that the Malaq were behind both the pandemic and the rise of infertility in the first place, and no amount of hard science ever put the rumour to rest. Most of the fighting and the violence over how to live with the hybrids involved humans; with the Malaq intervening only as a last resort.

There were other, tedious complications. The explicit link between technology and settlement led many governments to make unilateral offers of territory free of any UN interference, but the Illuvatar (pressured no doubt by Max) kept the UN at the forefront of all negotiations. By late June, amid what appeared to be, superficially at least, a restoration of 'normality' – Congressional then Presidential elections in the US, the final collapse of the British junta and an interim government supported by Scotland – twelve territories were identified; situated across all continents, some decidedly bleak, but the Malaq seemed to have few qualms about climate. The Australian government handed over vast swathes of their northern territories, most owned by aboriginal nations, and when the first transports arrived in August, the Malaq were confronted with unintelligible lawsuits by tribal authorities and forced evictions. The pattern was repeated elsewhere, with the newly elected US president handing over vast federal lands in Arizona and Montana without consulting individual states. North African governments ceded land that was basically uninhabitable to humans, a canny move by all since within a decade they were highly productive settlements, terraformed and lush.

But the return of 'normal politics' was an illusion. Human communities had divided so sharply between those who chose to resist, and those that collaborated, that no peace treaty ever held for long. Settlements were frequently attacked, and people who supported Malaq settlement murdered, sparking tit for tat reprisals that were hard to control as military and law enforcing agencies began to suffer crippling shortages of personnel. Clinics working on the 'hybridisation' program were frequently destroyed, as were the clinics attempting to reverse human sterility without submitting to 'alien occupation'. Malaq egg nurseries were destroyed. Each country faced a version of a civil war, without boundaries, fluid in its violence and often senseless. A small but influential number of the first born settlers decided to shun human contact on the grounds that we were dangerous and senseless, and best left to die quietly. These would become known as the *Illuvan*.

As for what Max referred to rather primly as the 'sex bit', things were obviously complex, and they got a lot more complex before the last humans moved into their own reservations to 'die pure'. The easiest route to restoring a substantially reconfigured human genome lay, ironically, in fertile gay men – although there were not a great many. Many gay men – myself included – paired with Malaq. Malaq physiology proved incredibly erotic, for the most part, and pregnant Malaq laid between five and ten eggs. As had been anticipated from UNCSAC's simulations, the eggs were not incubated but left in areas of suitable ambient temperature, rather as their distant raptor ancestors had done in the late Jurassic. They hatched within four months and the offspring grew dramatically; reaching physical maturity in four years.

The offspring – called Dura Malaq, meaning second born (or rather, born after the first) were only slightly more human than their parents, retaining the monomorphism and dual sexual reproductive system of the first hybrids. Yet many human genetic expressions turned out to be recessive; and by the third generation considerable variations began to occur. Eggs hatched to reveal very human looking hybrids, and although still lacking any obvious dimorphic features, many of these were placental and lacking in the symbiont algae that allowed Malaq and Dura Malaq to change the colour of their pigmentation on the neck and face. Many also grew hair on their scalps.

For women who were impregnated by a Malaq during their male cycle, the process was essentially the same but in reverse. Despite all the horror stories, women gave live birth to Dura Malaq – the only complication being that these were frequently multiple births. Rearing was problematic since these Dura Malaq were initially severely lactose intolerant while also growing rapidly, a process which required an extensive (and expensive) amount of nutrition. The offspring of Dura Malaq produced by human women reverted back to egg laying, until finally representing the classic recessive ration of 3:1 in subsequent generations. Based on data obtained in 2050, it was clear that placental births were replacing egg laying, although surprisingly the monomorphic physiology remained, as did the Malaq sex cycle; male genitalia was sheathed in the 'female' phase (varied for three to four months of the year); unsheathed for the rest. As such, the Dura Malaq retained the ability to be both 'mother' or 'father' to their offspring.

There were of course, especially before the settlements expanded into the empty spaces created by depopulated human territory, Malaq only pairings and these were by far the most common unions until the 2030s. These reproduced the so-called first-born physiology exactly. In sum, all these biological interactions produced considerable variation. Given that potential sexual preferences were between humans (fertile or not) and Malaq, Dura Malaq from women and Dura Malaq from men, simple debates on gender and sexuality collapsed. The Malaq Valka – a general term for nation or a possible equivalent for the word race – was luckily inclusive and made no distinctions, viewing human prejudice on appearance a curiosity, but the imbrication of human culture and religion was potent, and not even the Illuvatar could have foreseen the consequences. Eventually the ideas of Malaq purity amongst some of the first born were expressed in terms very close to 'race'.

Of the original 30 million settlers, these Malaq *Illuvan* – followers of the Illuvatar and presumably of its original mission – remained a minority. Their beliefs were eclectic and esoteric; mostly on the nature of form and thought, especially telepathy. Their exposure to human thoughts on the divine, derived unfortunately from Garen, produced the equivalent of the Christian trinity, with all its low Greek cunning and complexity. Max was a human emissary to an experiment that was divine, but in Malaq form and evidently mortal. The Illuvatar was Max, but Max was not the Illuvatar. He was also male in a world in which sex was no longer moored to biological dualism but this permanence fascinated them.

The Illuvan became, in effect, a phallocentric cult in which telepathy and meditation kept them male; evolving a monastic movement and eventually a curia as they co-opted the random, eclectic imagination of the Reconfigured Man. They even had their own heresy: that Max was a god after all. Unwilling to breed further, deliberately trapping themselves in a male form, the Illuvan survived through their extraordinary longevity; although it was widely believed that they could mate and lay in secret or that they had perfected immortality. To the Dura Malaq – which quickly became the dominant group – there was something contradictory and perverse about all this; but toleration remained if only because the Dura had no doctrinal faith and because the Illuvan would not proselytise their beliefs to any but themselves.

Although Max and I never discussed the experiment's use of religion, we often discussed its consequences. Max blamed the intense phobia and violence of the humans in the first years of their arrival, and the centrality sex had acquired in popular human culture before the fall. I did not necessarily disagree, but the Malaq suffered from an absence of a living culture themselves. The experiment guarded the secrets of their distant Seeth ancestors, but it was a dead archive of a dead race: human vibrancy was immediate and tangible, and its impact all pervasive. I think Garen should get more credit for the unintended consequences of his imagination.

For the human equivalents of the *Illuvan*, - the die hard leadership of Davies' movement – 'race' purity meant extinction. As each new generation of Malaq emerged, survivalists howled in outrage and disbelief at the demonic monstrosities spawned by the proliferating hybrids, retreating slowly as their population collapsed. Weakened by the deprivations and shortages that had followed the pandemic, and no longer able to sustain themselves, human populations that chose isolation retracted sharply. By 2025, the population of the UK was just under 30 million and dropping. In the US, continental Europe and China, the combined population figures was 900 million – by 2035 it had fallen to 600 million as the oldest cohorts died. By 2045 the global human population was a third of what it had been in 2018, and in 2060 there were more Malaq than humans. What Davies had once referred to as a mathematical certainty made it clear, even to the Earth for Humans movement, that repeated attempts to save themselves were indeed fruitless. No longer able to constitute a significant threat, the UN reconfigured the old UNCSAC into The United Nations Commission for Human Welfare, administering large tracts of land where humans sat out their final years. Exhausted, many reluctantly accepted the help offered by the skinks – still the most favoured term to describe all Malaq.

The last stronghold of human supremacy was in the old Arizona settlement zone, a place I joined in 2061 on my seventieth birthday. Adam was dead – killed alongside Jonathan in a bomb explosion at an irrigation facility, but although old I was still useful. It seems callous to say that I felt Jonathan's loss more keenly; but he had been an exceptional friend, and we had loved each other deeply.

With Adam I had a large, prosperous family, many working on the
newly built space orbital, scientists, explorers – and although not all
agreed with my decision, they understood it.

I pitied the last humans; perhaps I even pitied myself. Most of all I
wanted to show them that they were wrong about the Malaq, despite
all that they had done, that humanity's existence would live on in the
hybrids and its achievements, not only remembered but built upon in
ways that we would never have been capable of. Maybe the truth
was more painful; that at the end of days I wanted to be with my
own kind, linked to a world that was now rapidly passing away. I
worked as the reservation's doctor, caring for the growing infirm. I
liaised in secret with the Malaq Salliq, keeping our supplies coming
in and receiving some news from the last human outposts before
they faded. Many in the facility knew about my frequent, barely
secret meetings and I think in the end they were grateful.

There were so many ironies at the end, it would be futile to list them.
Perhaps the greatest was the rise of the UN to world government.
The replacement of national governments by the UN was almost
entirely to do with the proliferation of the Malaq, who since their
arrival had seen it as the only viable institution capable of protecting
them; and so it was that at the end of human dominion, an institution
created in 1944 to prevent states going to war, finally became the
seat of global power laid out in the covenant of 2040, with the
General Assembly becoming an elected parliament and the Security
Council the executive.

Finally, last as he was first, there was Max. His decision to leave was
a bitter loss to me, unable or unwilling to imagine the world without
him. This was, after all, his world; the world he had helped create.
But Max had not aged since his return, an anomaly that could only
be explained by his genetic oddity: his genome had no telomeres; not
protein code breakers that, in normal humans gradually cluttered up
the replication of the DNA coding in cell division, producing
increasing imperfection and error: the ravages of age being one of

them. He was also frustrated – perhaps even disappointed – by the behaviour of the Illuvan, uneasy as an object of veneration; a focus for a view of the universe that saw him as outside of the world, intimately linked to the concept of the divine. He had constant run ins with them, but he remained until his departure the only none first born who could enter their monasteries and talk with their elders. During one such conclave, it emerged that he had decided to leave earth. He had managed to persuade the experiment that its work was done here, and in the final days, four of the Illuvan orders went with them, back to the stars and the vast spaces of the universe. Max departed just over ten years ago. I do not expect to see him again, not in this life.

Printed in Great Britain
by Amazon